Doris Lessing

was born of British parents in Persia (now Iran) in 1919 and was taken to Southern Rhodesia (now Zimbabwe) when she was five. She spent her childhood on a large farm there and first came to England in 1949. She brought with her the manuscript of her first novel, *The Grass is Singing*, which was published in 1950 with outstanding success in Britain, in America, and in ten European countries. Since then her international reputation not only as a novelist but as a non-fiction and short-story writer has flourished. For her collection of short novels, *Five*, she was honoured with the 1954 Somerset Maugham Award. She was awarded the Austrian State Prize for European Literature in 1981, and the German Federal Republic Shakespeare Prize of 1982. Among her other celebrated novels are the five-volume *Children of Violence* series, *The Golden Notebook*, *The Summer Before the Dark* and *Memoirs of a Survivor*. Many of her short stories have been collected in two volumes entitled *To Room Nineteen* and *The Temptation of Jack Orkney*, while her African stories appear in *This Was the Old Chief's Country* and *The Sun Between Their Feet*. *Shikasta*, the first in the series of five novels with the overall title of *Canopus in Argos: Archives*, was published in 1979. Her novel *The Good Terrorist* won the W. H. Smith Literary Award for 1985, and the Mondello Prize in Italy that year. *The Fifth Child* won the Grinzane Cavour Prize in Italy, an award voted on by students in their final year at school. *The Making of the Representative for Planet 8* was made into an opera with Philip Glass, libretto by the author, and premièred in Houston. Her most recent works include *London Observed* and *African Laughter*.

By the same author:

DORIS LESSING

Winter in July

Flamingo
An Imprint of HarperCollins*Publishers*

Flamingo
An Imprint of HarperCollins*Publishers*
77–85 Fulham Palace Road,
Hammersmith, London W6 8JB

Published by Flamingo 1993
9 8 7 6 5 4 3 2 1

Previously published by Grafton Books 1966

First published in Great Britain by
Michael Joseph Ltd (as part of the
collection, *African Stories*) 1964

Copyright © Doris Lessing 1966

The Author asserts the moral right to
be identified as the author of this work

Author photograph copyright © Ingrid von Kruse

ISBN 0 00 654526 2

Set in Palatino

Printed in Great Britain by
HarperCollinsManufacturing Glasgow

All rights reserved. No part of this publication may be
reproduced, stored in a retrieval system, or transmitted,
in any form, or by any means, electronic, mechanical,
photocopying, recording or otherwise, without the prior
permission of the publishers.

This book is sold subject to the condition that it shall not,
by way of trade or otherwise, be lent, re-sold, hired out or
otherwise circulated without the publisher's prior consent
in any form of binding or cover other than that in which it
is published and without a similar condition including this
condition being imposed on the subsequent purchaser.

Contents

The Second Hut

Before that season and his wife's illness, he had thought things could get no worse; until then, poverty had meant not to deviate further than snapping point from what he had been brought up to think of as a normal life.

Being a farmer (he had come to it late in life, in his forties) was the first test he had faced as an individual. Before he had always been supported, invisibly perhaps, but none the less strongly, by what his family expected of him. He had been a regular soldier, not an unsuccessful one, but his success had been at the cost of a continual straining against his own inclinations; and he did not know himself what his inclinations were. Something stubbornly unconforming kept him apart from his fellow officers. It was an inward difference: he did not think of himself as a soldier. Even in his appearance, square, close-bitten, disciplined, there had been a hint of softness, or of strain, showing itself in his smile, which was too quick, like the smile of a deaf person afraid of showing incomprehension, and in the anxious look of his eyes. After he left the army he quickly slackened into an almost slovenly carelessness of dress and carriage. Now, in his farm clothes there was nothing left to suggest the soldier. With a loose, stained felt hat on the back of his head, khaki shorts a little too long and too wide, sleeves flapping over spare brown arms, his wispy moustache hiding a strained, set mouth, Major Carruthers looked what he was, a gentleman farmer going to seed.

The house had that brave, worn appearance of those struggling to keep up appearances. It was a four-roomed shack, its red roof dulling to streaky brown. It was the sort of house an apprentice farmer builds as a temporary shelter till he can afford better. Inside, good but battered furniture stood over worn places in the rugs; the piano was out of tune and the notes stuck; the silver tea things from the big narrow house in England where his brother (a lawyer) now lived were used as ornaments, and inside were bits of paper, accounts, rubber rings, old corks.

The room where his wife lay, in a greenish sun-lanced gloom, was a place of seedy misery. The doctor said it was her heart; and Major Carruthers knew this was true; she had broken down through heart-break over the conditions they lived in. She did not want to get better. The harsh light from outside was shut out with dark blinds, and she turned her face to the wall and lay there, hour after hour, inert and uncomplaining, in a stoicism of defeat nothing could penetrate. Even the children hardly moved her. It was as if she had said to herself: 'If I cannot have what I wanted for them, then I wash my hands of life.'

Sometimes Major Carruthers thought of her as she had been, and was filled with uneasy wonder and with guilt. That pleasant conventional pretty English girl had been bred to make a perfect wife for the professional soldier she had imagined him to be, but chance had wrenched her on to this isolated African farm, into a life which she submitted herself to, as if it had nothing to do with her. For the first few years she had faced the struggle humorously, courageously; it was a sprightly attitude towards life, almost flirtatious, as a woman flirts lightly with a man who means nothing to her. As the house grew shabby, and the furniture, and her clothes could not be replaced; when she looked into the mirror and saw her drying, untidy hair and roughening face, she would give a quick high laugh and say, 'Dear me, the things one comes to!' She was facing this poverty as she would have faced, in England, poverty of a narrowing, but socially accepted kind. What she could not face was a different kind of fear; and Major Carruthers understood that too well, for it was now his own fear.

The two children were pale, fine-drawn creatures, almost transparent-looking in their thin nervous fairness, with the defensive and wary manners of the young who have been brought up to expect a better way of life than they enjoy. Their anxious solicitude wore on Major Carruthers' already over-sensitized nerves. Children had no right to feel the aching pity which showed on their faces whenever they looked at him. They were too polite, too careful, too scrupulous. When they went into their mother's room she grieved sorrowfully over them, and they submitted patiently to her emotion. All those weeks of the school holidays after she was taken ill, they moved about the farm like two strained and anxious ghosts, and whenever he saw them his sense of guilt throbbed like a wound. He was glad they were going back to school soon, for then – so he thought – it would be easier to manage. It was an intolerable strain, running the farm and coming back to the neglected house and the problems of food and clothing, and a sick wife who would not get better until he could offer her hope.

But when they had gone back, he found that after all, things were not much easier. He slept little, for his wife needed attention in the night; and he became afraid for his own health, worrying over what he ate and wore. He learnt to treat himself as if his health was not what he was, what made him, but something apart, a commodity like efficiency, which could be estimated in terms of money at the end of a season. His health stood between them and complete ruin; and soon there were medicine bottles beside his bed, as well as beside his wife's

One day, while he was carefully measuring out tonics for himself in the bedroom, he glanced up and saw his wife's small reddened eyes staring incredulously but ironically at him over the bedclothes. 'What are you doing?' she asked.

'I need a tonic,' he explained awkwardly, afraid to worry her by explanations.

She laughed, for the first time in weeks; then the slack tears began welling under the lids, and she turned to the wall again.

He understood that some vision of himself had been destroyed, finally, for her. Now she was left with an ageing, rather fussy gentleman, carefully measuring medicine after meals. But he did not blame her; he never had blamed her; not even though he knew her illness was a failure of will. He patted her cheek uncomfortably, and said: 'It wouldn't do for me to get run down, would it?' Then he adjusted the curtains over the windows to shut out a streak of dancing light that threatened to fall over her face, set a glass nearer to her hand, and went out to arrange for her tray of slops to be carried in.

Then he took, in one swift, painful movement, as if he were leaping over an obstacle, the decision he had known for weeks he must take sooner or later. With a straightening of his shoulders, an echo from his soldier past, he took on the strain of an extra burden: he must get an assistant, whether he liked it or not.

So much did he shrink from any self-exposure, that he did not even consider advertising. He sent a note by native bearer to his neighbour, a few miles off, asking that it should be spread abroad that he was wanting help. He knew he would not have to wait long. It was 1931, in the middle of a slump, and there was unemployment, which was a rare thing for this new, sparsely-populated country.

He wrote the following to his two sons at boarding-school:

I expect you will be surprised to hear I'm getting another man on the place. Things are getting a bit too much, and as I plan to plant a bigger acreage of maize this year, I thought it would need two of us. Your mother is better this week, on the whole, so I think things are looking up. She is looking forward to your next holidays, and asks me to say she will write soon. Between you and me, I don't think she's up to writing at the moment. It will soon be getting cold, I think, so if you need any clothes, let me know, and I'll see what I can do . . .

A week later, he sat on the little verandah, towards evening, smoking, when he saw a man coming through the trees on a bicycle. He watched him closely, already trying to form an estimate of his character by the tests he had used all his life: the width between the eyes, the shape of the skull, the way the legs were set on to the body. Although he had been taken in a dozen times, his belief in these methods never wavered. He was an easy prey for any trickster, lending money he never saw again, taken in by professional adventurers who (it seemed to him, measuring others by his own decency and the quick warmth he felt towards people) were the essence of gentlemen. He used to say that being a gentleman was a question of instinct: one could not mistake a gentleman.

As the visitor stepped off his bicycle and wheeled it to the verandah, Major Carruthers saw he was young, thirty perhaps, sturdily built, with enormous strength in the thick arms and shoulders. His skin was burnt a healthy orange-brown colour. His close hair, smooth as the fur of an animal, reflected no light. His obtuse, generous features were set in a round face, and the eyes were pale grey, nearly colourless.

Major Carruthers instinctively dropped his standards of value as he looked, for this man was an Afrikaner, and thus came into an outside category. It was not that he disliked him for it, although his father had been killed in the Boer War, but he had never had anything to do with the Afrikaans people before, and his knowledge of them was hearsay, from Englishmen who had the old prejudice. But he liked the look of the man: he liked the honest and straightforward face.

As for Van Heerden, he immediately recognized his traditional enemy, and his inherited dislike was strong. For a moment he appeared obstinate and wary. But they needed each other too badly to nurse old hatreds, and Van Heerden sat down when he was asked, though awkwardly, suppressing reluctance, and began drawing patterns in the dust with a piece of straw he had held between his lips.

Major Carruthers did not need to wonder about the man's circumstances: his quick acceptance of what were poor terms spoke of a long search for work.

He said scrupulously: 'I know the salary is low and the living quarters are bad, even for a single man. I've had a patch of bad luck, and I can't afford more. I'll quite understand if you refuse.'

'What are the living quarters?' asked Van Heerden. His was the rough voice of the uneducated Afrikaner: because he was uncertain where the accent should fall in each sentence, his speech had a wavering, halting sound, though his look and manner were direct enough.

Major Carruthers pointed ahead of them. Before the house the bush sloped gently down to the fields. 'At the foot of the hill there's a hut I've been using as a storehouse. It's quite well-built. You can put up a place for a kitchen.'

Van Heerden rose. 'Can I see it?'

They set off. It was not far away. The thatched hut stood in uncleared bush. Grass grew to the walls and reached up to meet the slanting thatch. Trees mingled their branches overhead. It was round, built of poles and mud and with a stamped dung floor. Inside there was a stale musty smell because of the ants and beetles that had been at the sacks of grain. The one window was boarded over, and it was quite dark. In the confusing shafts of light from the door, a thick sheet of felted spider web showed itself, like a curtain halving the interior, as full of small flies and insects as a butcher-bird's cache. The spider crouched, vast and glittering, shaking gently, glaring at them with small red eyes, from the centre of the web. Van Heerden did what Major Carruthers would have died rather than do: he tore the web across with his bare hands, crushed the spider between his fingers, and brushed them lightly against the walls to free them from the clinging silky strands and the sticky mush of insect-body.

'It will do fine,' he announced.

He would not accept the invitation to a meal, thus making it clear this was merely a business arrangement. But he asked politely (hating that he had to beg a favour), for a month's salary in advance. Then he set off on his bicycle to the store, ten miles off, to buy what he needed for his living.

Major Carruthers went back to his sick wife with a burdened feeling, caused by his being responsible for another human being having to suffer such conditions. He could not have the man in the house: the idea came into his head and was quickly dismissed. They had nothing in common, they would make each other uncomfortable – that was how he put it to himself. Besides, there wasn't really any room. Underneath, Major Carruthers knew that if his new assistant had been an Englishman, with the same upbringing, he would have found a corner in his house and a welcome as a friend. Major Carruthers threw off these thoughts: he had enough to worry him without taking on another man's problems.

A person who had always hated the business of organization, which meant dividing responsibility with others, he found it hard to arrange with Van Heerden how the work was to be done. But as the Dutchman was good with cattle, Major Carruthers handed over all the stock on the farm to his care, thus relieving his mind of its most nagging care, for he was useless with beasts, and knew it. So they began, each knowing exactly where they stood. Van Heerden would make laconic reports at the end of each week, in the manner of an expert foreman reporting to a boss ignorant of technicalities – and Major Carruthers accepted this attitude, for he liked to respect people, and it was easy to respect Van Heerden's inspired instinct for animals.

For a few weeks Major Carruthers was almost happy. The fear of having to apply for another loan to his brother – worse, asking for the passage money to England and a job, thus justifying his family's belief in him as a failure, was pushed away; for while taking on a manager did not in itself improve things, it was an action, a decision, and there was nothing that he found more dismaying than decisions. The thought of his family in England, and particularly his elder brother, pricked him into slow burning passions of resentment. His brother's letters galled him so that he had grown to hate mail-days. They were crisp, affectionate letters, without condescension, but about money, bank-drafts, and insurance policies. Major Carruthers did not see life like that. He had not written to his brother for over a year. His wife, when she was well, wrote once a week, in the spirit of one propitiating fate.

Even she seemed cheered by the manager's coming; she

sensed her husband's irrational lightness of spirit during that short time. She stirred herself to ask about the farm; and he began to see that her interest in living would revive quickly if her sort of life came within reach again.

But some two months after Van Heerden's coming, Major Carruthers was walking along the farm road towards his lands, when he was astonished to see, disappearing into the bushes, a small flaxen-haired boy. He called, but the child froze as an animal freezes, flattening himself against the foliage. At last, since he could get no reply, Major Carruthers approached the child, who dissolved backwards through the trees, and followed him up the path to the hut. He was very angry, for he knew what he would see.

He had not been to the hut since he handed it over to Van Heerden. Now there was a clearing, and amongst the stumps of trees and the flattened grass, were half a dozen children, each as tow-headed as the first, with that bleached sapless look common to white children in the tropics who have been subjected to too much sun.

A lean-to had been built against the hut. It was merely a roof of beaten petrol tins, patched together like cloth with wire and nails and supported on two unpeeled sticks. There, holding a cooking pot over an open fire that was dangerously close to the thatch, stood a vast slatternly woman. She reminded him of a sow among her litter, as she lifted her head, the children crowding about her, and stared at him suspiciously from pale and white-lashed eyes.

'Where is your husband?' he demanded.

She did not answer. Her suspicion deepened into a glare of hate: clearly she knew no English.

Striding furiously to the door of the hut, he saw that it was crowded with two enormous native-style beds: strips of hide stretched over wooden poles embedded in the mud of the floor. What was left of the space was heaped with the stained and broken belongings of the family. Major Carruthers strode off in search of Van Heerden. His anger was now mingled with

14

the shamed discomfort of trying to imagine what it must be to live in such squalor.

Fear rose high in him. For a few moments he inhabited the landscape of his dreams, a grey country full of sucking menace, where he suffered what he would not allow himself to think of while awake: the grim poverty that could overtake him if his luck did not turn, and if he refused to submit to his brother and return to England.

Walking through the fields, where the maize was now waving over his head, pale gold with a froth of white, the sharp dead leaves scything crisply against the wind, he could see nothing but that black foetid hut and the pathetic futureless children. That was the lowest he could bring his own children to! He felt moorless, helpless, afraid: his sweat ran cold on him. And he did not hesitate in his mind; driven by fear and anger, he told himself to be hard; he was searching in his mind for the words with which he would dismiss the Dutchman who had brought his worst nightmares to life, on his own farm, in glaring daylight, where they were inescapable.

He found him with a screaming rearing young ox that was being broken to the plough, handling it with his sure understanding of animals. At a cautious distance stood the natives who were assisting; but Van Heerden, fearless and purposeful, was fighting the beast at close range. He saw Major Carruthers, let go the plunging horn he held, and the ox shot away backwards, roaring with anger, into the crowd of natives, who gathered loosely about it with sticks and stones to prevent it running away altogether.

Van Heerden stood still, wiping the sweat off his face, still grinning with the satisfaction of the fight, waiting for his employer to speak.

'Van Heerden,' said Major Carruthers, without preliminaries, 'why didn't you tell me you had a family?'

As he spoke the Dutchman's face changed, first flushing into guilt, then setting hard and stubborn. 'Because I've been out of work for a year, and I knew you would not take me if I told you.'

The two men faced each other, Major Carruthers tall, fly-away, shambling, bent with responsibility; Van Heerden stiff and defiant. The natives remained about the ox, to prevent its escape – for them this was a brief intermission in the real work of the farm – and their shouts mingled with the incessant bellowing. It was a hot day; Van Heerden wiped the sweat from his eyes with the back of his hand.

'You can't keep a wife and all those children here – how many children?'

'Nine.'

Major Carruthers thought of his own two, and his perpetual dull ache of worry over them; and his heart became grieved for Van Heerden. Two children, with all the trouble over everything they ate and wore and thought, and what would become of them, were too great a burden; how did this man, with nine, manage to look so young?

'How old are you?' he asked abruptly, in a different tone.

'Thirty-four,' said Van Heerden suspiciously, unable to understand the direction Major Carruthers followed.

The only marks on his face were sun-creases; it was impossible to think of him as the father of nine children and the husband of that terrible broken-down woman. As Major Carruthers gazed at him, he became conscious of the strained lines on his own face, and tried to loosen himself, because he took so badly what this man bore so well.

'You can't keep a wife and children in such conditions.'

'We were living in a tent in the bush on mealie meal and what I shot for nine months, and that was through the wet season,' said Van Heerden drily.

Major Carruthers knew he was beaten. 'You've put me in a false position, Van Heerden,' he said angrily. 'You know I can't afford to give you more money. I don't know where I'm going to find my own children's school fees, as it is. I told you the position when you came. I can't afford to keep a man with such a family.'

'Nobody can afford to have me either,' said Van Heerden sullenly.

'How can I have you living on my place in such a fashion? Nine children! They should be at school. Didn't you know there is a law to make them go to school? Hasn't anybody been to see you about them?'

'They haven't got me yet. They won't get me unless someone tells them.'

Against this challenge, which was also an unwilling appeal, Major Carruthers remained silent, until he said brusquely: 'Remember, I'm not responsible.' And he walked off, with all the appearance of anger.

Van Heerden looked after him, his face puzzled. He did not know whether or not he had been dismissed. After a few moments he moistened his dry lips with his tongue, wiped his hand again over his eyes, and turned back to the ox. Looking over his shoulder from the edge of the field, Major Carruthers could see his wiry stocky figure leaping and bending about the ox whose bellowing made the whole farm ring with anger.

Major Carruthers decided, once and for all, to put the family out of his mind. But they haunted him; he even dreamed of them; and he could not determine whether it was his own or the Dutchman's children who filled his sleep with fear.

It was a very busy time of the year. Harassed, like all his fellow-farmers, by labour difficulties, apportioning out the farm tasks was a daily problem. All day his mind churned slowly over the necessities; this fencing was urgent, that field must be reaped at once. Yet, in spite of this, he decided it was his plain duty to build a second hut beside the first. It would do no more than take the edge off the discomfort of that miserable family, but he knew he could not rest until it was built.

Just as he had made up his mind and was wondering how the thing could be managed, the bossboy came to him, saying that unless the Dutchman went, he and his friends would leave the farm.

'Why?' asked Major Carruthers, knowing what the answer would be. Van Heerden was a hard worker, and the cattle were improving week by week under his care, but he could not handle natives. He shouted at them, lost his temper, treated them like dogs. There was continual friction.

'Dutchmen are no good,' said the bossboy simply, voicing the hatred of the black man for that section of the white people he considers his most brutal oppressors.

Now, Major Carruthers was proud that at a time when most farmers were forced to buy labour from the contractors, he was able to attract sufficient voluntary labour to run his farm. He was a good employer, proud of his reputation for fair dealing. Many of his natives had been with him for years, taking a few months off occasionally for a rest in their kraals, but always returning to him. His neighbours were complaining of the sullen attitude of their labourers: so far Major Carruthers had kept this side of that form of passive resistance which could ruin a farmer. It was walking on a knife-edge, but his simple human relationship with his workers was his greatest asset as a farmer, and he knew it.

He stood and thought, while his bossboy, who had been on this farm twelve years, waited for a reply. A great deal was at stake. For a moment Major Carruthers thought of dismissing the Dutchman; he realized he could not bring himself to do it: what would happen to all those children? He decided on a course which was repugnant to him. He was going to appeal to his employee's pity.

'I have always treated you square?' he asked. 'I've always helped you when you were in trouble?'

The bossboy immediately and warmly assented.

'You know that my wife is ill, and that I'm having a lot of trouble just now? I don't want the Dutchman to go, just now when the work is so heavy. I'll speak to him, and if there is any more trouble with the men, then come to me and I'll deal with it myself.'

It was a glittering blue day, with a chill edge on the air, that stirred Major Carruthers' thin blood as he stood, looking in appeal into the sullen face of the native. All at once, feeling the fresh air wash along his cheeks, watching the leaves shake with a ripple of gold on the trees down the slope, he felt superior to his difficulties and able to face anything. 'Come,' he said, with his rare, diffident smile. 'After all these years, when we have been working together for so long, surely you can do this for me. It won't be for very long.'

He watched the man's face soften in response to his own; and wondered at the unconscious use of the last phrase, for there was no reason, on the face of things, why the situation should not continue as it was for a very long time.

They began laughing together; and separated cheerfully; the African shaking his head ruefully over the magnitude of the sacrifice asked of him, thus making the incident into a joke; and he dived off into the bush to explain the position to his fellow-workers.

Repressing a strong desire to go after him, to spend the lovely fresh day walking for pleasure, Major Carruthers went into his wife's bedroom, inexplicably confident and walking like a young man.

She lay as always, face to the wall, her protruding shoulders visible beneath the cheap pink bed-jacket he had bought for her illness. She seemed neither better nor worse. But as she turned her head, his buoyancy infected her a little; perhaps, too, she was conscious of the exhilarating day outside her gloomy curtains.

What kind of a miraculous release was she waiting for? he wondered, as he delicately adjusted her sheets and pillows and laid his hand gently on her head. Over the bony cage of the skull, the skin was papery and bluish. What was she thinking? He had a vision of her brain as a small frightened animal pulsating under his fingers.

With her eyes still closed, she asked in her querulous thin voice: 'Why don't you write to George?'

Involuntarily his fingers contracted on her hair, caused her to start and to open her reproachful, red-rimmed eyes. He waited for her usual appeal: the children, my health, our future. But she sighed and remained silent, still loyal to the man she had imagined she was marrying; and he could feel her thinking: *the lunatic stiff pride of men*.

Understanding that for her it was merely a question of waiting for his defeat, as her deliverance, he withdrew his hand, in dislike of her, saying: 'Things are not as bad as that yet.' The cheerfulness of his voice was genuine, holding still the courage and hope instilled into him by the bright day outside.

'Why, what has happened?' she asked swiftly, her voice suddenly strong, looking at him in hope.

'Nothing,' he said; and the depression settled down over him again. Indeed, nothing had happened; and his confidence was a trick of the nerves. Soberly he left the bedroom, thinking: I must get that well built; and when that is done, I must do the drains and then . . . He was thinking, too, that all these things must wait for the second hut.

Oddly, the comparatively small problem of that hut occupied his mind during the next few days. A slow and careful man, he set milestones for himself and overtook them one by one.

Since Christmas the labourers had been working a seven-day week in order to keep ahead in the race against the weeds. They resented it, of course, but that was the custom. Now that the maize was grown, they expected work to slack off, they expected their Sundays to be restored to them. To ask even half a dozen of them to sacrifice their weekly holiday for the sake of the hated Dutchman might precipitate a crisis. Major Carruthers took his time, stalking his opportunity like a hunter, until one evening he was talking with his bossboy as man to man, about farm problems; but when he broached the subject of a hut, Major Carruthers saw that it would be as he feared: the man at once turned stiff and unhelpful. Suddenly impatient, he said: 'It must be done next Sunday. Six men could finish it in a day, if they worked hard.'

The black man's glance became veiled and hostile. Responding to the authority in the voice he replied simply: 'Yes, baas.' He was accepting the order from above, and refusing responsibility: his co-operation was switched off: he had become a machine for transmitting orders. Nothing exasperated Major Carruthers more than when this happened.

He said sternly: 'I'm not having any nonsense. If that hut isn't built, there'll be trouble.'

'Yes, baas,' said the bossboy again. He walked away, stopped some natives who were coming off the fields with their hoes over their shoulders, and transmitted the order in a neutral voice. Major Carruthers saw them glance at him in fierce antagonism; then they turned away their heads, and walked off, in a group, towards their compound.

It would be all right, he thought, in disproportionate relief. It would be difficult to say exactly what it was he feared, for the question of the hut had loomed so huge in his mind that he was beginning to feel an almost superstitious foreboding. Driven downwards through failure after failure, fate was becoming real to him as a cold malignant force; the careful balancing of unfriendly probabilities that underlay all his planning had developed in him an acute sensitivity to the future; and he had learned to respect his dreams and omens. Now he wondered at the strength of his desire to see that hut built, and whatever danger it represented behind him.

He went to the clearing to find Van Heerden and tell him what had been planned. He found him sitting on a candle-box in the doorway of the hut, playing good-humouredly with his children, as if they had been puppies, tumbling them over, snapping his fingers in their faces, and laughing outright with boyish exuberance when one little boy squared up his fists at him in a moment of temper against this casual, almost contemptuous treatment of them. Major Carruthers heard that boyish laugh with amazement; he looked blankly at the young Dutchman, and then from him to his wife, who was standing, as usual, over a petrol tin that balanced on the small fire. A smell of meat and pumpkin filled the clearing. The woman seemed to Major Carruthers less a human being than the expression of an elemental, irrepressible force: he saw her, in her vast sagging fleshiness, with her slow stupid face, her instinctive responses to her children, whether for affection or temper, as the symbol of fecundity, a strong, irresistible heave of matter. She frightened him. He turned his eyes from her

21

and explained to Van Heerden that a second hut would be built here, beside the existing one.

Van Heerden was pleased. He softened into quick confiding friendship. He looked doubtfully behind him at the small hut that sheltered eleven human beings, and said that it was really not easy to live in such a small space with so many children. He glanced at the children, cuffing them affectionately as he spoke, smiling like a boy. He was proud of his family, of his own capacity for making children: Major Carruthers could see that. Almost, he smiled; then he glanced through the doorway at the grey squalor of the interior and hurried off, resolutely preventing himself from dwelling on the repulsive facts that such close-packed living implied.

The next Saturday evening he and Van Heerden paced the clearing with tape measure and spirit level, determining the area of the new hut. It was to be a large one. Already the sheaves of thatching grass had been stacked ready for the next day, shining brassily in the evening sun; and the thorn poles for the walls lay about the clearing, stripped of bark, the smooth inner wood showing white as kernels.

Major Carruthers was waiting for the natives to come up from the compound for the building before daybreak that Sunday. He was there even before the family woke, afraid that without his presence something might go wrong. He feared the Dutchman's temper because of the labourers' sulky mood.

He leaned against a tree, watching the bush come awake, while the sky flooded slowly with light, and the birds sang about him. The hut was, for a long time, silent and dark. A sack hung crookedly over the door, and he could glimpse huddled shapes within. It seemed to him horrible, a stinking kennel shrinking ashamedly to the ground away from the wide hall of fresh blue sky. Then a child came out, and another; soon they were spilling out of the doorway, in their little rags of dresses, or hitching khaki pants up over the bony jut of a hip. They smiled shyly at him, offering him friendship. Then came the woman, moving sideways to ease herself through the narrow door-frame – she was so huge it was almost a fit. She lumbered slowly, thick and stupid with sleep, over to the cold fire, raising her arms in a yawn, so that wisps of dull yellow hair fell over her shoulders and her dark slack dress lifted in creases under her neck. Then she saw Major Carruthers and smiled at him. For the first time he saw her as a human being and not as something fatally ugly. There was something shy, yet frank, in that smile; so that he could imagine the strong, laughing adolescent girl, with the frank, inviting, healthy sensuality of the young Dutchwoman – so she had been when she married Van Heerden. She stooped painfully to stir up the ashes, and soon the fire spurted up under the leaning patch of tin roof. For a while Van Heerden did not appear; neither did the natives who were supposed to be here a long while since; Major Carruthers continued to lean against a tree, smiling at the children, who nevertheless kept their distance from him, unable to play naturally because of his presence there, smiling at Mrs Van Heerden who was throwing handfuls of mealie meal into a petrol tin of boiling water, to make native-style porridge.

It was just on eight o'clock, after two hours of impatient waiting, that the labourers filed up the bushy incline, with the axes and picks over their shoulders, avoiding his eyes. He pressed down his anger: after all it was Sunday, and they had had no day off for weeks; he could not blame them.

They began by digging the circular trench that would hold the wall poles. As their picks rang out on the pebbly ground, Van Heerden came out of the hut, pushing aside the dangling sack with one hand and pulling up his trousers with the other, yawning broadly, then smiling at Major Carruthers apologetically. 'I've had my sleep out,' he said; he seemed to think his employer might be angry.

Major Carruthers stood close over the workers, wanting it to be understood by them and by Van Heerden that he was responsible. He was too conscious of their resentment, and knew that they would scamp the work if possible. If the hut was to be completed as planned, he would need all his tact and good-humour. He stood there patiently all morning, watching

23

the thin sparks flash up as the picks swung into the flinty earth. Van Heerden lingered nearby, unwilling to be thus publicly superseded in the responsibility for his own dwelling in the eyes of the natives.

When they flung down their picks and went to fetch the poles, they did so with a side glance at Major Carruthers, challenging him to say the trench was not deep enough. He called them back, laughingly, saying: 'Are you digging for a dog-kennel then, and not a hut for a man?' One smiled unwillingly in response; the other sulked. Perfunctorily they deepened the trench to the very minimum that Major Carruthers was likely to pass. By noon, the poles were leaning drunkenly in place, and the natives were stripping the binding from beneath the bark of nearby trees. Long fleshy strips of fibre, rose-coloured and apricot and yellow, lay tangled over the grass, and the wounded trees showed startling red gashes around the clearing. Swiftly the poles were laced together with natural rope, so that when the frame was complete it showed up against green trees and sky like a slender gleaming white cage, interwoven lightly with rosy-yellow. Two natives climbed on top to bind the roof poles into their conical shape, while the others stamped a slushy mound of sand and earth to form plaster for the walls. Soon they stopped – the rest could wait until after the midday break.

Worn out by the strain of keeping the balance between the fiery Dutchman and the resentful workers, Major Carruthers went off home to eat. He had one and a half hour's break. He finished his meal in ten minutes, longing to be able to sleep for once till he woke naturally. His wife was dozing, so he lay down on the other bed and at once dropped off to sleep himself. When he woke it was long after the time he had set himself. It was after three. He rose in a panic and strode to the clearing, in the grip of one of his premonitions.

There stood the Dutchman, in a flaring temper, shouting at the natives who lounged in front of him, laughing openly. They had only just returned to work. As Major Carruthers approached, he saw Van Heerden using his open palms in a series of quick swinging slaps against their faces, knocking them sideways against each other: it was as if he were cuffing his own children in a fit of anger. Major Carruthers broke into a run, erupting into the group before anything else could happen. Van Heerden fell back on seeing him. He was beef-red with fury. The natives were bunched together, on the point of throwing down their tools and walking off the job.

'Get back to work,' snapped Major Carruthers to the men: and to Van Heerden: 'I'm dealing with this.' His eyes were an appeal to recognize the need for tact, but Van Heerden stood squarely there in front of him, on planted legs, breathing heavily. 'But Major Carruthers . . .' he began, implying that as a white man, with his employer not there, it was right that he should take the command. 'Do as I say,' said Major Carruthers. Van Heerden, with a deadly look at his opponents, swung on his heel and marched off into the hut. The slapping swing of the grain-bag was as if a door had been slammed. Major Carruthers turned to the natives. 'Get on,' he ordered briefly, in a calm decisive voice. There was a moment of uncertainty. Then they picked up their tools and went to work.

Some laced the framework of the roof; others slapped the mud on to the walls. This business of plastering was usually a festival, with laughter and raillery, for there were gaps between the poles, and a handful of mud could fly through a space into the face of a man standing behind: the thing could become a game, like children playing snowballs. Today there was no pretence at good-humour. When the sun went down the men picked up their tools and filed off into the bush without a glance at Major Carruthers. The work had not prospered. The grass was laid untidily over the roof-frame, still uncut and reaching to the ground in long swatches. The first layer of mud had been unevenly flung on. It would be a shabby building.

His own fault, thought Major Carruthers, sending his slow, tired blue glance to the hut where the Dutchman was still cherishing the seeds of wounded pride. Next day, when Major Carruthers was in another part of the farm, the Dutchman got his own back in a fine flaming scene with the ploughboys: they came to complain to the bossboy, but not to Major Carruthers. This made him uneasy. All that week he waited for fresh complaints about the Dutchman's behaviour. So much was he keyed up, waiting for the scene between himself and a grudging bossboy, that when nothing happened his apprehensions deepened into a deep foreboding.

The building was finished the following Sunday. The floors were stamped hard with new dung, the thatch trimmed, and the walls grained smooth. Another two weeks must elapse before the family could move in, for the place smelled of damp. They were weeks of worry for Major Carruthers. It was unnatural for the Africans to remain passive and sullen under the Dutchman's handling of them, and especially when they knew he was on their side. There was something he did not like in the way they would not meet his eyes and in the over-polite attitude of the bossboy.

The beautiful clear weather that he usually loved so much, May weather, sharpened by cold, and crisp under deep clear skies, pungent with gusts of wind from the drying leaves and grasses of the veld, was spoilt for him this year: something was going to happen.

When the family eventually moved in, Major Carruthers became discouraged because the building of the hut had represented such trouble and worry, while now things seemed hardly better than before: what was the use of two small round huts for a family of eleven? But Van Heerden was very pleased, and expressed his gratitude in a way that moved Major Carruthers deeply: unable to show feeling himself, he was grateful when others did, so relieving him of the burden of his shyness. There was a ceremonial atmosphere on the evening when one of the great sagging beds was wrenched out of the floor of the first hut and its legs plastered down newly into the second hut.

That very same night he was awakened towards dawn by voices calling to him from outside his window. He started up, knowing that whatever he had dreaded was here, glad that the tension was over. Outside the back door stood his bossboy, holding a hurricane lamp which momentarily blinded Major Carruthers.

'The hut is on fire.'

Blinking his eyes, he turned to look. Away in the darkness flames were lapping over the trees, outlining branches so that as a gust of wind lifted them patterns of black leaves showed clear and fine against the flowing red light of the fire. The veld was illuminated with a fitful plunging glare. The two men ran off into the bush down the rough road, towards the blaze.

The clearing was lit up, as bright as morning, when they arrived. On the roof of the first hut squatted Van Heerden, lifting tins of water from a line of natives below, working from the water-butt, soaking the thatch to prevent it catching the flames from the second hut that was only a few yards off. That was a roaring pillar of fire. Its frail skeleton was still erect, but twisting and writhing incandescently within its envelope of flame, and it collapsed slowly as he came up, subsiding in a crash of sparks.

'The children,' gasped Major Carruthers to Mrs Van Heerden, who was watching the blaze fatalistically from where she sat on a scattered bundle of bedding, the tears soaking down her face, her arms tight round a swathed child.

As he spoke she opened the cloths to display the smallest infant. A swathe of burning grass from the roof had fallen across its head and shoulders. He sickened as he looked, for there was nothing but raw charred flesh. But it was alive: the limbs still twitched a little.

'I'll get the car and we'll take it in to the doctor.'

He ran out of the clearing and fetched the car. As he tore down the slope back again he saw he was still in his pyjamas, and when he gained the clearing for the second time, Van Heerden was climbing down from the roof, which dripped water as if there had been a storm. He bent over the burnt child.

'Too late,' he said.

'But it's still alive.'

Van Heerden almost shrugged; he appeared dazed. He continually turned his head to survey the glowing heap that had so recently sheltered his children. He licked his lips with a quick unconscious movement, because of their burning dryness. His face was grimed with smoke and inflamed from the great heat, so that his young eyes showed startlingly clear against the black skin.

'Get into the car,' said Major Carruthers to the woman. She automatically moved towards the car, without looking at her husband, who said: 'But it's too late, man.'

Major Carruthers knew the child would die, but his protest against the waste and futility of the burning expressed itself in this way: that everything must be done to save this life, even against hope. He started the car and slid off down the hill. Before they had gone half a mile he felt his shoulder plucked from behind, and, turning, saw the child was now dead. He reversed the car into the dark bush off the road, and drove back to the clearing. Now the woman had begun wailing, a soft, monotonous, almost automatic sound that kept him tight in his seat, waiting for the next cry.

The fire was now a dark heap, fanning softly to a glowing red as the wind passed over it. The children were standing in a half-circle, gazing fascinated at it. Van Heerden stood near them, laying his hands gently, restlessly, on their heads and shoulders, reassuring himself of their existence there, in the flesh and living, beside him.

Mrs Van Heerden got clumsily out of the car, still wailing, and disappeared into the hut, clutching the bundled dead child.

Feeling out of place among that bereaved family, Major Carruthers went up to his house, where he drank cup after cup of tea, holding himself tight and controlled, conscious of over-strained nerves.

Then he stooped into his wife's room, which seemed small and dark and airless. The cave of a sick animal, he thought, in disgust; then, ashamed of himself, he returned out of doors, where the sky was filling with light. He sent a message for the bossboy, and waited for him in a condition of tensed anger.

When the man came Major Carruthers asked immediately: 'Why did that hut burn?'

The bossboy looked at him straight and said: 'How should I know?' Then, after a pause, with guileful innocence: 'It was the fault of the kitchen, too close to the thatch.'

Major Carruthers glared at him, trying to wear down the straight gaze with his own accusing eyes.

'That hut must be rebuilt at once. It must be rebuilt today.'

The bossboy seemed to say that it was a matter of indifference to him whether it was rebuilt or not. 'I'll go and tell the others,' he said, moving off.

'Stop,' barked Major Carruthers. Then he paused, frightened, not so much at his rage, but his humiliation and guilt. He had foreseen it! He had foreseen it all! And yet, that thatch could so easily have caught alight from the small incautious fire that sent up sparks all day so close to it.

Almost, he burst out in wild reproaches. Then he pulled himself together and said: 'Get away from me.' What was the use? He knew perfectly well that one of the Africans whom Van Heerden had kicked or slapped or shouted at had fired that hut; no one could ever prove it.

He stood quite still, watching the bossboy move off, tugging at the long wisps of his moustache in frustrated anger.

And what would happen now?

He ordered breakfast, drank a cup of tea, and spoilt a piece of toast. Then he glanced in again at his wife, who would sleep for a couple of hours yet.

Again tugging fretfully at his moustache, Major Carruthers set off for the clearing.

Everything was just as it had been, though the pile of black débris looked low and shabby now that morning had come and heightened the wild colour of sky and bush. The children were playing nearby, their hands and faces black, their rags of clothing black – everything seemed patched and smudged with black, and on one side the trees hung withered and grimy and the soil was hot underfoot.

Van Heerden leaned against the framework of the first hut. He looked subdued and tired, but otherwise normal. He greeted Major Carruthers, and did not move.

'How is your wife?' asked Major Carruthers. He could hear a moaning sound from inside the hut.

'She's doing well.'

Major Carruthers imagined her weeping over the dead child; and said: 'I'll take your baby into town for you and arrange for the funeral.'

Van Heerden said: 'I've buried her already.' He jerked his thumb at the bush behind them.

'Didn't you register its birth?'

Van Heerden shook his head. His gaze challenged Major Carruthers as if to say: Who's to know if no one tells them? Major Carruthers could not speak: he was held in silence by the thought of that charred little body, huddled into a packing-case or wrapped in a piece of cloth, thrust into the ground, at the mercy of wild animals or of white ants.

'Well, one comes and another goes,' said Van Heerden at last, slowly reaching out for philosophy as a comfort, while his eyes filled with rough tears.

Major Carruthers stared: he could not understand. At last the meaning of the words came into him, and he heard the moaning from the hut with a new understanding.

The idea had never entered his head; it had been a complete failure of the imagination. If nine children, why not ten? Why not fifteen, for that matter, or twenty? Of course there would be more children.

'It was the shock,' said Van Heerden. 'It should be next month.'

Major Carruthers leaned back against the wall of the hut and took out a cigarette clumsily. He felt weak. He felt as if Van Heerden had struck him, smiling. This was an absurd and unjust feeling, but for a moment he hated Van Heerden for standing there and saying: this grey country of poverty that you fear so much, will take on a different look when you actually enter it. You will cease to exist; there is no energy left, when one is wrestling naked, with life, for your kind of fine feelings and scruples and regrets.

'We hope it will be a boy,' volunteered Van Heerden, with a tentative friendliness, as if he thought it might be considered a familiarity to offer his private emotions to Major Carruthers. 'We have five boys and four girls – three girls,' he corrected himself, his face contracting.

Major Carruthers asked stiffly: 'Will she be all right?'

'I do it,' said Van Heerden. 'The last was born in the middle of the night, when it was raining. That was when we were in the tent. It's nothing to her,' he added, with pride. He was listening, as he spoke, to the slow moaning from inside. 'I'd better be getting in to her,' he said, knocking out his pipe against the mud of the walls. Nodding to Major Carruthers, he lifted the sack and disappeared.

After a while Major Carruthers gathered himself together and forced himself to walk erect across the clearing under the curious gaze of the children. His mind was fixed and numb, but he walked as if moving to a destination. When he reached the house, he at once pulled paper and pen towards him and wrote, and each slow difficult word was a nail in the coffin of his pride as a man.

Some minutes later he went in to his wife. She was awake, turned on her side, watching the door for the relief of his coming. 'I've written for a job at Home,' he said simply, laying his hand on her thin dry wrist, and feeling the slow pulse beat up suddenly against his palm.

He watched curiously as her face crumpled and the tears of thankfulness and release ran slowly down her cheeks and soaked the pillow.

The Nuisance

Two narrow tracks, one of them deepened to a smooth dusty groove by the incessant padding of bare feet, wound from the farm compound to the old well through half a mile of tall blond grass that was soiled and matted because of the nearness of the clustering huts: the compound had been on that ridge for twenty years.

The native women with their children used to loiter down the track, and their shrill laughter and chattering sounded through the trees as if one might suddenly have come on a flock of brilliant noisy parrots. It seemed as if fetching water was more of a social event to them than a chore. At the well itself they would linger half the morning, standing in groups to gossip, their arms raised in that graceful, eternally moving gesture to steady glittering or rusted petrol tins balanced on head-rings woven of grass; kneeling to slap bits of bright cloth on slabs of stone blasted long ago from the depths of earth. Here they washed and scolded and dandled their children. Here they scrubbed their pots. Here they sluiced themselves and combed their hair.

Coming upon them suddenly there would be sharp exclamations; a glimpse of soft brown shoulders and thighs withdrawing to the bushes, or annoyed and resentful eyes. It was their well. And while they were there, with their laughter, and gossip and singing, their folded draperies, bright armbands, earthenware jars and metal combs, grouped in attitudes of head-slowed indolence, it seemed as if the bellowing of distant cattle, drone of tractor, all the noises of the farm, were simply lending themselves to form a background to this antique scene: Women, drawing water at the well.

When they left the ground would be scattered with the

bright-pink, fleshy skins of the native wild-plum which contracts the mouth shudderingly with its astringency, or with the shiny green fragments of the shells of kaffir oranges.

Without the women the place was ugly, paltry. The windlass, coiled with greasy rope, propped for safety with a forked stick, was sheltered by a tiny cock of thatch that threw across the track a long, intensely black shadow. For the rest, veld; the sere, flattened, sun-dried veld.

They were beautiful, these women. But she whom I thought of vaguely as 'The cross-eyed one', offended the sight. She used to lag behind the others on the road, either by herself, or in charge of the older children. Not only did she suffer from a painful squint, so that when she looked towards you it was with a confused glare of white eyeball; but her body was hideous. She wore the traditional dark-patterned blue stuff looped at the waist, and above it her breasts were loose, flat crinkling triangles.

She was a solitary figure at the well, doing her washing unaided and without laughter. She would strain at the windlass during the long slow ascent of the swinging bucket that clanged sometimes, far below, against the sides of naked rock until at that critical moment when it hung vibrating at the mouth of the well, she would set the weight of her shoulder in the crook of the handle and with a fearful snatching movement bring the water to safety. It would slop over, dissolving in a shower of great drops that fell tinkling to disturb the surface of that tiny, circular, dully-gleaming mirror which lay at the bottom of the plunging rock tunnel. She was clumsy. Because of her eyes her body lumbered.

She was the oldest wife of 'The Long One', who was our most skilful driver.

'The Long One' was not so tall as he was abnormally thin. It was the leanness of those driven by inner restlessness. He could never keep still. His hands plucked at pieces of grass, his shoulder twitched to a secret rhythm of the nerves. Set a-top of that sinewy, narrow, taut body was a narrow head, with wide-pointed ears, which give him an appearance of alert caution.

The expression of the face was always violent, whether he was angry, laughing, or – most usually – sardonically critical. He had a tongue that was feared by every labourer on the farm. Even my father would smile ruefully after an altercation with his driver and say: 'He's a man, that native. One must respect him, after all. He never lets you get away with anything.'

In his own line he was an artist – his line being cattle. He handled oxen with a delicate brutality that was fascinating and horrifying to watch. Give him a bunch of screaming, rearing three-year-olds, due to take their first taste of the yoke, and he would fight them for hours under a blistering sun with the sweat running off him, his eyes glowing with a wicked and sombre satisfaction. Then he would use his whip, grunting savagely as the lash cut down into flesh, his tongue stuck calculatingly between his teeth as he measured the exact weight of the blow. But to watch him handle a team of sixteen fat tamed oxen was a different thing. It was like watching a circus act; there was the same suspense in it: it was a matter of pride to him that he did not need to use the whip. This did not by any means imply that he wished to spare the beasts pain, not at all; he liked to feed his pride on his own skill. Alongside the double line of ponderous cattle that strained across acres of heavy clods, danced, raved and screamed the Long One, with his twelve-foot-long lash circling in black patterns over their backs; and though his threatening yells were the yells of an inspired madman, and the heavy whip could be heard clean across the farm, so that on a moonlight night when they were ploughing late it sounded like the crack and whine of a rifle, never did the dangerous metal-tipped lash so much as touch a hair of their hides. If you examined the oxen as they were outspanned, they might be exhausted, driven to staggering-point, so that my father had to remonstrate, but there was never a mark on them.

'He knows how to handle oxen, but he can't handle his woman.'

We gave our natives labels such as that, since it was impossible ever to know them as their fellows knew them, in the round. That phrase summarized for us what the Long One offered in entertainment during the years he was with us. Coming back to the farm, after an absence, one would say in humorous anticipation: 'And what has the Long One been up to now, with his harem?'

There was always trouble with his three wives. He used to come up to the house to discuss with my father, man to man, how the youngest wife was flirting with the bossboy from the neighbouring compound, six miles off; or how she had thrown a big pot of smoking mealie-pap at the middle wife, who was jealous of her.

We grew accustomed to the sight of the Long One standing at the back door, at the sunset hour, when my father held audience after work. He always wore long khaki trousers that slipped down over thin bony hips, and went bare-chested, and there would be a ruddy gleam on his polished black skin, and his spindly gesticulating form would be outlined against a sea of fiery colours. At the end of his tale of complaint he would relapse suddenly into a pose of resignation that was self-consciously weary. My father used to laugh until his face was wet and say: 'That man is a natural-born comedian. He would have been on the stage if he had been born another colour.'

But he was no buffoon. He would play up to my father's appreciation of the comic, but he would never play the ape, as some Africans did, for our amusement. And he was certainly no figure of fun to his fellows. That same thing in him that sat apart, watchfully critical, even of himself, gave his humour its mordancy, his tongue its sting. And he was terribly attractive to his women. I have seen him slouch down the road on his way from one team to another, his whip trailing behind in the dust, his trousers sagging in folds from hip-bone to ankle, his eyes broodingly directed in front of him, merely nodding as he passed a group of women among whom might be his wives. And it was as if he had lashed them with that whip. They would bridle and writhe; and then call provocatively after him, but with a note of real anger, to make him notice them. He would not so much as turn his head.

When the real trouble started, though, my father soon got tired of it. He liked to be amused, not seriously implicated in his labourers' problems. The Long One took to coming up not occasionally, as he had been used to do, but every evening. He was deadly serious, and very bitter. He wanted my father to persuade the old wife, the cross-eyed one, to go back home to her own people. The woman was driving him crazy. A nagging woman in your house was like having a flea on your body; you could scratch but it always moved to another place, and there was no peace till you killed it.

'But you can't send her back, just because you are tired of her.'

The Long One said his life had become insupportable. She grumbled, she sulked, she spoilt his food.

'Well, then your other wives can cook for you.'

But it seemed there were complications. The two younger women hated each other, but they were united in one thing, that the old wife should stay, for she was so useful. She looked after the children, she did the hoeing in the garden; she picked relishes from the veld. Besides, she provided endless amusement with her ungainliness. She was the eternal butt, the fool, marked by fate for the entertainment of the whole-limbed and the comely.

My father referred at this point to a certain handbook on native lore, which stated definitively that an elder wife was entitled to be waited on by a young wife, perhaps as compensation for having to give up the pleasures of her lord's favour. The Long One and his ménage cut clean across this amiable theory. And my father, being unable to find a prescribed remedy (as one might look for a cure for a disease in a pharmacopoeia) grew angry. After some weeks of incessant complaint from the Long One he was told to hold his tongue and manage his women himself. That evening the man stalked furiously down the path, muttering to himself between teeth clenched on a grass-stem, on his way home to his two giggling younger wives and the ugly sour-faced old woman, the mother of his elder children, the drudge of his household and the scourge of his life.

It was some weeks later that my father asked casually one day: 'And by the way, Long One, how are things with you? All right again?'

And the Long One answered simply: 'Yes, baas. She's gone away.'

'What do you mean, gone away?'

The Long One shrugged. She had just gone. She had left suddenly, without saying anything to anyone.

Now, the woman came from Nyasaland, which was days and days of weary walking away. Surely she hadn't gone by herself? Had a brother or an uncle come to fetch her? Had she gone with a band of passing Africans on their way home?

My father wondered a little, and then forgot about it. It wasn't his affair. He was pleased to have his most useful native back at work with an unharassed mind. And he was particularly pleased that the whole business was ended before the annual trouble over the water-carrying.

For there were two wells. The new one, used by ourselves, had fresh sparkling water that was sweet in the mouth; but in July of each year it ran dry. The water of the old well had a faintly unpleasant taste and was pale brown, but there was always plenty of it. For three or four months of the year, depending on the rains, we shared that well with the compound.

Now, the Long One hated fetching water three miles, four times a week, in the water-cart. The women of the compound disliked having to arrange their visits to the well so as not to get in the way of the water-carriers. There was always grumbling.

This year we had not even begun to use the old well when complaints started that the water tasted bad. The big baas must get the well cleaned.

My father said vaguely that he would clean the well when he had time.

Next day there came a deputation from the women of the

compound. Half a dozen of them stood at the back door, arguing that if the well wasn't cleaned soon, all their children would be sick.

'I'll do it next week,' he promised, with bad grace.

The following morning the Long One brought our first load of the season from the old well; and as we turned the taps on the barrels a foetid smell began to pervade the house. As for drinking it, that was out of the question.

'Why don't you keep the cover on the well?' my father said to the women, who were still loitering resentfully at the back door. He was really angry. 'Last time the well was cleaned there were fourteen dead rats and a dead snake. We never get things in our well because we remember to keep the lid on.'

But the women appeared to consider the lid being on, or off, was an act of God, and nothing to do with them.

We always went down to watch the well-emptying, which had the fascination of a ritual. Like the mealie-shelling, or the first rains, it marked a turning point in the year. It seemed as if a besieged city were laying plans for the conservation of supplies. The sap was falling in tree and grass-root; the sun was withdrawing high, high, behind a veil of smoke and dust; the fierce dryness of the air was a new element, parching foliage as the heat cauterized it. The well-emptying was an act of faith, and of defiance. For a whole afternoon there would be no water on the farm at all. One well was completely dry. And this one would be drained, dependent on the mysterious ebbing and flowing of underground rivers. What if they should fail us? There was an anxious evening, every year; and in the morning, when the Long One stood at the back door and said, beaming, that the bucket was bringing up fine new water, it was like a festival.

But this afternoon we could not stick it out. The smell was intolerable. We saw the usual complement of bloated rats, laid out on the stones around the well, and there was even the skeleton of a small buck that must have fallen in in the dark. Then we left, along the road that was temporarily a river whose source was that apparently endless succession of buckets, filled by greyish evil water.

It was the Long One himself that came to tell us the news. Afterwards we tried to remember what look that always expressive face wore as he told it.

It seemed that in the last bucket but one had floated a human arm, or rather the fragments of one. Piece by piece they had fetched her up, the Cross-eyed Woman, his own first wife. They recognized her by her bangles. Last of all, the Long One went down to fetch up her head, which was missing.

'I thought you said your wife had gone home?' said my father.

'I thought she had. Where else could she have gone?'

'Well,' said my father at last, disgusted by the whole thing, 'if she had to kill herself, why couldn't she hang herself on a tree, instead of spoiling the well?'

'She might have slipped and fallen,' said the Long One.

My father looked up at him suddenly. He stared for a few moments. Then: 'Ye-yes,' he said, 'I suppose she might.'

Later, we talked about the thing, saying how odd it was that natives should commit suicide; it seemed almost like an impertinence, as if they were claiming to have the same delicate feelings as ours.

But later still, apropos of nothing in particular, my father was heard to remark: 'Well, I don't know, I'm damned if I know, but in any case he's a damned good driver.'

The De Wets Come
to Kloof Grange

The verandah, which was lifted on stone pillars, jutted forward over the garden like a box in the theatre. Below were luxuriant masses of flowering shrubs, and creepers whose shiny leaves, like sequins, reflected light from a sky stained scarlet and purple and apple-green. This splendiferous sunset filled one half of the sky, fading gently through shades of mauve to a calm expanse of ruffling grey, blown over by tinted cloudlets; and in this still evening sky, just above a clump of darkening conifers, hung a small crystal moon.

There sat Major Gale and his wife, as they did every evening at this hour, side by side trimly in deck chairs, their sundowners on small tables at their elbows, critically watching, like connoisseurs, the pageant presented for them.

Major Gale said, with satisfaction: 'Good sunset tonight,' and they both turned their eyes to the vanquishing moon. The dusk drew veils across sky and garden; and punctually, as she did every day, Mrs Gale shook off nostalgia like a terrier shaking off water and rose, saying: 'Mosquitoes!' She drew her deck chair to the wall, where she neatly folded and stacked it.

'Here is the post,' she said, her voice quickening; and Major Gale went to the steps, waiting for the native who was hastening towards them through the tall shadowing bushes. He swung a sack from his back and handed it to Major Gale. A sour smell of raw meat rose from the sack. Major Gale said with the kindly contempt he used for his native servants: 'Did the spooks get you?' and laughed. The native, who had panted the last mile of his ten-mile journey through a bush filled with unnameable phantoms, ghosts of ancestors, wraiths of tree and beast, put on a pantomime of fear and chattered and shivered for a moment like an ape, to amuse his master. Major Gale dismissed the boy. He ducked thankfully around the corner of the house to the back, where there were lights and companionship.

Mrs Gale lifted the sack and went into the front room. There she lit the oil lamp and called for the houseboy, to whom she handed the groceries and meat for removal. She took a fat bundle of letters from the very bottom of the sack and wrinkled her nose slightly: blood from the meat had stained them. She sorted the letters into two piles; and then husband and wife sat themselves down opposite each other to read their mail.

It was more than the ordinary farm living-room. There were koodoo horns branching out over the fireplace, and a bundle of knobkerries hanging on a nail; but on the floor were fine rugs, and the furniture was two hundred years old. The table was a pool of softly-reflected lights; it was polished by Mrs Gale herself every day before she set on it an earthenware crock filled with thorny red flowers. Africa and the English eighteenth century mingled in this room and were at peace.

From time to time Mrs Gale rose impatiently to attend to the lamp, which did not burn well. It was one of those terrifying paraffin things that have to be pumped with air to a whiter-hot flame from time to time, and which in any case emit a continuous soft hissing noise. Above the heads of the Gales a light cloud of flying insects wooed their fiery death and dropped one by one, plop, plop, plop to the table among the letters.

Mrs Gale took an envelope from her own heap and handed it to her husband. 'The assistant,' she remarked abstractedly, her eyes bent on what she held. She smiled tenderly as she read. The letter was from her oldest friend, a woman doctor in London, and they had written to each other every week for thirty years, ever since Mrs Gale came to exile in Southern Rhodesia. She murmured half-aloud: 'Why, Betty's brother's daughter is going to study economics,' and though she had never met Betty's brother, let alone the daughter, the news seemed to please and excite her extraordinarily. The whole of the letter was about people she had never met and was not likely ever to meet – about the weather, about English politics. Indeed, there was not a sentence in it that would not have struck an outsider as having been written out of a sense of duty; but when Mrs Gale had finished reading it, she put it aside gently and sat smiling quietly: she had gone back half a century to her childhood.

Gradually sight returned to her eyes, and she saw her husband where previously she had sat looking through him. He appeared disturbed; there was something wrong about the letter from the assistant.

Major Gale was a tall and still military figure, even in his khaki bush-shirt and shorts. He changed them twice a day. His shorts were creased sharp as folded paper, and the six pockets of his shirt were always buttoned up tight. His small head, with its polished surface of black hair, his tiny jaunty black moustache, his farmer's hands with their broken but clean nails – all these seemed to say that it was no easy matter not to let oneself go, not to let this damned disintegrating gaudy, easy-going country get under one's skin. It wasn't easy, but he did it; he did it with the conscious effort that had slowed his movements and added the slightest touch of caricature to his appearance: one finds a man like Major Gale only in exile.

He rose from his chair and began pacing the room, while his wife watched him speculatively and waited for him to tell her what was the matter. When he stood up, there was something not quite right – what was it? Such a spruce and tailored man he was; but the disciplined shape of him was spoiled by a curious fatness and softness: the small rounded head was set on a thickening neck; the buttocks were fattening too, and quivered as he walked. Mrs Gale, as these facts assailed her, conscientiously excluded them: she had her own picture of her husband, and could not afford to have it destroyed.

At last he sighed, with a glance at her; and when she said: 'Well, dear?' he replied at once, 'The man has a wife.'

'Dear me!' she exclaimed, dismayed.

At once, as if he had been waiting for her protest, he

returned briskly: 'It will be nice for you to have another woman about the place.'

'Yes, I suppose it will,' she said humorously. At this most familiar note in her voice, he jerked his head up and said aggressively: 'You always complain I bury you alive.'

And so she did. Every so often, but not so often now, she allowed herself to overflow into a mood of gently humorous bitterness; but it had not carried conviction for many years; it was more, really, of an attention to him, like remembering to kiss him good night. In fact, she had learned to love her isolation, and she felt aggrieved that he did not know it.

'Well, but they can't come to the house. That I really couldn't put up with.' The plan had been for the new assistant – Major Gale's farming was becoming too successful and expanding for him to manage any longer by himself – to have the spare room, and share the house with his employers.

'No, I suppose not, if there's a wife.' Major Gale sounded doubtful; it was clear he would not mind another family sharing with them. 'Perhaps they could have the old house?' he enquired at last.

'I'll see to it,' said Mrs Gale, removing the weight of worry off her husband's shoulders. Things he could manage: people bothered him. That they bothered her, too, now, was something she had become resigned to his not understanding. For she knew he was hardly conscious of her; nothing existed for him outside his farm. And this suited her well. During the early years of their marriage, with the four children growing up, there was always a little uneasiness between them, like an unpaid debt. Now they were friends and could forget each other. What a relief when he no longer 'loved' her! (That was how she put it.) Ah, that 'love' – she thought of it with a small humorous distaste. Growing old had its advantages.

When she said, 'I'll see to it,' he glanced at her, suddenly, directly: her tone had been a little too comforting and maternal. Normally his gaze wavered over her, not seeing her. Now he really observed her for a moment; he saw an elderly Englishwoman, as thin and dry as a stalk of maize in

September, sitting poised over her letters, one hand touching them lovingly, and gazing at him with her small flower-blue eyes. A look of guilt in them troubled him. He crossed to her and kissed her cheek. 'There!' she said, inclining her face with a sprightly, fidgety laugh. Overcome with embarrassment he stopped for a moment, then said determinedly: 'I shall go and have my bath.'

After his bath, from which he emerged pink and shining like an elderly baby, dressed in flannels and a blazer, they ate their dinner under the wheezing oil lamp and the cloud of flying insects. Immediately the meal was over he said 'Bed,' and moved off. He was always in bed before eight and up by five. Once Mrs Gale had adapted herself to this routine. Now, with the four boys out sailing the seven seas in the navy, and nothing really to get her out of bed (her servants were perfectly trained), she slept until eight, when she joined her husband at breakfast. She refused to have that meal in bed; nor would she have dreamed of appearing in her dressing-gown. Even as things were she was guilty enough about sleeping those three daylight hours, and found it necessary to apologize for her slackness. So, when her husband had gone to bed she remained under the lamp, re-reading her letters, sewing, reading, or simply dreaming about the past, the very distant past, when she had been Caroline Morgan, living near a small country town, a country squire's daughter. That was how she liked best to think of herself.

Tonight she soon turned down the lamp and stepped on to the verandah. Now the moon was a large, soft, yellow fruit caught in the top branches of the blue-gums. The garden was filled with glamour, and she let herself succumb to it. She passed quietly down the steps and beneath the trees with one quick solicitous glance back at the bedroom window: her husband hated her to be out of the house by herself at night. She was on her way to the old house that lay half a mile distant over the veld.

Before the Gales had come to this farm, two brothers had it, South Africans by birth and upbringing. The houses had then been separated by a stretch of untouched bush, with not so much as a fence or a road between them; and in this state of guarded independence the two men had lived, both bachelors, both quite alone. The thought of them amused Mrs Gale. She could imagine them sending polite notes to each other, invitations to meals or to spend an evening. She imagined them loaning each other books by native bearer, meeting at a neutral point between their homes. She was amused, but she respected them for a feeling she could understand. She had made up all kinds of pretty ideas about these brothers, until one day she learned from a neighbour that in fact the two men had quarrelled continually, and had eventually gone bankrupt because they could not agree how the farm was to be run. After this discovery Mrs Gale ceased to think about them; a pleasant fancy had become a distasteful reality.

The first thing she did on arriving was to change the name of the farm from Kloof Nek to Kloof Grange, making a link with home. One of the houses was denuded of furniture and used as a storage space. It was a square, bare box of a place, stuck in the middle of the bare veld, and its shut windows flashed back light to the sun all day. But her own home had been added to and extended, and surrounded with verandahs and fenced; inside the fence were two acres of garden, that she had created over years of toil. And what a garden! These were what she lived for: her flowering African shrubs, her vivid English lawns, her water-garden with the goldfish and water lilies. Not many people had such a garden.

She walked through it this evening under the moon, feeling herself grow lightheaded and insubstantial with the influence of the strange greenish light, and of the perfumes from the flowers. She touched the leaves with her fingers as she passed, bending her face to the roses. At the gate, under the hanging white trumpets of the moonflower she paused, and lingered for a while, looking over the space of empty veld between her and the other house. She did not like going outside her garden at night. She was not afraid of natives, no:

she had contempt for women who were afraid, for she regarded Africans as rather pathetic children, and was very kind to them. She did not know what made her afraid. Therefore she took a deep breath, compressed her lips, and stepped carefully through the gate, shutting it behind her with a sharp click. The road before her was a glimmering white ribbon, the hard-crusted sand sending up a continuous small sparkle of light as she moved. On either side were sparse stumpy trees, and their shadows were deep and black. A nightjar cut across the stars with crooked trailing wings, and she set her mouth defiantly: why, this was only the road she walked over every afternoon, for her constitutional! These were the trees she had pleaded for, when her husband was wanting to have them cut for firewood: in a sense, they were her trees. Deliberately slowing her steps, as a discipline, she moved through the pits of shadow, gaining each stretch of clear moonlight with relief, until she came to the house. It looked dead, a dead thing with staring eyes, with those blank windows gleaming pallidly back at the moon. Nonsense, she told herself. Nonsense. And she walked to the front door, unlocked it, and flashed her torch over the floor. Sacks of grain were piled to the rafters, and the brick floor was scattered with loose mealies. Mice scurried invisibly to safety, and flocks of cockroaches blackened the walls. Standing in a patch of moonlight on the brick, so that she would not unwittingly walk into a spiderweb or a jutting sack she drew in deep breaths of the sweetish smell of maize, and made a list in her head of what had to be done; she was a very capable woman.

Then something struck her: if the man had forgotten, when applying for the job, to mention a wife, he was quite capable of forgetting children too. If they had children it wouldn't do; no, it wouldn't. She simply couldn't put up with a tribe of children – for Afrikaners never had less than twelve – running wild over her beautiful garden and teasing her goldfish. Anger spurted in her. De Wet – the name was hard on her tongue. Her husband should not have agreed to take on an Afrikaner. Really, really, Caroline, she chided herself humorously, standing there in the deserted moonlit house, don't jump to conclusions, don't be unfair.

She decided to arrange the house for a man and his wife, ignoring the possibility of children. She would arrange things, in kindness, for a woman who might be unused to living in loneliness; she would be good to this woman; so she scolded herself, to make atonement for her short fit of pettiness. But when she tried to form a picture of this woman who was coming to share her life, at least to the extent of taking tea with her in the mornings, and swapping recipes (so she supposed), imagination failed her. She pictured a large Dutch frau, all homely comfort and sweating goodness, and was repulsed. For the first time the knowledge that she must soon, next week, take another woman into her life, came home to her; and she disliked it intensely.

Why must she? Her husband would not have to make a friend of the man. They would work together, that was all; but because they, the wives, were two women on an isolated farm, they would be expected to live in each other's pockets. All her instincts towards privacy, the distance which she had put between herself and other people, even her own husband, rebelled against it. And because she rebelled, rejecting this imaginary Dutch woman, to whom she felt so alien, she began to think of her friend Betty, as if it were she who would be coming to the farm.

Still thinking of her friend Betty she returned through the silent veld to her home, imagining them walking together over this road and talking as they had been used to do. The thought of Betty, who had turned into a shrewd, elderly woman doctor with kind eyes, sustained her through the frightening silences. At the gate she lifted her head to sniff the heavy perfume of the moonflowers, and became conscious that something else was invading her dream: it was a very bad smell, an odour of decay mingled with the odour from the flowers. Something had died on the veld, and the wind had changed and was bringing the smell towards the house. She made a mental note: I must send the boy in the morning to see what it is. Then the conflict between her thoughts of her friend and her own life presented itself sharply to her. You are a silly woman, Caroline, she said to herself. Three years before they had gone on holiday to England, and she had found she and Betty had nothing to say to each other. Their lives were so far apart, and had been for so long, that the weeks they spent together were an offering to a friendship that had died years before. She knew it very well, but tried not to think of it. It was necessary to her to have Betty remain, in imagination at least, as a counter-weight to her loneliness. Now she was being made to realize the truth. She resented that too, and somewhere the resentment was chalked up against Mrs De Wet, the Dutch woman who was going to invade her life with impertinent personal claims.

And next day, and the days following, she cleaned and swept and tidied the old house, not for Mrs De Wet, but for Betty. Otherwise she could not have gone through with it. And when it was all finished she walked through the rooms which she had furnished with things taken from her own home, and said to a visionary Betty (but Betty as she had been thirty years before): 'Well, what do you think of it?' The place was bare but clean now, and smelling of sunlight and air. The floors had coloured coconut matting over the brick; the beds, standing on opposite sides of the room, were covered with gaily striped counterpanes. There were vases of flowers everywhere. 'You would like living here,' Mrs Gale said to Betty, before locking the house up and returning to her own, feeling as if she had won a victory over herself.

The De Wets sent a wire saying they would arrive on Sunday after lunch. Mrs Gale noted with annoyance that this would spoil her rest, for she slept every day, through the afternoon heat. Major Gale, for whom every day was a working day (he hated idleness and found odd jobs to occupy him on Sundays), went off to a distant part of the farm to look at his cattle. Mrs Gale laid herself down on her bed with her eyes shut and listened for a car, all her nerves stretched. Flies buzzed drowsily over the window-panes; the breeze from the garden was warm and scented. Mrs Gale slept uncomfortably, warring all the afternoon with the knowledge that she should be awake. When she woke at four she was cross and tired, and there was still no sign of a car. She rose and dressed herself, taking a frock from the cupboard without looking to see what it was: her clothes were often fifteen years old. She brushed her hair absentmindedly: and then, recalled by a sense that she had not taken enough trouble, slipped a large gold locket round her neck, as a conscientious mark of welcome. Then she left a message with the houseboy that she would be in the garden and walked away from the verandah with a strong excitement growing in her. This excitement rose as she moved through the crowding shrubs under the walls, through the rose garden with its wide green lawns where water sprayed all the year round, and arrived at her favourite spot among the fountains and the pools of water lilies. Her water-garden was an extravagance, for the pumping of the water from the river cost a great deal of money.

She sat herself on a shaded bench; and on one side were the glittering plumes of the fountains, the roses, the lawns, the house, and beyond them the austere wind-bitten high veld; on the other, at her feet, the ground dropped hundreds of feet sharply to the river. It was a rocky shelf thrust forward over the gulf, and here she would sit for hours, leaning dizzily outwards, her short grey hair blown across her face, lost in adoration of the hills across the river. Not of the river itself, no, she thought of that with a sense of danger, for there, below her, in that green-crowded gully, were suddenly the tropics: palm trees, a slow brown river that eddied into reaches of marsh or curved round belts of reeds twelve feet high. There were crocodiles, and leopards came from the rocks to drink. Sitting there on her exposed shelf, a smell of sun-warmed green, of hot decaying water, of luxurious growth, an intoxicating heady smell, rose in waves to her face. She had learned to ignore it, and to ignore the river, while she watched the hills. They were *her* hills: that was how she felt. For years she had sat here, hours every day, watching the cloud shadows move over them, watching them turn blue with distance or come close after rain so that she could see the exquisite brushwork of trees on the lower slopes. They were never the same half an hour together. Modulating light created them anew for her as she looked, thrusting one peak forward and withdrawing another, moving them back so that they were hazed on a smoky horizon, crouched in sullen retreat, or raising them so that they towered into a brillant cleansed sky. Sitting here, buffeted by winds, scorched by the sun or shivering with cold, she could challenge anything. They were her mountains; they were what she was; they had made her, had crystallized her loneliness into a strength, had sustained her and fed her.

And now she almost forgot the De Wets were coming, and were hours late. Almost, not quite. At last, understanding that the sun was setting (she could feel its warmth striking below her shoulders), her small irritation turned to anxiety. Something might have happened to them? They had taken the wrong road, perhaps? The car had broken down? And there was the Major, miles away with their own car, and so there was no means of looking for them. Perhaps she should send out natives along the roads? If they had taken the wrong turning, to the river, they might be bogged in mud to the axles. Down there, in the swampy heat, they could be bitten by mosquitoes and then . . .

Caroline, she said to herself severely (thus finally withdrawing from the mountains), don't let things worry you so. She stood up and shook herself, pushed her hair out of her face, and gripped her whipping skirts in a thick bunch. She stepped backwards away from the wind that raked the edges of the cliff, sighed a goodbye to her garden for that day, and returned to the house. There, outside the front door, was a car, an ancient jalopy bulging with luggage, its back doors tied with rope. And children! She could see a half-grown girl on the steps. No, really, it was too much. On the other side of the car stooped a tall, thin, fairheaded man, burnt as brown as toffee, looking for someone to come. He must be the father. She approached, adjusting her face to a smile, looking apprehensively about her for the children. The man slowly came forward, the girl after him. 'I expected you earlier,' began Mrs Gale briskly, looking reproachfully into the man's face. His eyes were cautious, blue, assessing. He looked her casually up and down, and seemed not to take her into account. 'Is Major Gale about?' he asked. 'I am Mrs Gale,' she replied. Then, again: 'I expected you earlier.' Really, four hours late, and not a word of apology!

'We started late,' he remarked. 'Where can I put our things?'

Mrs Gale swallowed her annoyance and said: 'I didn't know you had a family. I didn't make arrangements.'

'I wrote to the Major about my wife,' said De Wet. 'Didn't he get my letter?' He sounded offended.

Weakly Mrs Gale said: 'Your wife?' and looked in wonderment at the girl, who was smiling awkwardly behind her husband. It could be seen, looking at her more closely, that she might perhaps be eighteen. She was a small creature, with delicate brown legs and arms, a brush of dancing black curls, and large excited black eyes. She put both hands round her husband's arm, and said, giggling: 'I am Mrs De Wet.'

De Wet put her away from him, gently, but so that she pouted and said: 'We got married last week.'

'Last week,' said Mrs Gale, conscious of dislike.

The girl said, with an extraordinary mixture of effrontery and shyness: 'He met me in the cinema and we got married next day.' It seemed as if she were in some way offering herself to the older woman, offering something precious of herself.

'Really,' said Mrs Gale politely, glancing almost apprehensively at this man, this slow-moving, laconic, shrewd South African, who had behaved with such violence and folly. Distaste twisted her again.

Suddenly the man said, grasping the girl by the arm, and

gently shaking her to and fro, in a sort of controlled exasperation: 'Thought I had better get myself a wife to cook for me, all this way out in the blue. No restaurants here, hey, Doodle?'

'Oh, Jack,' pouted the girl, giggling. 'All he thinks about is his stomach,' she said to Mrs Gale, as one girl to another, and then glanced with delicious fear up at her husband.

'Cooking is what I married you for,' he said, smiling down at her intimately.

There stood Mrs Gale opposite them, and she saw that they had forgotten her existence; and that it was only by the greatest effort of will that they did not kiss. 'Well,' she remarked drily, 'this is a surprise.'

They fell apart, their faces changing. They became at once what they had been during the first moments: two hostile strangers. They looked at her across the barrier that seemed to shut the world away from them. They saw a middle-aged English lady, in a shapeless old-fashioned blue silk dress, with a gold locket sliding over a flat bosom, smiling at them coldly, her blue, misted eyes critically narrowed.

'I'll take you to your house,' she said energetically. 'I'll walk, and you go in the car – no, I walk it often.' Nothing would induce her to get into the bouncing rattle-trap that was bursting with luggage and half-suppressed intimacies.

As stiff as a twig, she marched before them along the road, while the car jerked and ground along in bottom gear. She knew it was ridiculous; she could feel their eyes on her back, could feel their astonished amusement; but she could not help it.

When they reached the house, she unlocked it, showed them briefly what arrangements had been made, and left them. She walked back in a tumult of anger, caused mostly because of her picture of herself walking along that same road, meekly followed by the car, and refusing to do the only sensible thing, which was to get into it with them.

She sat on her verandah for half an hour, looking at the sunset sky without seeing it, and writhing with various emotions, none of which she classified. Eventually she called the houseboy, and gave him a note, asking the two to come to dinner. No sooner had the boy left, and was trotting off down the bushy path to the gate, than she called him back. 'I'll go myself,' she said. This was partly to prove that she made nothing of walking the half mile, and partly from contrition. After all, it was no crime to get married, and they seemed very fond of each other. That was how she put it.

When she came to the house, the front room was littered with luggage, paper, pots and pans. All the exquisite order she had created was destroyed. She could hear voices from the bedroom.

'But, Jack, I don't want you to. I want you to stay with me.' And then his voice, humorous, proud, slow, amorous: 'You'll do what I tell you, my girl. I've got to see the old man and find out what's cooking. I start work tomorrow, don't forget.'

'But, Jack . . .' Then came sounds of scuffling, laughter, and a sharp slap.

'Well,' said Mrs Gale, drawing in her breath. She knocked on the wood of the door, and all sound ceased. 'Come in,' came the girl's voice. Mrs Gale hesitated, then went into the bedroom.

Mrs De Wet was sitting in a bunch on the bed, her flowered frock spread all around her, combing her hair. Mrs Gale noted that the two beds had already been pushed together. 'I've come to ask you to dinner,' she said briskly. 'You don't want to have to cook when you've just come.'

Their faces had already become blank and polite.

'Oh no, don't trouble, Mrs Gale,' said De Wet awkwardly. 'We'll get ourselves something, don't worry.' He glanced at the girl, and his face softened. He said, unable to resist it: 'She'll get busy with the tin-opener in a minute, I expect. That's her idea of feeding a man.'

'Oh, Jack,' pouted his wife.

De Wet turned back to the washstand, and proceeded to swab lather on his face. Waving the brush at Mrs Gale, he said: 'Thanks all the same. But tell the Major I'll be over after dinner to talk things over.'

'Very well,' said Mrs Gale, 'just as you like.'

She walked away from the house. Now she felt rebuffed. After all, they might have had the politeness to come: yet she was pleased they hadn't; yet if they preferred making love to getting to know the people who were to be their close neighbours for what might be years, it was their own affair . . .

Mrs De Wet was saying, as she painted her toenails, with her knees drawn up to her chin, and the bottle of varnish gripped between her heels: 'Who the hell does she think she is, anyway? Surely she could give us a meal without making such a fuss when we've just come.'

'She came to ask us, didn't she?'

'Hoping we would say no.'

And Mrs Gale knew quite well that this was what they were thinking, and felt it was unjust. She would have liked them to come: the man wasn't a bad sort, in his way: a simple soul, but pleasant enough; as for the girl, she would have to learn, that was all. They should have come; it was their fault. Nevertheless she was filled with that discomfort that comes of having done a job badly. If she had behaved differently they would have come. She was cross throughout dinner; and that meal was not half finished when there was a knock on the door. De Wet stood there, apparently surprised they had not finished, from which it seemed that the couple had, after all, dined off sardines and bread and butter.

Major Gale left his meal and went out to the verandah to discuss business. Mrs Gale finished her dinner in state, and then joined the two men. Her husband rose politely at her coming, offered her a chair, sat down and forgot her presence. She listened to them talking for some two hours. Then she interjected a remark (a thing she never did, as a rule, for women get used to sitting silent when men discuss farming) and did not know herself what made her say what she did about the cattle; but when De Wet looked round absently as if to say she should mind her own business, and her husband remarked absently, 'Yes, dear,' when a Yes dear did not fit her remark at all, she got up angrily and went indoors. Well, let them talk, then, she did not mind.

As she undressed for bed, she decided she was tired, because of her broken sleep that afternoon. But she could not sleep then, either. She listened to the sound of the men's voices, drifting brokenly round the corner of the verandah. They seemed to be thoroughly enjoying themselves. It was after twelve when she heard De Wet say, in that slow facetious way of his: 'I'd better be getting home. I'll catch it hot, as it is.' And, with rage, Mrs Gale heard her husband laugh. He actually laughed. She realized that she herself had been planning an acid remark for when he came to the bedroom; so when he did enter, smelling of tobacco smoke, and grinning, and then proceeded to walk jauntily about the room in his underclothes, she said nothing, but noted that he was getting fat, in spite of all the hard work he did.

'Well, what do you think of the man?'

'He'll do very well indeed,' said Major Gale, with satisfaction. 'Very well. He knows his stuff all right. He's been doing mixed farming in the Transvaal for years.' After a moment he asked politely, as he got with a bounce into his own bed on the other side of the room: 'And what is she like?'

'I haven't seen much of her, have I? But she seems pleasant enough.' Mrs Gale spoke with measured detachment.

'Someone for you to talk to,' said Major Gale, turning himself over to sleep. 'You had better ask her over to tea.'

At this Mrs Gale sat straight up in her own bed with a jerk of annoyance. Someone for her to talk to, indeed! But she composed herself, said good night with her usual briskness, and lay awake. Next day she must certainly ask the girl to morning tea. It would be rude not to. Besides, that would leave the afternoon free for her garden and her mountains.

Next morning she sent a boy across with a note, which read: 'I shall be so pleased if you will join me for morning tea.' She signed it: Caroline Gale.

She went herself to the kitchen to cook scones and cakes. At eleven o'clock she was seated on the verandah in the green-dappled shade from the creepers, saying to herself that she believed she was in for a headache. Living as she did, in a long, timeless abstraction of growing things and mountains and silence, she had become very conscious of her body's responses to weather and to the slow advance of age. A small ache in her ankle when rain was due was like a cherished friend. Or she would sit with her eyes shut, in the shade, after a morning's pruning in the violent sun, feeling waves of pain flood back from her eyes to the back of her skull, and say with satisfaction: 'You deserve it, Caroline!' It was right she should pay for such pleasure with such pain.

At last she heard lagging footsteps up the path, and she opened her eyes reluctantly. There was the girl, preparing her face for a social occasion, walking primly through the bougainvillaea arches, in a flowered frock as vivid as her surroundings. Mrs Gale jumped to her feet and cried gaily: 'I am so glad you had time to come.' Mrs De Wet giggled irresistibly and said: 'But I had nothing else to do, had I?' Afterwards she said scornfully to her husband: 'She's nuts. She writes me letters with stuck-down envelopes when I'm five minutes away, and says have I the time? What the hell else did she think I had to do?' And then, violently: 'She can't have anything to do. There was enough food to feed ten.'

'Wouldn't be a bad idea if you spent more time cooking,' said De Wet fondly.

The next day Mrs Gale gardened, feeling guilty all the time, because she could not bring herself to send over another note of invitation. After a few days, she invited the De Wets to dinner, and through the meal made polite conversation with the girl while the men lost themselves in cattle diseases. What could one talk to a girl like that about? Nothing! Her mind, as far as Mrs Gale was concerned, was a dark continent, which she had no inclination to explore. Mrs De Wet was not interested in recipes, and when Mrs Gale gave helpful advice about ordering clothes from England, which was so much cheaper than buying them in the local towns, the reply came that she had made all her own clothes since she was seven. After that there seemed nothing to say, for it was hardly possible to remark that these strapped sun-dresses and bright slacks were quite unsuitable for the farm, besides being foolish, since bare shoulders in this sun were dangerous. As for her shoes! She wore corded beach sandals which had already turned dust colour from the roads.

There were two more tea parties; then they were allowed to lapse. From time to time Mrs Gale wondered uneasily what on earth the poor child did with herself all day, and felt it was her duty to go and find out. But she did not.

One morning she was pricking seedlings into a tin when the houseboy came and said the little missus was on the verandah and she was sick.

At once dismay flooded Mrs Gale. She thought of a dozen tropical diseases, of which she had had unpleasant experience, and almost ran to the verandah. There was the girl, sitting screwed up in a chair, her face contorted, her eyes red, her whole body shuddering violently. Malaria, thought Mrs Gale at once, noting that trembling.

'What is the trouble, my dear?' Her voice was kind. She put her hand on the girl's shoulder. Mrs De Wet turned and flung her arms round her hips, weeping, weeping, her small curly head buried in Mrs Gale's stomach. Holding herself stiffly away from this dismaying contact, Mrs Gale stroked the head and made soothing noises.

'Mrs Gale, Mrs Gale . . .'

'What *is* it?'

'I can't stand it. I shall go mad. I simply can't stand it.'

Mrs Gale, seeing that this was not a physical illness, lifted her up, led her inside, laid her on her own bed, and fetched cologne and handkerchiefs. Mrs De Wet sobbed for a long while, clutching the older woman's hand, and then at last grew silent. Finally she sat up with a small rueful smile, and said pathetically: 'I am a fool.'

'But what *is* it, dear?'

'It isn't anything, really. I am so lonely. I wanted to get my
mother up to stay with me, only Jack said there wasn't room,
and he's quite right, only I got mad, because I thought he
might at least have had my mother . . .'

Mrs Gale felt guilt like a sword: she could have filled the
place of this child's mother.

'And it isn't anything, Mrs Gale, not really. It's not that I'm
not happy with Jack. I am, but I never see him. I'm not used
to this kind of thing. I come from a family of thirteen counting
my parents, and I simply can't stand it.'

Mrs Gale sat and listened, and thought of her own
loneliness when she first began this sort of life.

'And then he comes in late, not till seven sometimes, and I
know he can't help it, with the farm work and all that, and
then he has supper and goes straight off to bed. I am not
sleepy then. And then I get up sometimes and I walk along
the road with my dog . . .'

Mrs Gale remembered how, in the early days after her
husband had finished with his brief and apologetic embraces,
she used to rise with a sense of relief and steal to the front
room, where she lighted the lamp again and sat writing
letters, reading old ones, thinking of her friends and of
herself as a girl. But that was before she had her first child.
She thought: This girl should have a baby; and could not help
glancing downwards at her stomach.

Mrs De Wet, who missed nothing, said resentfully: 'Jack
says I should have a baby. That's all he says.' Then, since she
had to include Mrs Gale in this resentment, she transformed
herself all at once from a sobbing baby into a gauche but
armoured young woman with whom Mrs Gale could have no
contact. 'I am sorry,' she said formally. Then, with a grating
humour: 'Thank you for letting me blow off steam.' She
climbed off the bed, shook her skirts straight, and tossed her
head. 'Thank you. I am a nuisance.' With painful brightness
she added: 'So, that's how it goes. Who would be a woman,
eh?'

Mrs Gale stiffened. 'You must come and see me whenever

you are lonely,' she said, equally bright and false. It seemed to her incredible that this girl should come to her with all her defences down, and then suddenly shut her out with this facetious nonsense. But she felt more comfortable with the distance between them, she couldn't deny it.

'Oh, I will, Mrs Gale. Thank you so much for asking me.' She lingered for a moment, frowning at the brilliantly polished table in the front room, and then took her leave. Mrs Gale watched her go. She noted that at the gate the girl started whistling gaily, and smiled comically. Letting off steam! Well, she said to herself, well . . . And she went back to her garden.

That afternoon she made a point of walking across to the other house. She would offer to show Mrs De Wet the garden. The two women returned together, Mrs Gale wondering if the girl regretted her emotional lapse of the morning. If so, she showed no signs of it. She broke into bright chatter when a topic mercifully occurred to her; in between were polite silences full of attention to what she seemed to hope Mrs Gale might say.

Mrs Gale was relying on the effect of her garden. They passed the house through the shrubs. There were the fountains, sending up their vivid showers of spray, there the cool mats of water lilies, under which the coloured fishes slipped, there the irises, sunk in green turf.

'This must cost a packet to keep up,' said Mrs De Wet. She stood at the edge of the pool, looking at her reflection dissolving among the broad green leaves, glanced obliquely up at Mrs Gale, and dabbled her exposed red toenails in the water.

Mrs Gale saw that she was thinking of herself as her husband's employer's wife. 'It does, rather,' she said drily, remembering that the only quarrels she ever had with her husband were over the cost of pumping up water. 'You are fond of gardens?' she asked. She could not imagine anyone not being fond of gardens.

Mrs De Wet said sullenly: 'My mother was always too busy

having kids to have time for gardens. She had her last baby early this year.' An ancient and incommunicable resentment dulled her face. Mrs Gale, seeing that all this beauty and peace meant nothing to her companion that she would have it mean, said, playing her last card: 'Come and see my mountains.' She regretted the pronoun as soon as it was out – *so* exaggerated.

But when she had the girl safely on the rocky verge of the escarpment, she heard her say: 'There's my river.' She was leaning forward over the great gulf, and her voice was lifted with excitement. 'Look,' she was saying. 'Look, there it is.' She turned to Mrs Gale, laughing, her hair spun over her eyes in a fine iridescent rain, tossing her head back, clutching her skirts down, exhilarated by the tussle with the wind.

'Mind, you'll lose your balance.' Mrs Gale pulled her back. 'You have been down to the river, then?'

'I go there every morning.'

Mrs Gale was silent. The thing seemed preposterous. 'But it is four miles there and four back.'

'Oh, I'm used to walking.'

'But . . .' Mrs Gale heard her own sour, expostulating voice and stopped herself. There was after all no logical reason why the girl should not go to the river. 'What do you do there?'

'I sit on the edge of a big rock and dangle my legs in the water, and I fish, sometimes. I caught a barbel last week. It tasted foul, but it was fun catching it. And I pick water lilies.'

'There are crocodiles,' said Mrs Gale sharply. The girl was wrong-headed; anyone was who could like that steamy bath of vapours, heat, smells and – what? It was an unpleasant place. 'A native girl was taken there last year, at the ford.'

'There couldn't be a crocodile where I go. The water is clear, right down. You can see right under the rocks. It is a lovely pool. There's a kingfisher, and water-birds, all colours. They are so pretty. And when you sit there and look, the sky is a long narrow slit. From here it looks quite far across the river to the other side, but really it isn't. And the trees crowding close make it narrower. Just think how many millions of years it must have taken for the water to wear down the rock so deep.'

'There's bilharzia, too.'

'Oh, bilharzia!'

'There's nothing funny about bilharzia. My husband had it. He had injections for six months before he was cured.'

The girl's face dulled. 'I'll be careful,' she said irrationally, turning away, holding her river and her long hot dreamy mornings away from Mrs Gale, like a secret.

'Look at the mountains,' said Mrs Gale, pointing. The girl glanced over the chasm at the foothills, then bent forward again, her face reverent. Through the mass of green below were glimpses of satiny brown. She breathed deeply: 'Isn't it a lovely smell?' she said.

'Let's go and have some tea,' said Mrs Gale. She felt cross and put out; she had no notion why. She could not help being brusque with the girl. And so at last they were quite silent together; and in silence they remained on that verandah above the beautiful garden, drinking their tea and wishing it was time for them to part.

Soon they saw the two husbands coming up the garden. Mrs De Wet's face lit up; and she sprang to her feet and was off down the path, running lightly. She caught her husband's arm and clung there. He put her away from him, gently. 'Hullo,' he remarked good-humouredly. 'Eating again?' And then he turned back to Major Gale and went on talking. The girl lagged up the path behind her husband like a sulky small girl, pulling at Mrs Gale's beloved roses and scattering crimson petals everywhere.

On the verandah the men sank at once into chairs, took large cups of tea, and continued talking as they drank thirstily. Mrs Gale listened and smiled. Crops, cattle, disease; weather, crops and cattle. Mrs De Wet perched on the verandah wall and swung her legs. Her face was petulant, her lips trembled, her eyes were full of tears. Mrs Gale was saying silently under her breath, with ironical pity, in which there was also cruelty: You'll get used to it, my dear; you'll get used to it. But she respected the girl, who had courage: walking to the river and back, wandering round the dusty flowerbeds in the starlight, trying to find peace – at least, she was trying to find it.

She said sharply, cutting into the men's conversation: 'Mr De Wet, did you know your wife spends her mornings at the river?'

The man looked at her vaguely, while he tried to gather the sense of her words: his mind was on the farm. 'Sure,' he said at last. 'Why not?'

'Aren't you afraid of bilharzia?'

He said laconically: 'If we were going to get it, we would have got it long ago. A drop of water can infect you, touching the skin.'

'Wouldn't it be wiser not to let the water touch you in the first place?' she enquired with deceptive mildness.

'Well, I told her. She wouldn't listen. It is too late now. Let her enjoy it.'

'But . . .'

'About that red heifer,' said Major Gale, who had not been aware of any interruption.

'No,' said Mrs Gale sharply. 'You are not going to dismiss it like that.' She saw the three of them look at her in astonishment. 'Mr De Wet, have you ever thought what it means to a woman being alone all day, with not enough to do? It's enough to drive anyone crazy.'

Major Gale raised his eyebrows; he had not heard his wife speak like that for so long. As for De Wet, he said with a slack good-humour that sounded brutal: 'And what do you expect me to do about it?'

'You don't realize,' said Mrs Gale futilely, knowing perfectly well there was nothing he could do about it. 'You don't understand how it is.'

'She'll have a kid soon,' said De Wet. 'I hope so, at any rate. That will give her something to do.'

Anger raced through Mrs Gale like a flame along petrol. She was trembling. 'She might be that red heifer,' she said at last.

'What's the matter with having kids?' asked De Wet. 'Any objection?'

'You might ask me first,' said the girl bitterly.

Her husband blinked at her, comically bewildered. 'Hey, what is this?' he enquired. 'What have I done? You said you wanted to have kids. Wouldn't have married you otherwise.'

'I never said I didn't.'

'Talking about her as if she were . . .'

'What, then?' Mrs Gale and the man were glaring at each other.

'There's more to women than having children,' said Mrs Gale at last, and flushed because of the ridiculousness of her words.

De Wet looked her up and down, up and down. 'I want kids,' he said at last. 'I want a large family. Make no mistake about that. And when I married her' – he jerked his head at his wife – 'I told her I wanted them. She can't turn round now and say I didn't.'

'Who is turning round and saying anything?' asked the girl, fine and haughty, staring away over the trees.

'Well, if no one is blaming anyone for anything,' asked Major Gale, jauntily twirling his little moustache, 'what is all this about?'

'God knows, I don't,' said De Wet angrily. He glanced sullenly at Mrs Gale. 'I didn't start it.'

Mrs Gale sat silent, trembling, feeling foolish, but so angry she could not speak. After a while she said to the girl: 'Shall we go inside, my dear?' The girl, reluctantly, and with a lingering backward look at her husband, rose and followed Mrs Gale. 'He didn't mean anything,' she said awkwardly, apologizing for her husband to her husband's employer's wife. This room, with its fine old furniture, always made her apologetic. At this moment, De Wet stooped into the doorway and said: 'Come on, I am going home.'

'Is that an order?' asked the girl quickly, backing so that she came side by side with Mrs Gale: she even reached for the older woman's hand. Mrs Gale did not take it: this was going too far.

'What's got into you?' he said, exasperated. 'Are you coming, or are you not?'

'I can't do anything else, can I?' she replied, and followed him from the house like a queen who has been insulted.

Major Gale came in after a few moments. 'Lovers' quarrel,' he said, laughing awkwardly. This phrase irritated Mrs Gale. 'That man!' she exclaimed. 'That man!'

'Why, what is wrong with him?' She remained silent, pretending to arrange her flowers. This silly scene, with its hinterlands of emotion, made her furious. She was angry with herself, angry with her husband, and furious at that foolish couple who had succeeded in upsetting her and destroying her peace. At last she said: 'I am going to bed. I've such a headache, I can't think.'

'I'll bring you a tray, my dear,' said Major Gale, with a touch of exaggeration in his courtesy that annoyed her even more. 'I don't want anything, thank you,' she said, like a child, and marched off to the bedroom.

There she undressed and went to bed. She tried to read, found she was not following the sense of the words, put down the book, and blew out the light. Light streamed into the room from the moon; she could see the trees along the fence banked black against stars. From next door came the clatter of her husband's solitary meal.

Later she heard voices from the verandah. Soon her husband came into the room and said: 'De Wet is asking whether his wife has been here.'

'What!' exclaimed Mrs Gale, slowly assimilating the implications of this. 'Why, has she gone off somewhere?'

'She's not at home,' said the Major uncomfortably. For he always became uncomfortable and very polite when he had to deal with situations like this.

Mrs Gale sank back luxuriously on her pillows. 'Tell that

fine young man that his wife often goes for long walks by herself when he's asleep. He probably hasn't noticed it.' Here she gave a deadly look at her husband. 'Just as I used to,' she could not prevent herself adding.

Major Gale fiddled with his moustache, and gave her a look which seemed to say: 'Oh, Lord, don't say we are going back to all that business again?' He went out, and she heard him saying: 'Your wife might have gone for a walk, perhaps?' Then the young man's voice: 'I know she does sometimes, I don't like her being out at night, but she just walks around the house. And she takes the dogs with her. Maybe she's gone further this time – being upset, you know.'

'Yes, I know,' said Major Gale. Then they both laughed. The laughter was of a quite different quality from the sober responsibility of their tone a moment before: and Mrs Gale found herself sitting up in bed, muttering: 'How *dare* he?'

She got up and dressed herself. She was filled with premonitions of unpleasantness. In the main room her husband was sitting reading, and since he seldom read, it seemed he was also worried. Neither of them spoke. When she looked at the clock, she found it was just past nine o'clock.

After an hour of tension, they heard the footsteps they had been waiting for. There stood De Wet, angry, worried sick, his face white, his eyes burning.

'We must get the boys out,' he said, speaking directly to Major Gale, and ignoring Mrs Gale.

'I am coming too,' she said.

'No, my dear,' said the Major cajolingly. 'You stay here.'

'You can't go running over the veld at this time of night,' said De Wet to Mrs Gale, very blunt and rude.

'I shall do as I please,' she returned.

The three of them stood on the verandah, waiting for the natives. Everything was drenched in moonlight. Soon they heard a growing clamour of voices from over a ridge, and a little while later the darkness there was lightened by flaring torches held high by invisible hands: it seemed as if the night were scattered with torches advancing of their own accord. Then a crowd of dark figures took shape under the broken lights. The farm natives, excited by the prospect of a night's chasing over the veld, were yelling as if they were after a small buck or a hare.

Mrs Gale sickened. 'Is it necessary to have all these natives in it?' she asked. 'After all, have we even considered the possibilities? Where can a girl run *to* on a place like this?'

'That is the point,' said Major Gale frigidly.

'I can't bear to think of her being – pursued, like this, by a crowd of natives. It's horrible.'

'More horrible still if she has hurt herself and is waiting for help,' said De Wet. He ran off down the path, shouting to the natives and waving his arms. The Gales saw them separate into three bands, and soon there were three groups of lights jerking away in different directions through the hazy dark, and the yells and shouting came back to them on the wind.

Mrs Gale thought: She could have taken the road back to the station, in which case she could be caught by car, even now.

She commanded her husband: 'Take the car along the road and see.'

'That's an idea,' said the Major, and went off to the garage. She heard the car start off, and watched the rear light dwindle redly into the night.

But that was the least ugly of the possibilities. What if she had been so blind with anger, grief, or whatever emotion it was that had driven her away, that she had simply run off into the veld not knowing where she went? There were thousands of acres of trees, thick grass, gullies, kopjes. She might at this moment be lying with a broken arm or leg; she might be pushing her way through grass higher than her head, stumbling over roots and rocks. She might be screaming for help somewhere for fear of wild animals, for if she crossed the valley into the hills there were leopards, lions, wild dogs. Mrs Gale suddenly caught her breath in an agony of fear: the valley! What if she had mistaken her direction and walked over the edge of the escarpment in the dark? What if she had forded the river and been taken by a crocodile? There were so many things: she might even be caught in a game trap. Once, taking her walk, Mrs Gale herself had come across a tall sapling by the path where the spine and ribs of a large buck dangled, and on the ground were the pelvis and legs, fine eroded bones of an animal trapped and forgotten by its trapper. Anything might have happened. And worse than any of the actual physical dangers was the danger of falling a victim to fear: being alone on the veld, at night, knowing oneself lost: this was enough to send anyone off balance.

The silly little fool, the silly little fool: anger and pity and terror confused in Mrs Gale until she was walking crazily up and down her garden through the bushes, tearing blossoms and foliage to pieces in trembling fingers. She had no idea how time was passing; until Major Gale returned and said that he had taken the ten miles to the station at seven miles an hour, turning his lights into the bush this way and that. At the station everyone was in bed; but the police were standing on the alert for news.

It was long after twelve. As for De Wet and the bands of searching natives, there was no sign of them. They would be miles away by this time.

'Go to bed,' said Major Gale at last.

'Don't be ridiculous,' she said. After a while she held out her hand to him, and said: 'One feels so helpless.'

There was nothing to say; they walked together under the stars, their minds filled with horrors. Later she made some tea and they drank it standing; to sit would have seemed heartless. They were so tired they could hardly move. Then they got their second wind and continued walking. That night Mrs Gale hated her garden, that highly-cultivated patch of luxuriant growth, stuck in the middle of a country that could do this sort of thing to you suddenly. It was all the fault of the country! In a civilized sort of place, the girl would have caught the train to her mother, and a wire would have put everything right. Here, she might have killed herself, simply because of a passing fit of despair. Mrs Gale began to get hysterical. She was weeping softly in the circle of her husband's arm by the time the sky lightened and the redness of dawn spread over the sky.

As the sun rose, De Wet returned alone over the veld. He said he had sent the natives back to their huts to sleep. They had found nothing. He stated that he also intended to sleep for an hour, and that he would be back on the job by eight. Major Gale nodded: he recognized this as a necessary discipline against collapse. But after the young man had walked off across the veld towards his house, the two older people looked at each other and began to move after him. 'He must not be alone,' said Mrs Gale sensibly. 'I shall make him some tea and see that he drinks it.'

'He wants sleep,' said Major Gale. His own eyes were red and heavy.

'I'll put something in his tea,' said Mrs Gale. 'He won't know it is there.' Now she had something to do, she was much more cheerful. Planning De Wet's comfort, she watched him turn in at his gate and vanish inside the house: they were some two hundred yards behind.

Suddenly there was a shout, and then a commotion of screams and yelling. The Gales ran fast along the remaining distance and burst into the front room, white-faced and expecting the worst, in whatever form it might choose to present itself.

There was De Wet, his face livid with rage, bending over his wife, who was huddled on the floor and shielding her head with her arms, while he beat her shoulders with his closed fists.

Mrs Gale exclaimed: 'Beating your wife!'

De Wet flung the girl away from him, and staggered to his feet. 'She was here all the time,' he said, half in temper, half in sheer wonder. 'She was hiding under the bed. She told me so. When I came in she was sitting on the bed and laughing at me.'

The girl beat her hands on the floor and said, laughing and crying together: 'Now you have to take some notice of me. Looking for me all night over the veld with your silly natives! You looked so stupid, running about like ants, looking for me.'

'My God,' said De Wet simply, giving up. He collapsed backwards into a chair and lay there, his eyes shut, his face twitching.

'So now you have to notice me,' she said defiantly, but beginning to look scared. 'I have to pretend to run away, but then you sit up and take notice.'

'Be quiet,' said De Wet, breathing heavily. 'Be quiet, if you don't want to get hurt bad.'

'Beating your wife,' said Mrs Gale. 'Savages behave better.'

'Caroline, my dear,' said Major Gale awkwardly. He moved towards the door.

'Take that woman out of here if you don't want me to beat her too,' said De Wet to Major Gale.

Mrs Gale was by now crying with fury. 'I'm not going,' she said. 'I'm not going. This poor child isn't safe with you.'

'But what was it all about?' said Major Gale, laying his hand kindly on the girl's shoulder. 'What was it, my dear? What did you have to do it for, and make us all so worried?'

She began to cry. 'Major Gale, I am so sorry. I forgot myself. I got so mad. I told him I was going to have a baby. I told him when I got back from your place. And all he said was: That's fine. That's the first of them, he said. He didn't love me, or say he was pleased, or nothing.'

'Dear Christ in hell,' said De Wet wearily, with the exasperation strong in his voice, 'what do you make me do these things for? Do you think I want to beat you? Did you think I wasn't pleased: I keep telling you I want kids, I love kids.'

'But you don't care about me,' she said, sobbing bitterly.

'Don't I?' he said helplessly.

'Beating your wife when she is pregnant,' said Mrs Gale. 'You ought to be ashamed of yourself.' She advanced on the young man with her own fists clenched, unconscious of what she was doing. 'You ought to be beaten yourself, that's what you need.'

Mrs De Wet heaved herself off the floor, rushed on Mrs Gale, pulled her back so that she nearly lost balance, and then flung herself on her husband. 'Jack,' she said, clinging to him desperately, 'I am so sorry, I am so sorry, Jack.'

He put his arms round her. 'There,' he said simply, his voice thick with tiredness, 'don't cry. We got mixed up, that's all.'

Major Gale who had caught and steadied his wife as she staggered back, said to her in a low voice: 'Come, Caroline. Come. Leave them to sort it out.'

'And what if he loses his temper again and decides to kill her this time?' demanded Mrs Gale, her voice shrill.

De Wet got to his feet, lifting his wife with him. 'Go away now, Mrs Major,' he said. 'Get out of here. You've done enough damage.'

'I've done enough damage?' she gasped. 'And what have I done?'

'Oh nothing, nothing at all,' he said with ugly sarcasm. 'Nothing at all. But please go and leave my wife alone in future, Mrs Major.'

'Come, Caroline, *please*,' said Major Gale.

She allowed herself to be drawn out of the room. Her head was aching so that the vivid morning light invaded her eyes in a wave of pain. She swayed a little as she walked.

'Mrs Major,' she said, 'Mrs Major!'

'He was upset,' said her husband judiciously.

She snorted. Then, after a silence: 'So, it was all my fault.'

'He didn't say so.'

'I thought that was what he was saying. He behaves like a brute and then says it is my fault.'

'It was no one's fault,' said Major Gale, patting her vaguely on shoulders and back as they stumbled home.

They reached the gate, and entered the garden, which was now musical with birds.

'A lovely morning,' remarked Major Gale.

'Next time you get an assistant,' she said finally, 'get people of our kind. These might be savages, the way they behave.'

And that was the last word she would ever say on the subject.

Little Tembi

Jane McCluster, who had been a nurse before she married, started a clinic on the farm within a month of arriving. Though she had been born and brought up in town, her experience of natives was wide, for she had been a sister in the native wards of the city hospital, by choice, for years; she liked nursing natives, and explained her feeling in the words: 'They are just like children, and appreciate what you do for them.' So, when she had taken a thorough, diagnosing kind of look at the farm natives, she exclaimed, 'Poor things!' and set about turning an old dairy into a dispensary. Her husband was pleased; it would save money in the long run by cutting down illness in the compound.

Willie McCluster who had also been born and raised in South Africa was nevertheless unmistakably and determinedly Scottish. His accent might be emphasized for loyalty's sake, but he had kept all the fine qualities of his people unimpaired by a slowing and relaxing climate. He was shrewd, vigorous, earthy, practical and kind. In appearance he was largely built, with a square bony face, a tight mouth, and eyes whose fierce blue glance was tempered by the laughter wrinkles about them. He became a farmer young, having planned the step for years: he was not one of those who drift on to the land because of discontent with an office, or because of failure, or vague yearnings towards 'freedom'. Jane, a cheerful and competent girl who knew what she wanted, trifled with her numerous suitors with one eye on Willie, who wrote her weekly letters from the farming college in the Transvaal. As soon as his four years' training were completed, they married.

They were then twenty-seven, and felt themselves well-equipped for a useful and enjoyable life. Their house was planned for a family. They would have been delighted if a baby had been born the old-fashioned nine months after marriage. As it was, a baby did not come; and when two years had passed Jane took a journey into the city to see a doctor. She was not so much unhappy as indignant to find she needed an operation before she could have children. She did not associate illness with herself, and felt as if the whole thing were out of character. But she submitted to the operation, and to waiting a further two years before starting a family, with her usual practical good sense. But it subdued her a little. The uncertainty preyed on her, in spite of herself; and it was because of her rather wistful, disappointed frame of mind at this time that her work in the clinic became so important to her. Whereas, in the beginning, she had dispensed medicines and good advice as a routine, every morning for a couple of hours after breakfast, she now threw herself into it, working hard, keeping herself at full stretch, trying to attack causes rather than symptoms.

The compound was the usual farm compound of insanitary mud and grass huts; the diseases she had to deal with were caused by poverty and bad feeding.

Having lived in the country all her life, she did not make the mistake of expecting too much; she had that shrewd, ironical patience that achieves more with backward people than any amount of angry idealism.

First she chose an acre of good soil for vegetables, and saw to the planting and cultivating herself. One cannot overthrow the customs of centuries in a season, and she was patient with the natives who would not at first touch food they were not used to. She persuaded and lectured. She gave the women of the compound lessons in cleanliness and baby care. She drew up diet sheets and ordered sacks of citrus from the big estates; in fact, it was not long before it was Jane who organized the feeding of Willie's two-hundred-strong labour force, and he was glad to have her help. Neighbours laughed at them; for it is even now customary to feed natives

on maize meal only, with an occasional slaughtered ox for a
feasting; but there was no doubt Willie's natives were
healthier than most and he got far more work out of them.
On cold winter mornings Jane would stand dispensing cans
of hot cocoa from a petrol drum with a slow fire burning
under it to the natives before they went to the fields; and if a
neighbour passed and laughed at her, she set her lips and
said good-humouredly: 'It's good sound common sense,
that's what it is. Besides – poor things, poor things!' Since
the McClusters were respected in the district, they were
humoured in what seemed a ridiculous eccentricity.

But it was not easy, not easy at all. It was of no use to cure
hookworm-infested feet that would become reinfested in a
week, since none wore shoes; nothing could be done about
bilharzia, when all the rivers were full of it; and the natives
continued to live in the dark and smoky huts.

But the children could be helped; Jane most particularly
loved the little black piccanins. She knew that fewer children
died in her compound than in any for miles around, and this
was her pride. She would spend whole mornings explaining
to the women about dirt and proper feeding; if a child became
ill, she would sit up all night with it, and cried bitterly
if it died. The name for her among the natives was The
Goodhearted One. They trusted her. Though mostly they
hated and feared the white man's medicines,* they let Jane
have her way, because they felt she was prompted by
kindness; and day by day the crowds of natives waiting for
medical attention became larger. This filled Jane with pride;
and every morning she made her way to the big stone-
floored, thatched building at the back of the house that
smelled always of disinfectants and soap, accompanied by
the houseboy who helped her, and spent there many hours
helping the mothers and the children and the labourers who
had hurt themselves at work.

Little Tembi was brought to her for help at the time when
she knew she could not hope to have a child of her own for at

* This story was written in 1950.

least two years. He had what the natives call 'the hot weather sickness'. His mother had not brought him soon enough, and by the time Jane took him in her arms he was a tiny wizened skeleton, loosely covered with harsh greyish skin, the stomach painfully distended. 'He will die,' moaned the mother from outside the clinic door, with that fatalistic note that always annoyed Jane. 'Nonsense!' she said briskly – even more briskly because she was so afraid he would.

She laid the child warmly in a lined basket, and the houseboy and she looked grimly into each other's faces. Jane said sharply to the mother, who was whimpering helplessly from the floor where she squatted with her hands to her face: 'Stop crying. That doesn't do any good. Didn't I cure your first child when he had the same trouble?' But that other little boy had not been nearly as sick as this one.

When Jane had carried the basket into the kitchen, and set it beside the fire for warmth, she saw the same grim look on the cookboy's face as she had seen on the houseboy's – and could feel on her own. 'This child is *not* going to die,' she said to herself. 'I won't let it! I won't let it.' It seemed to her that if she could pull little Tembi through, the life of the child she herself wanted so badly would be granted her.

She sat beside the basket all day, willing the baby to live, with medicines on the table beside her, and the cookboy and the houseboy helping her where they could. At night the mother came from the compound with her blanket; and the two women kept vigil together. Because of the fixed, imploring eyes of the black woman Jane was even more spurred to win through; and the next day, and the next, and through the long nights, she fought for Tembi's life even when she could see from the faces of the house natives that they thought she was beaten. Once, towards dawn of one night when the air was cold and still, the little body chilled to the touch, and there seemed no breath in it, Jane held it close to the warmth of her own breast murmuring fiercely over and over again: You *will* live, you *will* live – and when the sun rose the infant was breathing deeply and its feet were pulsing in her hand.

When it became clear that he would not die, the whole house was pervaded with a feeling of happiness and victory. Willie came to see the child, and said affectionately to Jane: 'Nice work, old girl, I never thought you'd do it.' The cookboy and the houseboy were warm and friendly towards Jane, and brought her gratitude presents of eggs and ground meal. As for the mother, she took her child in her arms with trembling joy and wept as she thanked Jane.

Jane herself, though exhausted and weak, was too happy to rest or sleep: she was thinking of the child she would have. She was not a superstitious person, and the thing could not be described in such terms: she felt that she had thumbed her nose at death, that she had sent death slinking from her door in defeat, and now she would be strong to make life, fine strong children of her own; she could imagine them springing up beside her, lovely children conceived from her own strength and power against sneaking death.

Little Tembi was brought by his mother up to the house every day for a month, partly to make sure he would not relapse, partly because Jane had grown to love him. When he was quite well, and no longer came to the clinic, Jane would ask the cookboy after him, and sometimes sent a message that he should be fetched to see her. The native woman would then come smiling to the back door with the little Tembi on her back and her older child at her skirts, and Jane would run down the steps, smiling with pleasure, waiting impatiently as the cloth was unwound from the mother's back revealing Tembi curled there, thumb in mouth, with great black solemn eyes, his other hand clutching the stuff of his mother's dress for security. Jane would carry him indoors to show Willie. 'Look,' she would say tenderly. 'Here's my little Tembi. Isn't he a sweet little piccanin?'

He grew into a fat shy little boy, staggering uncertainly from his mother's arms to Jane's. Later, when he was strong on his legs, he would run to Jane and laugh as she caught him up. There was always fruit or sweets for him when he visited the house, always a hug from Jane and a good-humoured, amused smile from Willie.

He was two years old when Jane said to his mother: 'When the rains come this year I shall also have a child.' And the two women, forgetting the difference in colour, were happy together because of the coming children: the black woman was expecting her third baby.

Tembi was with his mother when she came to visit the cradle of the little white boy. Jane held out her hand to him and said: 'Tembi, how are you?' Then she took her baby from the cradle and held it out, saying: 'Come and see my baby, Tembi.' But Tembi backed away, as if afraid, and began to cry. 'Silly Tembi,' said Jane affectionately; and sent the houseboy to fetch some fruit as a present. She did not make the gift herself, as she was holding her child.

She was absorbed by this new interest, and very soon found herself pregnant again. She did not forget little Tembi, but thought of him rather as he had been, the little toddler whom she had loved wistfully when she was childless. Once she caught sight of Tembi's mother walking along one of the farm roads, leading a child by the hand, and said: 'But where's Tembi?' Then she saw the child was Tembi. She greeted him; but afterwards said to Willie: 'Oh dear, it's such a pity when they grow up, isn't it?' 'He could hardly be described as grown-up,' said Willie, smiling indulgently at her where she sat with her two infants on her lap. 'You won't be able to have them climbing all over you when we've a dozen,' he teased her – they had decided to wait another two years and then have some more; Willie came from a family of nine children. 'Who said a dozen?' exclaimed Jane tartly, playing up to him. 'Why not?' asked Willie. 'We can afford it.' 'How do you think I can do everything?' grumbled Jane pleasantly. For she was very busy. She had not let the work at the clinic lapse; it was still she who did the ordering and planning of the labourers' food; and she looked after her children without help – she did not even have the customary native nanny. She could not really be blamed for losing touch with little Tembi.

He was brought to her notice one evening when Willie was having the usual weekly discussion with the bossboy over the farm work. He was short of labour again and the rains had been heavy and the lands were full of weeds. As fast as the gangs of natives worked through a field it seemed that the weeds were higher than ever. Willie suggested that it might be possible to take some of the older children from their mothers for a few weeks. He already employed a gang of piccanins, of between about nine and fifteen years old, who did lighter work; but he was not sure that all the available children were working. The bossboy said he would see what he could find.

As a result of this discussion Willie and Jane were called one day to the front door by a smiling cookboy to see Little Tembi, now about six years old, standing proudly beside his father, who was also smiling. 'Here is a man to work for you,' said Tembi's father to Willie, pushing forward Tembi, who jibbed like a little calf, standing with his head lowered and his fingers in his mouth. He looked so tiny, standing all by himself, that Jane exclaimed compassionately: 'But, Willie, he's just a baby still!' Tembi was quite naked, save for a string of blue beads cutting into the flesh of his fat stomach. Tembi's father explained that his older child, who was eight, had been herding the calves for a year now, and that there was no reason why Tembi should not help him.

'But I don't need two herdboys for the calves,' protested Willie. And then, to Tembi: 'And now, my big man, what money do you want?' At this Tembi dropped his head still lower, twisted his feet in the dust, and muttered: 'Five shillings.' 'Five shillings a month!' exclaimed Willie indignantly. 'What next? Why, the ten-year-old piccanins get that much.' And then, feeling Jane's hand on his arm, he said hurriedly: 'Oh, all right, four and sixpence. He can help his big brother with the calves.' Jane, Willie, the cookboy and Tembi's father stood laughing sympathetically as Tembi lifted his head, stuck out his stomach even further, and swaggered off down the path, beaming with pride. 'Well,' sighed Jane, 'I never would have thought it. Little Tembi! Why, it seems only the other day . . .'

Tembi, promoted to a loincloth, joined his brother with the calves; and as the two children ran alongside the animals, everyone turned to look smiling after the tiny black child, strutting with delight, and importantly swishing the twig his father had cut him from the bush as if he were a full-grown driver with his team of beasts.

The calves were supposed to stay all day near the kraal; when the cows had been driven away to the grazing, Tembi and his brother squatted under a tree and watched the calves, rising to run, shouting, if one attempted to stray. For a year Tembi was apprentice to the job; and then his brother joined the gang of older piccanins who worked with the hoe. Tembi was then seven years old, and responsible for twenty calves, some standing higher than he. Normally a much older child had the job; but Willie was chronically short of labour, as all the farmers were, and he needed every pair of hands he could find, for work in the fields.

'Did you know your Tembi is a proper herdboy now?' Willie said to Jane, laughing, one day. 'What!' exclaimed Jane. 'That baby! Why, it's absurd.' She looked jealously at her own children, because of Tembi; she was the kind of woman who hates to think of her children growing up. But now she had three, and was very busy indeed. She forgot the little black boy.

Then one day a catastrophe happened. It was very hot, and Tembi fell asleep under the trees. His father came up to the house, uneasily apologetic, to say that some of the calves had got into the mealie fields and trampled down the plants. Willie was angry. It was that futile, simmering anger that cannot be assuaged, for it is caused by something that cannot be remedied; children had to herd the calves because adults were needed for more important work, and one could not be really angry with a child of Tembi's age. Willie had Tembi fetched to the house, and gave him a stern lecture about the terrible thing he had done. Tembi was crying when he turned away; he stumbled off to the compound with his father's hand resting on his shoulder, because the tears were streaming so fast he could not have directed his own steps. But in spite of the tears, and his contrition, it all happened again not very long afterwards. He fell asleep in the drowsily-warm shade, and when he woke, towards evening, all the calves had strayed into the fields and flattened acres of mealies. Unable to face punishment he ran away, crying, into the bush. He was found that night by his father who cuffed him lightly round the head for running away.

And now it was a very serious matter indeed. Willie was angry. To have happened once – that was bad, but forgivable. But twice, and within a month! He did not at first summon Tembi, but had a consultation with his father. 'We must do something he will not forget, as a lesson,' said Willie. Tembi's father said the child had already been punished. 'You have beaten him?' asked Willie. But he knew that Africans do not beat their children, or so seldom it was not likely that Tembi had really been punished. 'You say you have beaten him?' he insisted: and saw, from the way the man turned away his eyes and said, 'Yes, baas,' that it was not true. 'Listen,' said Willie. 'Those calves straying must have cost me about thirty pounds. There's nothing I can do. I can't get it back from Tembi, can I? And now I'm going to stop it happening again.' Tembi's father did not reply. 'You will fetch Tembi up here, to the house, and cut a switch from the bush, and I will give him a beating.' 'Yes, baas,' said Tembi's father, after a pause.

When Jane heard of the punishment she said: 'Shame! Beating my little Tembi . . .'

When the hour came, she took away her children so that they would not have such an unpleasant thing in their memories. Tembi was brought up to the verandah, clutching his father's hand and shivering with fear. Willie said he did not like the business of beating; he considered it necessary, however, and intended to go through with it. He took the long light switch from the cookboy, who had cut it from the bush, since Tembi's father had come without it, and ran the sharply-whistling thing loosely through the air to frighten Tembi. Tembi shivered more than ever, and pressed his face against his father's thighs. 'Come here, Tembi.' Tembi did not move; so his father lifted him close to Willie. 'Bend down.' Tembi did not bend down, so his father bent him down, hiding the small face against his own legs. Then Willie glanced smilingly but uncomfortably at the cookboy, the houseboy and Tembi's father, who were all regarding him with stern, unresponsive faces, and swished the wand backwards and forwards over Tembi's back; he wanted them to see he was only trying to frighten Tembi for the good of his upbringing. But they did not smile at all. Finally Willie said in an awful, solemn voice: 'Now, Tembi!' And then, having made the occasion solemn and angry, he switched Tembi lightly, three times, across the buttocks, and threw the switch away into the bush. 'Now you will never do it again, Tembi, will you?' he said. Tembi stood quite still, shuddering, in front of him, and would not meet his eyes. His father gently took his hand and led him away back home.

'Is it over?' asked Jane appearing from the house. 'I didn't hurt him,' said Willie crossly. He was annoyed, because he felt the black men were annoyed with him. 'They want to have it both ways,' he said. 'If the child is old enough to earn money, then he's old enough to be responsible. Thirty pounds!'

'I was thinking of our little Freddie,' said Jane emotionally. Freddie was their first child. Willie said impatiently: 'And what's the good of thinking of him?' 'Oh no good, Willie. No good at all,' agreed Jane tearfully. 'It does seem awful, though. Do you remember him, Willie? Do you remember what a sweet little thing he was?' Willie could not afford to remember the sweetness of the baby Tembi at that moment; and he was displeased with Jane for reminding him; there was a small constriction of feeling between them for a little while, which soon dissolved, for they were good friends, and were in the same mind about most things.

The calves did not stray again. At the end of the month, when Tembi stepped forward to take his four shillings and sixpence wages, Willie smiled at him and said: 'Well, Tembi, and how are things with you?' 'I want more money,' said Tembi boldly. 'Wha-a-at!' exclaimed Willie, astounded. He called to Tembi's father, who stepped out of the gang of waiting Africans, to hear what Willie wanted to say. 'This little rascal of yours lets the cattle stray twice, and then says he wants more money.' Willie said this loudly, so that everyone could hear; and there was laughter from the labourers. But Tembi kept his head high, and said defiantly: 'Yes, baas, I want more money.' 'You'll get your bottom tanned,' said Willie, only half-indignant: and Tembi went off sulkily, holding his silver in his hand, with amused glances following him.

He was now about seven, very thin and lithe, though he still carried his protuberant stomach before him. His legs were flat and spindly, and his arms broader below the elbow than above. He was not crying now, nor stumbling. His small thin shape was straight, and – so it seemed – angry. Willie forgot the incident.

But next month the child stood his ground and argued stubbornly for an increase. Willie raised him to five and sixpence, saying resignedly that Jane had spoiled him. Tembi bit his lips in triumph, and as he walked off gave little joyous skipping steps, finally breaking into a run as he reached the trees. He was still the youngest of the working children, and was now earning as much as some three or four years older than he: this made them grumble but it was recognized, because of Jane's attitude, that he was a favourite.

Now, in the normal run of things, it would have been a year, at least, before he got any more money. But the very month following he claimed the right to another increase. This time the listening natives made sounds of amused protest; the lad was forgetting himself. As for Willie, he was really annoyed. There was something insistent, something demanding, in the child's manner that was almost impertinent. He said sharply: 'If you don't stop this nonsense, I'll tell your father to teach you a lesson where it hurts.' Tembi's eyes glowed angrily, and he attempted to argue, but Willie dismissed him curtly, turning to the next labourer.

A few minutes later Jane was fetched to the back door by the cook, and there stood Tembi, shifting in embarrassment from foot to foot, but grinning at her eagerly. 'Why, Tembi . . .' she said vaguely. She had been feeding the children, and her mind was filled with thoughts of bathing and getting them to bed – thoughts very far from Tembi. Indeed, she had to look twice before she recognized him, for she carried always in the back of her mind the picture of that sweet fat black baby who bore, for her, the name Tembi. Only his eyes were the same: large dark glowing eyes, now imploringly fixed on her. 'Tell the boss to give me more money,' he beseeched.

Jane laughed kindly. 'But, Tembi, how can I do that? I've nothing to do with the farm. You know that.'

'Tell him, missus. Tell him, my missus,' he beseeched.

Jane felt the beginnings of annoyance. But she chose to laugh again, and said, 'Wait a minute, Tembi.' She went inside and fetched from the children's supper table some slices of cake, which she folded into a piece of paper and thrust into Tembi's hand. She was touched to see the child's face spread into a beaming smile: he had forgotten about the wages, the cake did as well or better. 'Thank you, thank you,' he said; and, turning, scuttled off into the trees.

And now Jane was given no chance of forgetting Tembi. He would come up to the house on a Sunday with quaint little mud toys for the children, or with the feather from a brilliant bird he had found in the bush; even a handful of wild flowers tied with wisps of grass. Always Jane welcomed him, talked to him, and rewarded him with small gifts. Then she had another child, and was very busy again. Sometimes she was too occupied to go herself to the back door. She would send her servant with an apple or a few sweets.

Soon after, Tembi appeared at the clinic one morning with his toe bound up. When Jane removed the dirty bit of cloth, she saw a minute cut, the sort of thing no native, whether child or adult, would normally take any notice of at all. But she bound it properly for him, and even dressed it good-naturedly when he appeared again, several days later. Then, only a week afterwards, there was a small cut on his finger. Jane said impatiently: 'Look here, Tembi, I don't run this clinic for nonsense of this kind.' When the child stared up at her blankly, those big dark eyes fixed on her with an intensity that made her uncomfortable, she directed the houseboy to translate the remark into dialect, for she thought Tembi had not understood. He said, stammering: 'Missus, my missus, I come to see you only.' But Jane laughed and sent him away. He did not go far. Later, when all the other patients had gone, she saw him standing a little way off, looking hopefully at her. 'What *is* it?' she asked, a little crossly, for she could hear the new baby crying for attention inside the house.

'I want to work for you,' said Tembi. 'But, Tembi, I don't need another boy. Besides, you are too small for housework. When you are older, perhaps.' 'Let me look after the children.' Jane did not smile, for it was quite usual to employ small piccanins as nurses for children not much younger than themselves. She might even have considered it, but she said: 'Tembi, I have just arranged for a nanny to come and help me. Perhaps later on. I'll remember you, and if I need someone to help the nanny I'll send for you. First you must learn to work well. You must work well with the calves and not let them stray; and then we'll know you are a good boy, and you can come to the house and help me with the children.'

Tembi departed on this occasion with lingering steps, and some time later Jane, glancing from the window, saw him standing at the edge of the bush gazing towards the house. She despatched the houseboy to send him away, saying that she would not have him loitering round the house doing nothing.

Jane, too, was now feeling that she had 'spoiled' Tembi, that he had 'got above himself'.

And now nothing happened for quite a long time.

Then Jane missed her diamond engagement ring. She used often to take it off when doing household things; so that she was not at first concerned. After several days she searched thoroughly for it, but it could not be found. A little later a pearl brooch was missing. And there were several small losses, a spoon used for the baby's feeding, a pair of scissors, a silver christening mug. Jane said crossly to Willie that there must be a poltergeist. 'I had the thing in my hand and when I turned round it was gone. It's just silly. Things don't vanish like that.' 'A black poltergeist, perhaps,' said Willie. 'How about the cook?' 'Don't be ridiculous,' said Jane, a little too quickly. 'Both the houseboys have been with us since we came to the farm.' But suspicion flared in her, nevertheless. It was a well-worn maxim that no native, no matter how friendly, could be trusted; scratch any one of them, and you found a thief. Then she looked at Willie, understood that he was feeling the same, and was as ashamed of his feelings as she was. The houseboys were almost personal friends. 'Nonsense,' said Jane firmly. 'I don't believe a word of it.' But no solution offered itself, and things continued to vanish.

One day Tembi's father asked to speak to the boss. He untied a piece of cloth, laid it on the ground – and there were all the missing articles. 'But not Tembi, *surely*,' protested Jane. Tembi's father, awkward in his embarrassment, explained that he had happened to be passing the cattle kraals, and had happened to notice the little boy sitting on his antheap, in the shade, playing with his treasures. 'Of course he had no idea of their value,' appealed Jane. 'It was just because they were so shiny and glittering.' And indeed, as they stood there, looking down at the lamplight glinting on the silver and the diamonds, it was easy to see how a child could be fascinated. 'Well, and what are we going to do?'

asked Willie practically. Jane did not reply directly to the question; she exclaimed helplessly: 'Do you realize that the little imp must have been watching me doing things round the house for weeks, nipping in when my back was turned for a moment – he must be quick as a snake.' 'Yes, but what are we going to do?' 'Just give him a good talking-to,' said Jane, who did not know why she felt so dismayed and lost. She was angry; but far more distressed – there was something ugly and persistent in this planned, deliberate thieving, that she could not bear to associate with little Tembi, whom she had saved from death.

'A talking-to won't do any good,' said Willie. Tembi was whipped again; this time properly, with no nonsense about making the switch whistle for effect. He was made to expose his bare bottom across his father's knees, and when he got up, Willie said with satisfaction: 'He's not going to be comfortable sitting down for a week.' 'But, Willie, there's blood,' said Jane. For as Tembi walked off stiffly, his legs straddled apart from the pain, his fists thrust into his streaming eyes, reddish patches appeared on the stuff of his trousers. Willie said angrily: 'Well, what do you expect me to do – make him a present of it and say: How clever of you?'

'But *blood*, Willie!'

'I didn't know I was hitting so hard,' admitted Willie. He examined the long flexible twig in his hands, before throwing it away, as if surprised at its effectiveness. 'That must have hurt,' he said doubtfully. 'Still, he deserved it. Now stop crying, Jane. He won't do that again.'

But Jane did not stop crying. She could not bear to think of the beating; and Willie, no matter what he said, was uncomfortable when he remembered it. They would have been pleased to let Tembi slip from their minds for a while, and have him reappear later, when there had been time for kindness to grow in them again.

But it was not a week before he demanded to be made nurse to the children: he was now big enough, he said; and Jane had promised. Jane was so astonished she could not speak to him. She went indoors, shutting the door on him; and when she knew he was still lingering there for speech with her, she sent out the houseboy to say she was not having a thief as nurse for her children.

A few weeks later he asked again; and again she refused. Then he took to waylaying her every day, sometimes several times a day: 'Missus, my missus, let me work near you, let me work near you.' Always she refused, and always she grew more angry.

At last, the sheer persistence of the thing defeated her. She said: 'I won't have you as a nurse, but you can help me with the vegetable garden.' Tembi was sullen, but he presented himself at the garden next day, which was not the one near the house, but the fenced patch near the compound, for the use of the natives. Jane employed a garden boy to run it, telling him when was the time to plant, explaining about compost and the proper treatment of soil. Tembi was to help him.

She did not often go to the garden; it ran of itself. Sometimes, passing, she saw the beds full of vegetables were running to waste; this meant that a new batch of Africans were in the compound, natives who had to be educated afresh to eat what was good for them. But now she had had her last baby, and employed two nannies in the nurseries, she felt free to spend more time at the clinic and at the garden. Here she made a point of being friendly to Tembi. She was not a person to bear grudges, though a feeling that he was not to be trusted barred him as a nurse. She would talk to him about her own children, and how they were growing, and would soon be going to school in the city. She would talk to him about keeping himself clean, and eating the right things; how he must earn good money so that he could buy shoes to keep his feet from the germ-laden dust; how he must be honest, always tell the truth and be obedient to the white people. While she was in the garden he would follow her around, his hoe trailing forgotten in his hand, his eyes fixed on her. 'Yes, missus; yes, my missus,' he repeated continually. And when she left, he would implore: 'When are you coming again? Come again soon, my missus.' She took to bringing him her own children's books, when they were too worn for use in the nursery. 'You must learn to read, Tembi,' she would say. 'Then, when you want to get a job, you will earn more wages if you can say: "Yes, missus, I can read and write." You can take messages on the telephone then, and write down orders so that you don't forget them.' 'Yes, missus,' Tembi would say, reverently taking the books from her. When she left the garden, she would glance back, always a little uncomfortably, because of Tembi's intense devotion, and see him kneeling on the rich red soil, framed by the bright green of the vegetables, knitting his brows over the strange coloured pictures and the unfamiliar print.

This went on for about two years. She said to Willie: 'Tembi seems to have got over that funny business of his. He's really useful in that garden. I don't have to tell him when to plant things. He knows as well as I do. And he goes round the huts in the compound with the vegetables, persuading the natives to eat them.' 'I bet he makes a bit on the side,' said Willie, chuckling. 'Oh no, Willie, I'm sure he wouldn't do that.'

And, in fact, he didn't. Tembi regarded himself as an apostle of the white man's way of life. He would say earnestly, displaying the baskets of carefully displayed vegetables to the native women: 'The Goodhearted One says it is right we should eat these things. She says eating them will save us from sickness.' Tembi achieved more than Jane had done in years of propaganda.

He was nearly eleven when he began giving trouble again. Jane sent her two elder children to boarding-school, dismissed her nannies, and decided to engage a piccanin to help with the children's washing. She did not think of Tembi; but she engaged Tembi's younger brother.

Tembi presented himself at the back door, as of old, his eyes flashing, his body held fine and taut, to protest. 'Missus, missus, you promised I should work for you.' 'But Tembi, you are working for me, with the vegetables.' 'Missus, my missus, you said when you took a piccanin for the house, that piccanin would be me.' But Jane did not give way. She still felt as if Tembi were on probation. And the demanding, insistent, impatient thing in Tembi did not seem to her a good quality to be near her children. Besides, she liked Tembi's little brother, who was a softer, smiling, chubby Tembi, playing good-naturedly with the children in the garden when he had finished the washing and ironing. She saw no reason to change, and said so.

Tembi sulked. He no longer took baskets of green stuff from door to door in the compound. And he did as little work as he need without actually neglecting it. The spirit had gone out of him.

'You know,' said Jane half indignantly, half amused, to Willie: 'Tembi behaves as if he had some sort of claim on us.'

Quite soon, Tembi came to Willie and asked to be allowed to buy a bicycle. He was then earning ten shillings a month, and the rule was that no native earning less than fifteen shillings could buy a bicycle. A fifteen-shilling native would keep five shillings of his wages, give ten to Willie, and undertake to remain on the farm till the debt was paid. That might take two years, or even longer. 'No,' said Willie. 'And what does a piccanin like you want with a bicycle? A bicycle is for big men.'

Next day, their eldest child's bicycle vanished from the house, and was found in the compound leaning against Tembi's hut. Tembi had not even troubled to conceal the theft; and when he was called for an interview kept silent. At last he said: 'I don't know why I stole it. I don't know.' And he ran off, crying, into the trees.

'He must go,' said Willie finally, baffled and angry.

'But his father and mother and the family live in our compound,' protested Jane.

'I'm not having a thief on the farm,' said Willie. But getting rid of Tembi was more than dismissing a thief: it was pushing aside a problem that the McClusters were not equipped to handle. Suddenly Jane knew that when she no longer saw

Tembi's burning, pleading eyes, it would be a relief; though she said guiltily: 'Well, I suppose he can find work on one of the farms nearby.'

Tembi did not allow himself to be sacked so easily. When Willie told him he burst into passionate tears, like a very small child. Then he ran round the house and banged his fists on the kitchen door till Jane came out. 'Missus, my missus, don't let the baas send me away.' 'But Tembi, you must go, if the boss says so.' 'I work for you, missus, I'm your boy, let me stay. I'll work for you in the garden and I won't ask for any more money.' 'I'm sorry, Tembi,' said Jane. Tembi gazed at her while his face hollowed into incredulous misery: he had not believed she would not take his part. At this moment his little brother came round the corner of the house carrying Jane's youngest child, and Tembi flew across and flung himself on them, so that the little black child staggered back, clutching the white infant to himself with difficulty. Jane flew to rescue her baby, and then pulled Tembi off his brother, who was bitten and scratched all over his face and arms.

'That finishes it,' she said coldly. 'You will be off this farm in an hour, or the police will chase you off.'

They asked Tembi's father, later, if the lad had found work; the reply was that he was garden boy on a neighbouring farm. When the McClusters saw these neighbours they asked after Tembi, but the reply was vague: on this new farm Tembi was just another labourer without a history.

Later still, Tembi's father said there had been 'trouble', and that Tembi had moved to another farm, many miles away. Then, no one seemed to know where he was; it was said he had joined a gang of boys moving south to Johannesburg for work in the gold mines.

The McClusters forgot Tembi. They were pleased to be able to forget him. They thought of themselves as good masters; they had a good name with their labourers for kindness and fair dealing; while the affair of Tembi left something hard and unassimilable in them, like a grain of sand in a mouthful of food. The name 'Tembi' brought uncomfortable emotions with it; and there was no reason why it should, according to their ideas of right and wrong. So at last they did not even remember to ask Tembi's father what had become of him: he had become another of those natives who vanish from one's life after seeming to be such an intimate part of it.

It was about four years later that the robberies began again. The McClusters' house was the first to be rifled. Someone climbed in one night and took the following articles: Willie's big winter coat, his stick, two old dresses belonging to Jane, a quantity of children's clothing and an old and battered child's tricycle. Money left lying in a drawer was untouched. 'What extraordinary things to take,' marvelled the McClusters. For except for Willie's coat, there was nothing of value. The theft was reported to the police, and a routine visit was made to the compound. It was established that the thief must be someone who knew the house, for the dogs had not barked at him; and that it was not an experienced thief, who would certainly have taken money and jewellery.

Because of this, the first theft was not connected with the second, which took place at a neighbouring farmhouse. There, money and watches and a gun were stolen. And there were more thefts in the district of the same kind. The police decided it must be a gang of thieves, not the ordinary pilferer, for the robberies were so clever and it seemed as if several people had planned them. Watchdogs were poisoned; times were chosen when servants were out of the house; and on two occasions someone had entered through bars so closely set together that no one but a child could have forced his way through.

The district gossiped about the robberies; and because of them, the anger lying dormant between white and black, always ready to flare up, deepened in an ugly way. There was hatred in the white people's voices when they addressed their servants, that futile anger, for even if their personal servants were giving information to the thieves, what could be done about it? The most trusted servant could turn out to be a thief. During these months when the unknown gang terrorized the district, unpleasant things happened; people were fined more often for beating their natives; a greater number of labourers than usual ran away over the border to Portuguese territory; the dangerous, simmering anger was like heat growing in the air. Even Jane found herself saying one day: 'Why do we do it? Look how I spend my time nursing and helping these natives! What thanks do I get? They aren't grateful for anything we do for them.' This question of gratitude was in every white person's mind during that time.

As the thefts continued, Willie put bars in all the windows of the house, and bought two large fierce dogs. This annoyed Jane, for it made her feel confined and a prisoner in her own home.

To look at a beautiful view of mountains and shaded green bush through bars, robs the sight of joy; and to be greeted on her way from house to storeroom by the growling of hostile dogs who treated everyone, black and white, as an enemy, became daily more exasperating. They bit everyone who came near the house, and Jane was afraid for her children. However, it was not more than three weeks after they were bought that they were found lying stretched in the sun, quite dead, foam at their mouths and their eyes glazing. They had been poisoned. 'It looks as if we can expect another visit,' said Willie crossly; for he was by now impatient of the whole business. 'However,' he said impatiently, 'if one chooses to live in a damned country like this, one has to take the consequences.' It was an exclamation that meant nothing that could not be taken seriously by anyone. During that time, however, a lot of settled and contented people were talking with prickly anger about 'the damned country'. In short, their nerves were on edge.

Not long after the dogs were poisoned, it became necessary for Willie to make the trip into town, thirty miles off. Jane did not want to go; she disliked the long, hot, scurrying day in the streets. So Willie went by himself.

In the morning, Jane went to the vegetable garden with her

younger children. They played around the water-butt, by themselves, while she staked out a new row of beds; her mind was lazily empty, her hands working quickly with twine and wooden pegs. Suddenly, however, an extraordinary need took her to turn around sharply, and she heard herself say: 'Tembi!' She looked wildly about her; afterwards it seemed to her she had heard him speak her name. It seemed to her that she would see a spindly earnest-faced black child kneeling behind her between the vegetable beds, poring over a tattered picture book. Time slipped and swam together; she felt confused; and it was only by looking determinedly at her two children that she regained a knowledge of how long it had been since Tembi followed her around this garden.

When she got back to the house, she sewed on the verandah. Leaving her chair for a moment to fetch a glass of water, she found her sewing basket had gone. At first she could not believe it. Distrusting her own senses, she searched the place for her basket, which she knew very well had been on the verandah not a few moments before. It meant that a native was lingering in the bush, perhaps a couple of hundred yards away, watching her movements. It wasn't a pleasant thought. An old uneasiness filled her; and again the name 'Tembi' rose into her mind. She took herself into the kitchen and said to the cookboy: 'Have you heard anything of Tembi recently?' But there had been no news, it seemed. He was 'at the gold mines'. His parents had not heard from him for years.

'But why a sewing basket?' muttered Jane to herself, incredulously. 'Why take such a risk for so little? It's insane.'

That afternoon, when the children were playing in the garden and Jane was asleep on her bed, someone walked quietly into the bedroom and took her big garden hat, her apron, and the dress she had been wearing that morning. When Jane woke and discovered this, she began to tremble, half with anger, half with fear. She was alone in the house, and she had the prickling feeling of being watched. As she moved from room to room, she kept glancing over her shoulder behind the angles of wardrobe and cupboard, and fancied that Tembi's great imploring eyes would appear there, as unappeasable as a dead person's eyes, following her.

She found herself watching the road for Willie's return. If Willie had been there, she could have put the responsibility on to him and felt safe: Jane was a woman who depended very much on that invisible support a husband gives. She had not known, before that afternoon, just how much she depended on him; and this knowledge – which it seemed the thief shared – made her unhappy and restless. She felt that she should be able to manage this thing by herself, instead of waiting helplessly for her husband. I must do something, I must do something, she kept repeating.

It was a long, warm, sunny afternoon. Jane, with all her nerves standing to attention, waited on the verandah, shading her eyes as she gazed along the road for Willie's car. The waiting preyed on her. She could not prevent her eyes from returning again and again to the bush immediately in front of the house, which stretched for mile on mile, a low, dark scrubby green, darker because of the lengthening shadows of approaching evening. An impulse pulled her to her feet, and she marched towards the bush through the garden. At its edge she stopped, peering everywhere for those dark and urgent eyes, and called 'Tembi, Tembi.' There was no sound. 'I won't punish you, Tembi,' she implored. 'Come here to me.' She waited, listening delicately, for the slightest movement of branch or dislodged pebble. But the bush was silent under the sun; even the birds were drugged by the heat; and the leaves hung without trembling. 'Tembi!' she called again; at first peremptorily, and then with a quaver in her voice. She knew very well that he was there, flattening himself behind some tree or bush, waiting for her to say the right word, to find the right things to say, so that he could trust her. It maddened her to think he was so close and she could no more reach him than she could lay her hands on a shadow. Lowering her voice persuasively she said: 'Tembi, I know you are there. Come here and talk to me. I won't tell the police. Can't you trust me, Tembi?'

Not a sound, not the whisper of a reply. She tried to make her mind soft and blank, so that the words she needed would appear there, ready for using. The grass was beginning to shake a little in the evening breeze, and the hanging leaves tremored once or twice; there was a warm mellowing of the light that meant the sun would soon sink; a red glow showed on the foliage, and the sky was flaring high with light. Jane was trembling so she could not control her limbs; it was a deep internal trembling, welling up from inside, like a wound bleeding invisibly. She tried to steady herself. She said: This is silly. I can't be afraid of little Tembi! How could I be? She made her voice firm and loud and said: 'Tembi, you are being very foolish. What's the use of stealing things like a stupid child? You can be clever about stealing for a little while, but sooner or later the police will catch you and you will go to prison. You don't want that, do you? Listen to me, now. You come out now and let me see you; and when the boss comes I'll explain to him, and I'll say you are sorry, and you can come back and work for me in the vegetable garden. I don't like to think of you as a thief, Tembi. Thieves are bad people.' She stopped. The silence settled around her; she felt the silence like a coldness, as when a cloud passes overhead. She saw that the shadows were thick about her and the light had gone from the leaves, that had a cold grey look. She knew Tembi would not come out to her now. She had not found the right things to say. 'You are a silly little boy,' she announced to the still listening bush. 'You make me very angry, Tembi.' And she walked very slowly back to the house, holding herself calm and dignified, knowing that Tembi was watching her, with some plan in his mind she could not conjecture.

When Willie returned from town, tired and irritable as he always was after a day of traffic, and interviewing people, and shopping, she told him carefully, choosing her words, what had happened. When she told how she had called to

Tembi from the verges of the bush, Willie looked gently at her and said: 'My dear, what good do you think that's going to do?' 'But Willie, it's all so awful . . .' Her lips began to tremble luxuriously, and she allowed herself to weep comfortably on his shoulder. 'You don't know it is Tembi,' said Willie. 'Of course it's Tembi. Who else could it be? The silly little boy. My silly little Tembi . . .'

She could not eat. After supper she said suddenly: 'He'll come here tonight. I'm sure of it.' 'Do you think he will?' said Willie seriously, for he had a great respect for Jane's irrational knowledge. 'Well, don't worry, we'll be ready for him.' 'If he'd only let me talk to him,' said Jane. 'Talk to him!' said Willie. 'Like hell! I'll have him in prison. That's the only place for him.' 'But *Willie* . . .' Jane protested, knowing perfectly well that Tembi must go to prison.

It was then not eight o'clock. 'I'll have my gun beside the bed,' planned Willie. 'He stole a gun, didn't he, from the farm over the river? He might be dangerous.' Willie's blue eyes were alight; he was walking up and down the room, his hands in his pockets, alert and excited: he seemed to be enjoying the idea of capturing Tembi, and because of this Jane felt herself go cold against him. It was at this moment that there was a sound from the bedroom next door. They sprang up, and reached the entrance together. There stood Tembi, facing them, his hands dangling empty at his sides. He had grown taller, but still seemed the same lithe, narrow child, with the thin face and great eloquent eyes. At the sight of those eyes Jane said weakly: 'Willie . . .'

Willie, however, marched across to Tembi and took that unresisting criminal by the arm. 'You young rascal,' he said angrily, but in a voice appropriate, not to a dangerous thief, who had robbed many houses, but rather to a naughty child caught pilfering fruit. Tembi did not reply to Willie: his eyes were fixed on Jane. He was trembling; he looked no more than a boy.

'Why didn't you come when I called you?' asked Jane. 'You are so foolish, Tembi.'

'I was afraid, missus,' said Tembi, in a voice just above a whisper. 'But I said I wouldn't tell the police,' said Jane.

'Be quiet, Jane,' ordered Willie. 'Of course we're calling the police. What are you thinking of?' As if feeling the need to remind himself of this important fact, he said: 'After all, the lad's a criminal.'

'I'm not a bad boy,' whispered Tembi imploringly to Jane. 'Missus, my missus, I'm not a bad boy.'

But the thing was out of Jane's hands; she had relinquished it to Willie.

Willie seemed uncertain what to do. Finally he strode purposefully to the wardrobe, and took his rifle from it, and handed it to Jane. 'You stay here,' he ordered. 'I'm calling the police on the telephone.' He went out, leaving the door open, while Jane stood there holding the big gun, and waiting for the sound of the telephone.

She looked helplessly down at the rifle, set it against the bed, and said in a whisper: 'Tembi, why did you steal?'

Tembi hung his head and said, 'I don't know, missus.' 'But you must know.' There was no reply. The tears poured down Tembi's cheeks.

'Tembi, did you like Johannesburg?' There was no reply. 'How long were you there?' 'Three years, missus.' 'Why did you come back?' 'They put me in prison, missus.' 'What for?' 'I didn't have a pass.' 'Did you get out of prison?' 'No, I was there one month and they let me go.' 'Was it you who stole all the things from the houses around here?' Tembi nodded, his eyes cast down to the floor.

Jane did not know what to do. She repeated firmly to herself: 'This is a dangerous boy, who is quite unscrupulous, and very clever,' and picked up the rifle again. But the weight of it, a cold hostile thing, made her feel sorry. She set it down sharply. 'Look at me, Tembi,' she whispered. Outside, in the passage, Willie was saying in a firm confident voice: 'Yes, Sergeant, we've got him here. He used to work for us, years ago. Yes.'

'Look, Tembi,' whispered Jane quickly. 'I'm going out of

the room. You must run away quickly. How did you get in?'
This thought came to her for the first time. Tembi looked at
the window. Jane could see how the bars had been forced
apart, so that a very slight person could squeeze in,
sideways. 'You must be strong,' she said. 'Now, there isn't
any need to go out that way. Just walk out of that door,' she
pointed at the door to the living-room, 'and go through into
the verandah, and run into the bush. Go to another district
and get yourself an honest job and stop being a thief. I'll talk
to the baas. I'll tell him to tell the police we made a mistake.
Now then, Tembi . . .' she concluded urgently and went into
the passage, where Willie was at the telephone, with his back
to her.

He lifted his head, looked at her incredulously, and said:
'Jane, you're crazy.' Into the telephone he said: 'Yes, come
quickly.' He set down the receiver, turned to Jane and said:
'You know he'll do it again, don't you?' He ran back to the
bedroom.

But there had been no need to run. There stood Tembi,
exactly where they had left him, his fists in his eyes, like a
small child.

'I told you to run away,' said Jane angrily.

'He's nuts,' said Willie.

And now, just as Jane had done, Willie picked up the rifle,
seemed to feel foolish holding it, and set it down again.

Willie sat on the bed and looked at Tembi with the look of
one who has been outwitted. 'Well, I'm damned,' he said.
'It's got me beat, this has.'

Tembi continued to stand there in the centre of the floor,
hanging his head and crying. Jane was crying too. Willie was
getting angrier, more and more irritable. Finally he left the
room, slamming the door, and saying: 'God damn it,
everyone is mad.'

Soon the police came, and there was no more doubt about
what should be done. Tembi nodded at every question: he
admitted everything. The handcuffs were put on him, and he
was taken away in the police car.

At last Willie came back into the bedroom, where Jane lay crying on the bed. He patted her on the shoulder and said: 'Now stop it. The thing is over. We can't do anything.'

Jane sobbed out: 'He's only alive because of me. That's what's so awful. And now he's going to prison.'

'They don't think anything of prison. It isn't a disgrace as it is for us.'

'But he's going to be one of those natives who spend all their lives in and out of prison.'

'Well, what of it?' said Willie. With the gentle, controlled exasperation of a husband, he lifted Jane and offered her his handkerchief. 'Now stop it, old girl,' he reasoned. 'Do stop it. I'm tired. I want to go to bed. I've had hell up and down those damned pavements all day, and I've got a heavy day tomorrow with the tobacco.' He began pulling off his boots.

Jane stopped crying, and also undressed. 'There's something horrible about it all,' she said restlessly. 'I can't forget it.' And finally, 'What did he *want*, Willie? What is it he was *wanting*, all this time?'

Old John's Place

The people of the district, mostly solidly established farmers who intended to live and die on their land, had become used to a certain kind of person buying a farm, settling on it with a vagabond excitement, but with one eye always on the attractions of the nearest town, and then flying off again after a year or so, leaving behind them a sense of puzzled failure, a desolation even worse than usual, for the reason that they had taken no more than a vagabond's interest in homestead and stock and land.

It soon became recognized that the Sinclairs were just such persons in spite of, even because of, their protestations of love for the soil and their relief at the simple life. Their idea of the simple was not shared by their neighbours, who felt they were expected to measure up to standards which were all very well when they had the glamour of distance, but which made life uncomfortably complicated if brought too close.

The Sinclairs bought Old John's Farm, and that was an unlucky place, with no more chance of acquiring a permanent owner than a restless dog has. Although this part of the district had not been settled for more than forty years, the farm had changed hands so often no one could remember how it had got its name. Old John, if he had ever existed, had become merely a place, as famous people may do.

Mr Sinclair had been a magistrate before he retired, and was known to have private means. Even if this had not been known – he referred to himself humorously as 'another of these damned cheque-book farmers' – his dilettante's attitude towards farming would have proved the fact: he made no attempt at all to make money and did not so much as plough a field all the time he was there. Mrs Sinclair gardened and gave parties. Her very first party became a legend, remembered with admiration, certainly, but also with that grudging tolerance that is accorded to spendthrifts who can afford to think of extravagance as a necessary. It was a weekend affair, very highly organized, beginning with tennis on Saturday morning and ending on Sunday night with a lengthy formal dinner for forty people. It was not that the district did not enjoy parties, or give plenty of their own; rather it was, again, that they were expected to enjoy themselves in a way that was foreign to them. Mrs Sinclair was a realist. Her parties, after that, followed a more familiar routine. But it became clear, from her manner, that in settling here she had seen herself chiefly as a hostess, and now felt that she had not chosen her guests with discrimination. She took to spending two or three days of each week in town; and went for prolonged visits to farms in other parts of the country. Mr Sinclair, too, was seen in the offices of estate agents. He did not mention these visits; Mrs Sinclair was reticent when she returned from those other farms.

When people began to say that the Sinclairs were leaving, and for the most familiar reasons, that Mrs Sinclair was not cut out for farm life, their neighbours nodded and smiled, very politely. And they made a point of agreeing earnestly with Mrs Sinclair when she said town life was after all essential to her.

The Sinclairs' farewell party was attended by perhaps fifty people who responded with beautiful tact to what the Sinclairs expected of them. The men's manner towards Mr Sinclair suggested a sympathy which the women, for once, regarded with indulgence. In the past many young men, angry and frustrated, had been dragged back to offices in town by their wives; and there had been farewell parties that left hostility between husbands and wives for days. The wives were unable to condemn a girl who was genuinely unable 'to take the life', as the men condemned her. They championed her, and something always happened then which was what those farmers perhaps dreaded most; for dig deep enough into any one of those wives, and one would find a willing martyr alarmingly apt to expose a bleeding heart in an effort to win sympathy from a husband supposed – for the purposes of this argument – not to have one at all.

But this substratum of feeling was not reached that evening. Here was no tragedy. Mrs Sinclair might choose to repeat, sadly, that she was not cut out for the life; Mr Sinclair could sigh with humorous resignation as much as he liked; but the whole thing was regarded as a nicely acted play. In corners people were saying tolerantly: 'Yes, they'll be much happier there.' Everyone knew the Sinclairs had bought another farm in a district full of cheque-book farmers, where they would be at home. The fact that they kept this secret – or thought they had – was yet another evidence of unnecessary niceness of feeling. Also, it implied that the Sinclairs thought them fools.

In short, because of the guards on everyone's tongue, the party could not take wings, in spite of all the drink and good food.

It began at sundown, on Old John's verandah, which might have been designed for parties. It ran two sides of the house, and was twenty feet deep.

Old John's house had been built on to and extended so often, by so many people with differing tastes and needs, that of all the houses in the district it was the most fascinating for children. It had rambling creeper-covered wings, a staircase climbing to the roof, a couple of rooms raised up a flight of steps here, another set of rooms sunk low, there; and through all these the children ran wild till they began to grow tired and fretful. They then gathered round their parents' chairs, where they were a nuisance, and the women roused themselves unwillingly from conversation, and began to look for places where they might sleep. By eight o'clock it was impossible to move anywhere without watching one's feet – children were bedded down on floors, in the bath, on sofas, any place, in fact, that had room for a child.

That done, the party was free to start properly, if it could.

But there was always a stage when the women sat at one end of the verandah and the men at the other. The host would set bottles of whisky freely on window-ledges and on tables among them. As for the women, it was necessary, in order to satisfy convention, to rally them playfully so that they could expostulate, cover their glasses, and exclaim that really, they couldn't drink another mouthful. The bottles were then left unobtrusively near them, and they helped themselves, drinking no less than the men.

During this stage Mrs Sinclair played the game and sat with the women, but it was clear that she felt defeated because she had been unable to dissolve the ancient convention of the segregation of the sexes. She frequently rose, when it was quite unnecessary, to attend to the food and to the servants who were handing it round; and each time she did so, glances followed her which were as ambiguous as she was careful to keep her own.

Between the two separate groups wandered a miserable child, who was too old to be put to bed with the infants, and too young to join the party; unable to read because that was considered rude; unable to do anything but loiter on the edge of each group in turn, until an impatient look warned her that something was being suppressed for her benefit that would otherwise add to the gaiety of the occasion. As the evening advanced and the liquor fell in the bottles, these looks became more frequent. Seeing the waif's discomfort, Mrs Sinclair took her hand and said: 'Come and help me with the supper,' thus giving herself a philanthropic appearance in removing herself and the child together.

The big kitchen table was covered with cold roast chickens, salads and trifles. These were the traditional party foods of the district; and Mrs Sinclair provided them; though at that first party, two years before, the food had been exotic.

'If I give you a knife, Kate, you won't cut yourself?' she enquired; and then said hastily, seeing the child's face, which protested, as it had all evening, that such consideration was not necessary: 'Of course you won't. Then help me joint these chickens . . . not that the cook couldn't do it perfectly well, I suppose.'

While they carved, Mrs Sinclair chatted determinedly; and only once said anything that came anywhere near to what they were both thinking, when she remarked briskly: 'It is a shame. Really, arrangements should be made for you. Having you about is unfair to you and to the grown-ups.'

'What could they do with me?' enquired Kate reasonably.

'Heaven knows,' acknowledged Mrs Sinclair. She patted Kate's shoulder encouragingly, and said in a gruff and friendly voice: 'Well, I can't say anything helpful, except that you are *bound* to grow up. It's an awful age, being neither one thing nor the other.' Kate was thirteen; and it was an age for which no social provision was made. She was thankful to have the excuse to be here in the kitchen, with at least an appearance of something to do. After a while Mrs Sinclair left her, saying without any attempt at disguising her boredom, even though Kate's parents were among those who bored her: 'I've got to go back, I suppose.'

Kate sat on a hard kitchen chair, and waited for something to happen though she knew she could expect nothing in the way of amusement save those odd dropped remarks which for the past year or so had formed her chief education.

In the meantime she watched the cook pile the pieces of chicken on platters, and hand trays and jugs and plates to the waiters, who were now hurrying between this room and the verandah. The sound of voices was rising steadily; Kate judged that the party must be moving towards its second phase, in which case she must certainly stay where she was, for fear of the third.

During the second phase the men and women mingled, pulling their chairs together in a wide circle; and it was likely that some would dance, calling for music, when the host would wind up an old portable gramophone. It was at this stage that the change in the atmosphere took place which Kate acknowledged by the phrase: 'It is breaking up.' The sharply-defined family units began to dissolve, and they dissolved always in the same way, so that during the last part of each evening, from about twelve o'clock, the same couples could be seen together dancing, talking, or even moving discreetly off into dark rooms or the night outside. This pattern was to Kate as if a veil had been gently removed from the daytime life of the district, revealing another truth, and one that was bare and brutal. Also quite irrevocable, and this was acknowledged by the betrayed themselves (who were also, in their own times and seasons, betrayers) for nothing was more startling than the patient discretion with which the whole thing was treated.

Mrs Wheatley, for instance, a middle-aged lady who played the piano at church services and ran the Women's Institute, known as a wonderful mother and prize cook, seemed on these occasions not to notice how her husband always sought out Mrs Fowler (her own best friend) and how his partnership seemed to strike sparks out of the eyes of everyone present. When Andrew Wheatley emerged from the dark with Nan Fowler, their eyes heavy, their sides pressed close together, Mrs Wheatley would simply avert her eyes and remark patiently (her lips tightened a little, perhaps): 'We ought to be going quite soon.' And so it was with everyone else. There was something recognized as dangerous, that had to be given latitude, emerging at these parties, and existing only because if it were forbidden it would be even more dangerous.

Kate, after many such parties, had learned that after a certain time, no matter how bored she might be, she must take herself out of sight. This was consideration for the grown-ups, not for her; since she did not have to be present in order to understand. There was a fourth stage, reached very rarely, when there was an explosion of raised voices, quarrels and ugliness. It seemed to her that the host and hostess were always acting as sentinels in order to prevent this fourth stage being reached: no matter how much the others drank, or how husbands and wives played false for the moment, they had to remain on guard: at all costs Mrs

Wheatley must be kept tolerant, for everything depended on her tolerance.

Kate had not been in the kitchen alone for long, before she heard the shrill thin scraping of the gramophone; and only a few minutes passed before both Mr and Mrs Sinclair came in. The degree of Kate's social education could have been judged by her startled look when she saw that neither was on guard and that anything might happen. Then she understood from what they said that tonight things were safe.

Mrs Sinclair said casually: 'Have something to eat, Kate?' and seemed to forget her. 'My God, they are a sticky lot,' she remarked to her husband.

'Oh, I don't know, they get around in their own way.'

'Yes, but what a way!' This was a burst of exasperated despair. 'They don't get going tonight, thank heavens. But one expects . . .' Here Mrs Sinclair's eyes fell on Kate, and she lowered her voice. 'What I can't stand is the sameness of it all. You press a button – that's sufficient alcohol – and then the machinery begins to turn. The same things happen, the same people, never a word said – it's awful.' She filled her glass liberally from a bottle that stood among the denuded chicken carcases. 'I needed that,' she remarked, setting the glass down. 'If I lived here much longer I'd begin to feel that I couldn't enjoy myself unless I were drunk.'

'Well, my dear, we are off tomorrow.'

'How did I stick two years of it? It really is awful,' she pursued petulantly. 'I don't know why I should get so cross about it. After all,' she added reasonably, 'I'm no puritan.'

'No, dear, you are not,' said Mr Sinclair drily; and the two looked at each other with precisely that brand of discretion which Kate had imagined Mrs Sinclair was protesting against. The words opened a vista with such suddenness that the child was staring in speculation at this plain, practical lady whose bread and butter air seemed to leave even less room for the romance which it was hard enough to associate with people like the Wheatleys and the Fowlers.

'Perhaps it is that I like a little more – what? – grace? with my sin?' enquired Mrs Sinclair, neatly expressing Kate's own thought; and Mr Sinclair drove it home by saying, still very dry-voiced: 'Perhaps at our age we ought not to be so demanding?'

Mrs Sinclair coloured and said quickly: 'Oh, you know what I mean.' For a moment this couple's demeanour towards each other was unfriendly; then they overcame it in a gulp of laughter. 'Cat,' commented Mrs Sinclair, wryly appreciative; and her husband slid a kiss on her cheek.

'You know perfectly well,' said Mrs Sinclair, slipping her arm through her husband's, 'that what I meant was . . .'

'Well, we'll be gone tomorrow,' Mr Sinclair repeated.

'I think, on the whole,' said Mrs Sinclair after a moment, 'that I prefer worthies like the Copes to the others; they at any rate have the discrimination to know what wouldn't become them . . . except that one knows it is sheer, innate dullness . . .'

Mr Sinclair made a quick warning movement; Mrs Sinclair coloured, looked confused, and gave Kate an irritated glance, which meant: That child here again!

To hear her parents described as 'worthies' Kate took, defiantly, as a compliment; but the look caused the tears to suffuse her eyes, and she turned away.

'I am sorry, my dear,' said kindhearted Mrs Sinclair penitently. 'You dislike being your age as I do being mine, I daresay. We must make allowances for each other.'

With her hand still resting on Kate's shoulder, she remarked to her husband: 'I wonder what Rosalind Lacey will make of all this?' She laughed, with pleasurable maliciousness.

'I wouldn't be surprised if they didn't do very well.' His dryness now was astringent enough to sting.

'How could they?' asked Mrs Sinclair, really surprised. 'I shall be really astonished if they last six months. After all, she's not the type – I mean, she has at least *some* idea.'

'Which idea?' enquired Mr Sinclair blandly, grinning spitefully; and though Mrs Sinclair exclaimed: 'You are horrid, darling,' Kate saw that she grinned no less spitefully.

While Kate was wondering how much more 'different' (the word in her mind to distinguish the Sinclairs from the rest of the district) the coming Laceys would be from the Sinclairs, they all became aware that the music had stopped, and with it the sounds of scraping feet.

'Oh dear,' exclaimed Mrs Sinclair, 'you had better take out another case of whisky. What is the matter with them tonight? Say what you like, but it is exactly like standing beside a machine with an oil-can waiting for it to make grinding noises.'

'No, let them go. We've done what we should.'

'We must join them, nevertheless.' Mrs Sinclair hastily swallowed some more whisky, and sighing heavily, moved to the door. Kate could see through a vista of several open doors to the verandah, where people were sitting about with bored expressions which suggested surreptitious glances at the clock. Among them were her own parents, sitting side by side, their solidity a comment (which was not meant) on the way the others had split up. Mr Cope, who was described as The Puritan by his neighbours, a name he considered a great compliment, managed to enjoy his parties because it was quite possible to shut one's eyes to what went on at them. He was now smiling at Andrew Wheatley and Nan Fowler, as if the way they were interlaced was no more than roguish good fun. I like to see everyone enjoying themselves, his expression said, defiant of the gloom which was in fact settling over everyone.

Kate heard Mrs Sinclair say to her husband, this time impatiently: 'I suppose those Lacey people are going to spoil everything we have done here?' and this remark was sufficient food for thought to occupy her during the time she knew must elapse before she would be called to the car.

What had the Sinclairs, in fact, done here? Nothing – at least, to the mind of the district.

Kate supposed it might be something in the house; but, in fact, nothing had been built on, nothing improved; the place had not even been painted. She began to wander through the rooms, cautious of the sleeping children whose soft breathing could be heard from every darkened corner. The Sinclairs had brought in a great deal of heavy dark furniture, which everyone knew had to be polished by Mrs Sinclair herself, as the servants were not to be trusted with it. There was silver, solid and cumbersome stuff. There were brass trays and fenders and coal scuttles which were displayed for use even in the warm weather. And there were inordinate quantities of water-colours, engravings and oils whose common factor was a pervading heaviness, a sort of brownish sigh in paint. All these things were now in their packing-cases, and when the lorries came in the morning, nothing would be left of the Sinclairs. Yet the Sinclairs grieved for the destruction of something they imagined they had contributed. This paradox slowly cleared in Kate's mind as she associated it with that suggestion in the Sinclairs' manner that everything they did or said referred in some way to a standard that other people could not be expected to understand, a standard that had nothing to do with beauty, ugliness, evil or goodness. Looked at in this light, the couple's attitude became clear. Their clothes, their furniture, even their own persons, all shared that same attribute, which was a kind of expensive and solid ugliness that could not be classified in any terms that had yet been introduced to Kate.

So the child shelved that problem and considered the Laceys, who were to arrive next week. They, presumably, would be even more expensive and ugly, yet kind and satisfactory, than the Sinclairs themselves.

But she did not have time to think of the Laceys for long; for the house began to stir into life as the parents came to rouse their children, and the family units separated themselves off in the dark outside the house, where the cars were parked. For this time, that other pattern was finished with, for now ordinary life must go on.

In the back of the car, heavily covered by blankets, for the night was cold, Kate lay half asleep, and heard her father say: 'I wonder who we'll get this time?'

'More successful, I hope,' said Mrs Cope.

'Horses, I heard,' Mr Cope tested the word.

Mrs Cope confirmed the doubt in his voice by saying decisively: 'Just as bad as the rest, I suppose. This isn't the place for horses on that scale.'

Kate gained an idea of something unrespectable. Not only the horses were wrong; what her parents said was clearly a continuation of other conversations, held earlier in the evening. So it was that long before they arrived the Laceys were judged, and judged as vagrants.

Mr Cope would have preferred to have the kind of neighbours who become a kind of second branch of one's own family, with the children growing up together, and a continual borrowing back and forth of farm implements and books and so forth. But he was a gentle soul, and accepted each new set of people with a courtesy that only his wife and Kate understood was becoming an effort . . . it was astonishing the way all the people who came to Old John's Place were so much *not* the kind the Copes would have liked.

Old John's House was three miles away, a comparatively short distance, and the boundary between the farms was a vlei which was described for the sake of grandness as a river, though most of the year there was nothing but a string of potholes caked with cracked mud. The two houses exchanged glances, as it were, from opposite ridges. The slope on the Copes' side was all ploughed land, of a dull yellow colour which deepened to glowing orange after rain. On the other side was a fenced expanse that had once been a cultivated field, and which was now greening over as the young trees spread and strengthened.

During the very first week of the Laceys' occupation this land became a paddock filled with horses. Mr Cope got out his binoculars, gazed across at the other slope, and dropped them after a while, remarking: 'Well, I suppose it is all right.'

It was a grudging acceptance. 'Why shouldn't they have horses?' asked Kate curiously.

'Oh, I don't know, I don't know. Let's wait and see.' Mr Cope had met Mr Lacey at the station on mail day, and his report of the encounter had been brief, because he was a man who hated to be unfair, and he could not help disliking everything he heard about the Laceys. Kate gathered that the Laceys included a Mr Hackett. They were partners, and had been farming in the Argentine, in the Cape, and in England. It was a foursome, for there was also a baby. The first wagon load of furniture had consisted of a complete suite of furniture for the baby's nurseries and many cases of saddles and stable equipment; and while they waited for the next load the family camped on the verandah without even so much as a teapot or a table for a meal. This tale was already making people smile. But because there was a baby the women warmed towards Mrs Lacey before they had seen her; and Mrs Cope greeted her with affectionate welcome when she arrived to make friends.

Kate understood at first glance that it was not Mrs Lacey's similarity to Mrs Sinclair that had caused the latter to accept her, in advance, as a companion in failure.

Mrs Lacey was not like the homely mothers of the district. Nor did she – like Mrs Sinclair – come into that category of leathery-faced and downright women who seemed more their husbands' partners than their wives. She was a tall, smooth-faced woman, fluidly moving, bronze hair coiled in her neck with a demureness that seemed a challenge, taken with her grace, and with the way she used her eyes. These were large, grey, and very quick; and Kate thought of the swift glances, retreating immediately behind smooth lowered lids, as spies sent out for information. Kate was charmed, as her mother was; as her father was, too – though against his will; but she could not rid herself of distrust. All this wooing softness was an apology for something of which her parents had a premonition, while she herself was in the dark. She knew it was not the fact of the horses, in itself, that created disapproval; just as she knew that it was not merely Mrs Lacey's caressing manner that was upsetting her father.

When Mrs Lacey left, she drew Kate to her, kissed her on both cheeks, and asked her to come and spend the day. Warmth suddenly enveloped the child, so that she was head over ears in love, but distrusting the thing as a mature person does. Because the gesture was so clearly aimed, not at her, but at her parents, that first moment resentment was born with the love and the passionate admiration; and she understood her father when he said slowly, Mrs Lacey having left: 'Well, I suppose it is all right, but I can't say I like it.'

The feeling over the horses was explained quite soon: Mr Lacey and Mr Hackett kept these animals as other people might keep cats. They could not do without them. As with the Sinclairs, there was money somewhere. In this district people did not *farm* horses; they might keep a few for the races or to ride round the lands. But at Old John's Place now there were dozens of horses, and if they were bought and sold it was not for the sake of the money, but because these people enjoyed the handling of them, the business of attending sales and the slow, shrewd talk of men as knowledgeable as themselves. There was, in fact, something excessive and outrageous about the Laceys' attitude towards horses: it was a passionate business, to be disapproved of, like gambling or women.

Kate went over to 'spend the day' a week after she was first asked; and that week was allowed to elapse only because she was too shy to go sooner. Walking up the road beside the paddock she saw the two men, in riding breeches, their whips looped over their arms, moving among the young animals with the seriousness of passion. They were both lean, tough, thin-flanked men, slow-moving and slow-spoken; and they appeared to be gripping invisible sadness with their knees even when they were walking. They turned their heads to stare at Kate, in the manner of those so deeply engrossed in what they are doing that outside things take a long time to grow in to their sight, but finally their whips cut a greeting in the air, and they shouted across to her. Their voices had a burr to them conveying again the exciting sense of things foreign; it was not the careful English voice of the Sinclairs, nor the lazy South African slur. It was an accent that had taken its timbre from many places and climates, and its effect on Kate was as if she had suddenly smelt the sea or heard a quickening strain of music.

She arrived at Old John's Place in a state of exaltation; and was greeted perfunctorily by Mrs Lacey, who then seemed to remind herself of something, for Kate once more found herself enveloped. Then, since the rooms were still scattered with packing-cases, she was asked to help arrange furniture and clear things up. By the end of that day her resentment was again temporarily pushed to the background by the necessity for keeping her standards sharp in her mind; for the Laceys, she knew, were to be resisted; and yet she was being carried away with admiration.

Mrs Sinclair might have brought something intangible here that to her was valuable, and she was right to have been afraid that Mrs Lacey would destroy it. The place was transformed. Mrs Lacey had colour-washed the walls sunny yellow, pale green and rose, and added more light by the sort of curtains and hangings that Kate knew her own mother would consider frivolous. Such rooms were new in this district. As for Mrs Lacey's bedroom, it was outrageous. One wall had been ripped away and it was now a sheet of glass; and across it had been arranged fifty yards of light transparent material that looked like crystallized sunlight. The floor was covered right over from wall to wall with a deep white carpet. The bed, standing out into the room in a way that drew immediate notice, was folded and looped into oyster-coloured satin. It was a room which had nothing to do with the district, nothing to do with the drifts of orange dust outside and the blinding sunlight, nothing to do with anything Kate had ever experienced. Standing just outside the door (for she was afraid she might leave orange-coloured footprints on that fabulous carpet) she stood and stared, and was unable to tear her eyes away even though she knew Mrs Lacey's narrowed grey gaze was fixed on her. 'Pretty?' she asked lightly, at last; and Kate knew she was being used as a test for what the neighbours might later say. 'It's lovely,' said Kate doubtfully; and saw Mrs Lacey smile. 'You'll never keep it clean,' she added, as her mother would certainly do, when she saw this room. 'It will be difficult, but it's worth it,' said Mrs Lacey, dismissing the objection far too lightly, as Kate could see when she looked obliquely along the walls, for already there were films of dust in the grain of the plaster. But all through that day Kate felt as if she were continually being brought face to face with something new, used, and dismissed: she had never been so used; she had never been so ravaged by love, criticism, admiration and doubt.

Using herself (as Mrs Lacey was doing) as a test for other people's reactions, Kate could already hear the sour criticisms which would eventually defeat the Laceys. When she saw the nursery, however, she felt differently. This was something that the women of the district would appreciate. There were, in fact, three rooms for the baby, all conveying a sense of discipline and hygiene, with white enamel, thick cork floors and walls stencilled all over with washable coloured animals. The baby himself, at the crawling stage, was still unable to appreciate his surroundings. His nanny, a very clean, white-aproned native girl, sat several paces away and watched him. Mrs Lacey explained that this nanny had orders not to touch the baby; she was acting as a guard; it was against the principles which were bringing the child up that the germs (which certainly infested every native, washed or not) should come anywhere near him.

Kate's admiration grew; the babies she had known were carried about by piccanins or by the cook's wife. They did not have rooms to themselves, but cots set immediately by their mothers' beds. From time to time they were weighed on the kitchen scales, for feeding charts and baby scales had been encountered only in the pages of women's magazines that arrived on mail days from England.

When she went home that evening she told her mother first about the nurseries and then about the bedroom: as she expected, the first fact slightly outweighed the second. 'She must be a good mother,' said Mrs Cope, adding immediately: 'I should like to know how she's going to keep the dust out of that carpet.' Mr Cope said: 'Well, I'm glad they've got money, because they are certainly going to need it.' These comments acted as temporary breakwaters to the flood that would later sweep through such very modified criticism.

For a while people discussed nothing but the Laceys. The horses were accepted with a shrug and the remark: 'Well, if they've money to burn . . .' Besides, that farm had never been properly used; this was merely a perpetuation of an existing fact. The word found for Mrs Lacey was that she was 'clever'. This was not often a compliment; in any case it was a tentative one. Mrs Lacey made her own clothes, but not in the way the other women made theirs. She cut out patterns from brown paper by some kind of an instinct; she made the desserts and salads from all kinds of unfamiliar substances; she grew vegetables profusely, and was generous with them. People were always finding a native at the back door, with a basket full of fresh things and Mrs Lacey's compliments. In fact, the women were going to Old John's House these days as they might have gone to raid a treasure cave; for they always returned with some fresh delight: mail order catalogues from America, new recipes, patterns for night-dresses. Mrs Lacey's nightdresses were discussed in corners at parties by the women, while the men called out across the room: 'What's that, eh? Let us in on the fun.' For a while it remained a female secret, for it was not so often that something new offered itself as spice to these people who knew each other far, far too well. At last, and it was at the Copes' house, one of the women stood up and demonstrated how Mrs Lacey's nightdresses were cut, while everyone applauded. For the first time Kate could feel a stirring, a quickening in the air; she could almost see it as a man slyly licking his lips. This was the first time, too, that Mr Cope openly disapproved of anything. He might be laughed at, but he was also a collective conscience; for when he said irritably: 'But it is so unnecessary, so *unnecessary*, this kind of thing . . .' everyone became quiet, and talked of something else. He always used that word when he did not want to condemn, but when he was violently uncomfortable. Kate remembered afterwards how the others looked over at him while they talked: their faces showed no surprise at his attitude, but also, for the moment, no agreement; it was as if a child looked at a parent to see how far it might go before forfeiting approval, for there was a lot of fun to be had out of the Laceys yet.

Mrs Lacey did not give her housewarming party until the place was finished, and that took several weeks. She did all the work herself. Kate, who was unable to keep away, helped her, and saw that Mrs Lacey was pleased to have her help. Mr Lacey was not interested in the beautiful house his wife was making; or, at any rate, he did not show it. Provided he was left enough room for books on horses, equipment for horses, and collections of sombreros, belts and saddles, he did not mind what she did. He once remarked: 'Well, it's your money, if you want to pour it down the sink.' Kate thought this sounded as if he wished to stop her; but Mrs Lacey merely returned, sharply: 'Quite. Don't let's go into that again, now.' And she looked meaningly at Kate. Several times she said: 'At last I can feel that I have a home. No one can understand what that is like.' At these moments Kate felt warm and friendly with her, for Mrs Lacey was confiding in her; although she was unable to see Old John's Place as anything but a kind of resthouse. Even the spirit of Mrs Sinclair was still strong in it, after all; for Kate summoned her, often, to find out what she would think of all this. She could positively see Mrs Sinclair standing there looking on, an ironical, pitying ghost. Kate was certain of the pity; because she herself could now hardly bear to look at Mrs Lacey's face when Mr Lacey and Mr Hackett came in to meals, and did not so much as glance at the work that had been done since they left. They would say: 'I heard there was a good thing down in Natal,' or 'that letter from old Perry, in California, made me think . . .' and they were so clearly making preparations for when the restless thing in them that had already driven them from continent to continent spoke again, that she wondered how Mrs Lacey could go on sewing curtains and ordering paints from town. Besides, Mrs Sinclair had known when she was defeated: she had chosen, herself, to leave. Turning the words over on her tongue that she had heard Mrs Sinclair use, she found the right ones for Mrs Lacey. But in the meantime, for the rest of the district, she was still 'clever'; and everyone looked forward to that party.

The Copes arrived late. As they climbed out of the car and moved to the door, they looked for the familiar groups on the verandah, but there was no one there, although laughter came from inside. Soon they saw that the verandah had been cleared of furniture, and the floor had been highly polished. There was no light, save for what fell through the windows; but this gave an appearance, not so much of darkness, but of hushed preparedness. There were tubs of plants set round the walls, forming wells of shadow, and chairs had been set in couples, discreetly, behind pillars and in corners.

Inside the room that opened from the verandah, there were men, but no women. Kate left her parents to assimilate themselves into the group (Mrs Cope protesting playfully that she was the only woman, and felt shy) and passed through the house to the nurseries. The women were putting the children to bed, under the direction of Mrs Lacey. The three rooms were arranged with camp-beds and stretchers, so that they looked like improvised dormitories, and the children were subdued and impressed, for they were not used to such organization. What Mrs Lacey represented, too, subdued them, as it was temporarily subduing their mothers.

Mrs Lacey was in white lace, and very pretty; but not only was she in evening dress and clearly put out because the other women were in their usual best dresses of an indeterminate floral crêpiness that was positively a uniform for such occasions, there was that contrast, stronger now than ever, between what she seemed to want to appear, and what everyone felt of her. Those heavy down-looping, demure coils of hair, the discreet eyelids, the light white dress with childish puffed sleeves, were a challenge, but a challenge that was being held in reserve, for it was not directed at the women.

They were talking with the hurried forced laughter of nervousness. 'You have got yourself up, Rosalind,' said one of them; and this released a chorus of admiring remarks. What was behind the admiration showed itself when Mrs Lacey left the nurseries for a moment to call the native nanny. The same sycophantic lady said tentatively, as if throwing a bird into the air to be shot at: 'It is a sort of madonna look, isn't it? That oval face and smooth hair, I mean . . .' After a short silence someone said pointedly: 'Some madonna,' and then there was laughter, of a kind that sickened Kate, torn as she was between passionate partisanship and the knowledge that here was a lost cause.

Mrs Lacey returned with the native girl; and her brief glance at the women was brave; Kate could have sworn she had heard the laughter and the remark that prompted it. It was with an air of womanly dignity that fitted perfectly with her dress and appearance that she said: 'Now we have got the children into bed, we'll leave the girl to watch them and feel safe.' But this was not how she had said previously: 'Let's get them out of the way, and then we can enjoy ourselves.' The women, however, filed obediently out; ignoring the small protests of the children, who were not at all sleepy, since it was before their proper bedtime.

In the big room Mrs Lacey arranged her guests in what was clearly a planned compromise between the family pattern and the thing she intended should grow out of it. Husbands and wives were put together, yes; but in such a way that they had only to turn their heads to find other partners. Kate was astonished that Mrs Lacey could have learned so much about these people in such a short time. The slightest suggestion of an attraction, which had merited no more than a smile or a glance, was acknowledged frankly by Mrs Lacey in the way she placed her guests. For instance, while the Wheatleys were sitting together, Nan Fowler was beside Andrew Wheatley, and an elderly farmer, who had flirted mildly with Mrs Wheatley on a former occasion, was beside her. Mrs Lacey sat herself by Mr Fowler, and cried gaily: 'Now I shall console you, my dear – no, I shall be jealous if you take any notice of your wife tonight.' For a moment there was a laughing, but uneasy pause, and then Mr Lacey came forward with bottles, and Kate saw that everything was working as Mrs Lacey had intended. In half an hour she saw she must leave, if she wanted to avoid that uncomfortable conviction of being a nuisance. By now Mrs Lacey was beside Mr Lacey at the sideboard, helping him with the drinks; there was no help here – she had been forgotten by her hostess.

Kate slipped away to the kitchens. Here were tables laden with chicken and trifles, certainly; but everything was a little dressed up; this was the district's party food elaborated to a stage where it could be admired and envied without causing suspicion.

Kate had had no time to do more than look for signs of the fatal aspics, sauces and creams when Mrs Lacey entered. Kate had to peer twice to make sure it was Mr Hackett and not Mr Lacey who came with her; the two men seemed to her so very alike. Mrs Lacey asked gaily: 'Having a good tuck-in?' and then the two passed through into the pantries. Here there was a good deal of laughter. Once Kate heard: 'Oh, do be careful . . .' and then Mrs Lacey looked cautiously into the kitchen. Seeing Kate she assumed a good-natured smile and said, 'You'll burst,' and then withdrew her head. Kate had eaten nothing; but she did what seemed to be expected of her, and left the kitchen, wondering just what this thing was that sprang up suddenly between men and women – no, not *what* it was, but what prompted it. The word love, which had already stretched itself to include so many feelings, atmospheres and occasions, had become elastic enough for

Kate not to astonish her. It included, for instance, Mr Lacey and Mrs Lacey helping each other to pour drinks, with an unmistakable good feeling; and Mrs Lacey flirting with Mr Hackett in the pantry while they pretended to be looking for something. To look at Mrs Lacey this evening – that was no problem, for the bright expectancy of love was around her like sunlight. But why Mr Hackett, or Mr Lacey; or why either of them? And then Nan Fowler, that fat, foolish, capable dame who flushed scarlet at a word: what drew Andrew Wheatley to her, of all women, through years of parties, and kept him there?

Kate drifted across the intervening rooms to the door of the big living-room, feeling as if someone had said to her: 'Yes, this house is yours, go in,' but had forgotten to give her the key, or even to tell her where the door was. And when she reached the room she stopped again; through the hazing cigarette smoke, the hubbub, the leaning, laughing faces, the hands lying along chair-arms, grasping glasses, she could see her parents sitting side by side, and knew at once, from their faces, that they wanted only to go home, and that if she entered now, putting her to bed would be made an excuse for going. She went back to the nurseries; as she passed the kitchen door she saw Mr Hackett, Mr Lacey and Mrs Lacey, arms linked from waist to waist, dancing along between the heaped tables and singing: All I want is a *lit*tle bit of love, a *lit*tle bit of love, a *lit*tle bit of love. Both men were still in their riding things, and their boots thumped and clattered on the floor. Mrs Lacey looked like a species of fairy who had condescended to appear to cowhands – cowhands who, however, were cynical about fairies, for at the end of the dance Mr Lacey smacked her casually across her behind and said, 'Go and do your stuff, my girl,' and Mrs Lacey went laughing to her guests, leaving the men raiding the chickens in what appeared to be perfect good fellowship.

In the nurseries Kate was struck by the easy manner in which some twenty infants had been so easily disposed of: they were all asleep. The silence here was deepened by the soft, regular sounds of breathing, and the faint sound of music from beyond the heavy baize doors. Even now, with the extra beds, and the little piles of clothing at the foot of each, everything was so extraordinarily tidy. A great cupboard, with its subdued gleaming paint, presented to Kate an image of Mrs Lacey herself; and she went to open it. Inside it was orderly, and on the door was a list of its contents, neatly typed; but if a profusion of rich materials, like satin and velvet, had tumbled out as the door opened, she would not have been in the least surprised. On the contrary, her feeling of richness restrained and bundled out of the way would have been confirmed, but there was nothing of the kind, not an article out of place anywhere, and on the floor sat the smiling native nanny, apologizing by her manner for her enforced uselessness, for the baby was whimpering and she was forbidden to touch it.

'Have you told Mrs Lacey?' asked Kate, looking doubtfully at the fat pink and white creature, which was exposed in a brief vest and napkin, for it was too hot an evening for anything more. The nanny indicated that she had told Mrs Lacey, who had said she would come when she could.

Kate sat beside the cot to wait, surrendering herself to self-pity: the grown-ups were rid of her, and she was shut into the nursery with the tiny children. Her tears gathered behind her eyes as the baby's cries increased. After some moments she sent the nanny again for Mrs Lacey, and when neither of them returned, she rather fearfully fetched a napkin from the cupboard and made the baby comfortable. Then she held it on her knee, for consolation. She did not much like small babies, but the confiding warmth of this one soothed her. When the nursery door swung open soundlessly, so that Mrs Lacey was standing over her before she knew it, she could not help wriggling guiltily up and exclaiming: 'I changed him. He was crying.' Mrs Lacey said firmly: 'You should never take a child out of bed once it is in. You should never alter a time-table.' She removed the baby and put it back into the cot. She was afloat with happiness, and could not be really angry, but went on: 'If you don't keep them strictly to a routine, they take advantage of you.' This was so like what Kate's own mother always said about her servants, that she could not help laughing; and Mrs Lacey said good-humouredly, turning round from the business of arranging the baby's limbs in an orderly fashion: 'It is all very well, but he is perfectly trained, isn't he? He never gives me any trouble. I am quite certain you have never seen such a well-trained baby around here before.' Kate admitted this was so, and felt appeased: Mrs Lacey had spoken as if there was at least a possibility of her one day reaching the status of being able to profit by the advice: she was speaking as if to an equal.

Kate watched her move to the window, adjust the angle of a pane so that the starlight no longer gleamed in it, and use it as a mirror: there was no looking-glass in the nurseries. The smooth folds of hair were unruffled, but the usually guarded, observant eyes were bright and reckless. There was a vivid flow about Mrs Lacey that made her an exotic in the nursery; even her presence there was a danger to the sleeping children. Perhaps she felt it herself, for she smoothed her forefinger along an eyebrow and said: 'Are you going to stay here?' Kate hesitated. Mrs Lacey said swiftly: 'I don't see why you shouldn't come in. It's your father, though. He's such an old . . .' She stopped herself, and smiled sourly. 'He doesn't approve of me. However, I can't help that.' She was studying Kate. 'Your mother has no idea, no idea at all,' she remarked impatiently, turning Kate about between her hands. Kate understood that had Mrs Lacey been her mother, her clothes would have been graded to suit her age. As it was, she wore a short pink cotton frock, reaching half-way down her thighs, that a child of six might have worn. That frock caused her anguished embarrassment, but loyalty made her say: 'I like pink,' very defiantly. Her eyes, though, raised in appeal to Mrs Lacey's, gained the dry reply: 'Yes, so I see.'

On her way out, Mrs Lacey remarked briskly: 'I've got a lot of old dresses that could be cut down for you. I'll help you with them.' Kate felt that this offer was made because Mrs Lacey truly loved clothes and materials; for a moment her manner to Kate had not been adjusted with an eye to the ridiculous but powerful Mr Cope. She said gratefully: 'Oh, Mrs Lacey . . .'

'And that hair of yours . . .' she heard, as the door swung, and went on swinging, soundlessly. There was the crisp sound of a dress moving along the passage, and the sweet homely smell of the nursery had given way to a perfume as unsettling as the music that poured strongly through the house. The Laceys had a radiogram and the newest records. Feet were swishing and sliding, the voices were softer now, with a reckless note. The laughter, on the other hand, swept by in great gusts. Peering through the doors, Kate tried to determine what 'stage' the party had reached; she saw there had been no stages; Mrs Lacey had fused these people together from the beginning, by the force of wanting to do it, and because her manner seemed to take the responsibility for whatever might happen. Now her light gay voice sounded above the others; she was flirting with everyone, dancing with everyone. Now there was no criticism; they were all in love with her.

Kate could see that while normally at this hour the rooms would be half empty, tonight they were all there. Couples were moving slowly in the subdued light of the verandah, very close together, or sitting at the tables, looking on. Then she suddenly saw someone walking towards her, by herself, in a violent staggering way; and peering close, saw it was Mrs Wheatley. She was crying. 'I want to go home, I want to go home,' she was saying, her tongue loose in her mouth. She did not see Kate, who ran quickly back to the baby, who was now asleep, lying quite still in its white cot, hands flexed at a level with its head, its fingers curled loosely over. Darling baby, whispered Kate, the tears stinging her cheeks. Darling, darling baby. The painful wandering emotion that had filled her for weeks, even since before the Laceys came, when she had felt held safe in Mrs Sinclair's gruff kindliness, spilled now into the child. With a fearful, clutching pounce, she lifted the sleeping child, and cuddled it. Darling, darling baby . . . Later, very much later, she woke to find Mr Lacey, looking puzzled, taking the baby from her; they had been lying asleep on the floor together. 'Your father wants you,' stated Mr Lacey carefully, the sickly smell of whisky coming strong from his mouth. Kate staggered up and gained the door on his arm; but it was not as strong a support as she needed, for he was holding on to tables and chairs as he passed them.

For a moment Kate's sleep-dazed eyes could find nothing to hold them, for the big room was quite empty; so, it seemed, was the verandah. Then she saw Mrs Lacey, dancing by herself down the dim shadowed space, weaving her arms and bending her body, and leaning her head to watch her white reflection move on the polished floor beside her. 'Who is going to dance with me?' she crooned. 'Who is going to dance?'

'You've worn us out,' said a man's voice from Kate's feet; and looking hazily round she saw that couples were sitting around the edges of the space, with their arms about each other. Another voice, a woman's this time, said: 'Oh what a beautiful dress, what a beautiful dress,' repeating it with drunken intensity; and someone answered in a low tone: 'Yes, and not much beneath it, either, I bet.'

Suddenly Kate's world was restored for her by her father's comment at her shoulder: 'So unnecessary!' And she felt herself pushed across the verandah in the path of the dancing Mrs Lacey, whose dim white skirts flung out and across her legs in a crisp caress. But she took no notice of Kate at all; nor did she answer Mr Cope when he said stiffly: 'Goodbye, Mrs Lacey, I am afraid we must take this child to bed.' She continued to dance, humming to herself, a drowsy happy look on her face.

In the car Kate lay wrapped in blankets and looked through the windows at the sky moving past. There was a white blaze of moonlight and the stars were full and bright. It could not be so very late after all, for the night still had the solemn intensity of midnight; that feeling of glacial withdrawal that comes into the sky towards dawn was not yet there. But in the hollow of the veld, where the cold lay congealed, she shivered and sat up. Her parents' heads showed against the stars, and they were being quite silent for her benefit. She was waiting for them to say something; she wanted her confused, conflicting impressions sorted and labelled by them. In her mind she was floating with Mrs Lacey down the polished floor; she was also in the nursery with the fat and lovable baby; she could feel the grip of Mr Lacey's hand on her shoulder. But not a word was said, not a word; though she could almost feel her mother thinking: 'She has to learn for herself,' and her father answering it with a 'Yes, but how unpleasant!'

The next day Kate waited until her father had gone down to the lands in order to watch his labourers at their work, and her mother was in the vegetable garden. Then she said to the cook: 'Tell the missus I have gone to Old John's Place.' She walked away from her home and down to the river with the feeling that large accusing eyes were fixed on her back, but it was essential that she should see Mrs Lacey that day: she was feverish with terror that Mr Lacey had given her away – worse, that the baby had caught cold from lying on the floor beside her, and was ill. She walked slowly, as if dragged by invisible chains: if she left behind her unspoken disapproval, in front of her she sensed cruel laughter and anger.

Guilt, knowledge of having behaved ridiculously, and defiance churned through her; above the tumult another emotion rose like a full moon over a sky of storm. She was possessed by love; she was in love with the Laceys, with the house and its new luxuries, with Mrs Lacey and the baby – even with Mr Lacey and Mr Hackett, who took lustre from Mrs Lacey. By the time she neared the place, her fear had subsided in her to a small wariness, lurking like a small trapped animal with bared teeth; she could think of nothing but that in a moment she would again have entered the magical circle. The drowsy warmth of a September morning, the cooing of pigeons in the trees all about, the dry smell of sunscorched foliage – all these familiar scents and sounds bathed her, sifted through her new sensitiveness and were reissued as it were, in a fresh currency: around Mrs Lacey's house the bush was necessarily more exciting than it could be anywhere else.

The picture in her mind of the verandah and the room behind it, as she had seen them the night before, dissolved like the dream it had appeared to be as she stepped through the screen door. Already at ten in the morning, there was not a sign of the party. The long space of floor had been polished anew to a dull gleaming red; the chairs were in their usual circle at one end, against a bank of ferns, and at the other Mrs Lacey sat sewing, the big circular table beside her heaped with materials and neatly-folded patterns. For a moment she did not notice Kate, who was free to stand and gaze in devoted wonder. Mrs Lacey was in fresh green linen, and her head was bent over the white stuff in her lap in a charming womanly pose. This, surely, could never have been that wild creature who danced down this same verandah last night? She lifted her head and looked towards Kate; her long eyes narrowed, and something hardened behind them until, for a brief second, Kate was petrified by a vision of a boredom so intense that it was as if Mrs Lacey had actually said: 'What! Not you again?' Then down dropped those lids, so that her face wore the insufferable blank piety of a primitive Madonna. Then she smiled. Even that forced smile won Kate; and she moved towards Mrs Lacey with what she knew was an uncertain and apprehensive grin. 'Sit down,' said Mrs Lacey cordially, and spoiled the effect by adding immediately: 'Do your parents know you are here?' She watched Kate obliquely as she put the question. 'No,' said Kate honestly, and saw the lids drop smoothly downwards.

She was stiff with dislike; she could not help but want to accept this parody of welcome as real; but not when the illusion was destroyed afresh every time Mrs Lacey spoke.

She asked timidly: 'How is the baby?' This time Mrs Lacey's look could not possibly be misinterpreted: she had been told by her husband; she had chosen, for reasons of her own, to say nothing. 'The baby's very well,' she said neutrally, adding after a moment: 'Why did you come without telling your mother?' Kate could not give any comfort. 'They would be angry if they knew I was here. I left a message.' Mrs Lacey frowned, laughed with brave, trembling gaiety, and then reached over and touched the bell behind her. Far away in the kitchens of that vast house there was a shrill peal; and soon a padding of bare feet announced the coming of the servant. 'Tea,' ordered Mrs Lacey. 'And bring some cakes for the little missus.' She rearranged her sewing, put her hand to her eyes, laughed ruefully and said: 'I've got such a hangover I won't be able to eat for a week. But it was worth it.' Kate could not reply. She sat fingering the materials heaped on the table; and wondered if any of these were what Mrs Lacey had intended to give her; she even felt a preliminary gratitude, as it were. But Mrs Lacey seemed to have forgotten her promise. The white stuff was for the baby. They discussed suitable patterns for children's vests: it went without saying that Mrs Lacey's pattern was one Kate had never seen before, combining all kinds of advantages, so that it appeared that not a binding, a tape or a fastener had escaped the most far-sighted planning.

The long hot morning had to pass at last; at twelve Mrs Lacey glanced at the folding clock which always stood beside her, and fetched the baby from where he lay in the shade under a big tree. She fed him orange juice, spoon by spoon, without taking him from the pram, while Kate watched him with all the nervousness of one who has betrayed emotion and is afraid it may be unkindly remembered. But the baby ignored her. He was a truly fine child, fat, firm, dimpled. When the orange juice was finished he allowed himself to be wheeled back to the tree without expostulating; and no one could have divined, from his placid look, the baffled affection that Kate was projecting into him.

That done, she accompanied Mrs Lacey to the nursery, where the cup and the spoon and the measuring-glass were boiled for germs and set to cool under a glass bell. The baby's rooms had a cool, ordered freshness; when the curtains blew out into the room, Kate looked instinctively at Mrs Lacey to see if she would check such undisciplined behaviour, but she was looking at the time-table which hung on the inside of the baize door. This time-table began with: 'Six a.m., orange juice'; continued through 'six-thirty, rusk and teething ring, seven, wash and dress'; and ended at 'five p.m., mothering hour and bed'. Somewhere inside of Kate bubbled a disloyal and incredulous laughter, which astonished her; the face she turned towards Mrs Lacey was suddenly so guilty that it was met with a speculative lift of the smooth wide brows. 'What is wrong with you now, Kate?' said Mrs Lacey.

Soon after, the men appeared, in their breeches and trailing their whips behind them across the polished floors. They smiled at Kate, but for a moment their pupils narrowed as Mrs Lacey's had done. Then they all sat on the verandah, not at the sewing end, but at the social part, where the big grass chairs were. The servant wheeled out a table stacked with drinks; Kate could not think of any other house where gin and vermouth were served as a routine, before meals. The men were discussing a gymkhana that was due shortly; Mrs Lacey did not interrupt. When they moved indoors to the dining-room, Kate again felt the incongruity between the orderly charm created by Mrs Lacey and the casual way the men took it, even destroying it by refusing to fit in. Lunch was a cool, lazy affair, with jugs of frosted drinks and quantities of chilled salads. Mr Lacey and Mr Hackett were scribbling figures on pieces of paper and talking together all through the meal; and it was not until it was over that Kate understood that the scene had been like a painted background to the gymkhana which to the men was far more real than anything Mrs Lacey said or did.

As soon as it was over, they offered their wide, lazy good-humoured grin, and slouched off again to the paddock. Kate could have smiled; but she knew there would be no answering smile from Mrs Lacey.

In silence they took their places at the sewing-table; and at two o'clock to the minute Mrs Lacey looked at the clock and brought the baby in for his nap, leaving the nanny crouched on the floor to guard him.

Afterwards Kate's discomfort grew acute. In the district 'coming over for the day' meant either one of two things: something was arranged, like tennis or swimming, with plenty to eat and drink; or the women came by themselves to sew and cook and knit, and this sharing of activity implied a deeper sharing. Kate used to think that her mother came back from a day with one of her women friends wearing the same relaxed softened expression as she did after a church service.

But Kate was at a hopelessly loose end, and Mrs Lacey did not show it only because it suited her book better not to. She offered to sew, and did not insist when Mrs Lacey rather uncomfortably protested. Mrs Lacey sewed exquisitely, and anything she could do would be bungling in comparison.

At last the baby woke. Kate knew the time-table said: 'Three to five: walk or playpen,' and offered to push the pram. Again she had to face up to the shrewd, impatient look, while Mrs Lacey warned: 'Remember, babies don't like being messed about.' 'I know,' said Kate consciously, colouring. When the baby was strapped in and arranged, Kate was allowed to take the handles of the pram. Leading away from the house in the opposite direction from the river was a long avenue of trees where the shade lay cool and deep. 'You mustn't go away from the trees,' directed Mrs Lacey; and Kate saw her return to the house, her step quickening with relief; whatever her life was, the delicious, devoted, secret life that Kate imagined, she was free to resume it now that Kate was gone: it seemed impossible this lovely and secret thing should not exist: for it was the necessary complement to the gross practicality of her husband and Mr Hackett. But when Kate returned at five o'clock, after two hours of steady walking up and down the avenue, pushing the pram and suppressing her passionate desire to cuddle the indifferent baby, Mrs Lacey was baking tarts in the kitchen.

If she was to be back home before it grew dark, she must leave immediately. She lingered, however, till five past five: during those two hours she had, in fact, been waiting for the moment when Mrs Lacey would 'mother' the baby. But Mrs Lacey seated herself with a book and left the child to crawl on a rug at her feet. Kate set off on the road home; and this time the eyes she felt follow her were irritated and calculating.

At the gate stood her mother. 'You shouldn't have gone off without telling me!' she exclaimed reproachfully. Now, Kate was free to roam as she willed over the farm, so this was unjust, and both sides knew it to be so. 'I left a message,' said Kate, avoiding her mother's eyes.

Next morning she was loitering about the gate looking out over the coloured slopes to the Laceys' house, when her mother came up behind her, apparently cutting zinnias, but in fact looking for an opportunity to express her grievance. 'You would live there if you could, wouldn't you, dear?' she said, smiling painfully. 'All those fashions and new clothes and things, we can't compete, can we?' Kate's smile was as twistingly jealous as hers; but she did not go to the Laceys' that day. After all, she couldn't very well: there were limits. She remained in that part of the farm which lay beside the Laceys', and looked across at the trees whose heavy greenness seemed to shed a perfume that was more than the scent of sun-heated leaves, and where the grass beckoned endlessly as the wind moved along it. Love, still unrecognized, still unaccepted in her, flooded this way and that, leaving her limp with hatred or exalted with remembrance. And through it all she thought of the baby while resentment grew in her. Whether she stood with the binoculars stuck to her eyes, hour after hour, hoping for a glimpse of Mrs Lacey on the verandah, or watching the men lean against the fence as the horses moved about them, the baby was in the back of her mind; and the idea of it was not merely the angry pity that is identification with suffering, but also a reflection of what other people were thinking. Kate knew, from a certain tone in her mother's voice when she mentioned that child, that she was not wholly convinced by time-tables and hygiene.

The ferment of the last party had not settled before Mrs Lacey issued invitations for another; there had only been a fortnight's interval. Mr Cope said, looking helplessly across at his wife: 'I suppose we ought to go?' and Mrs Cope replied guardedly: 'We can't very well not, when they are our nearest neighbours, can we?' 'Oh Lord!' exclaimed Mr Cope, moving irritably in his chair. Then Kate felt her parents' eyes come to rest on her; she was not surprised when Mr Cope asked: 'When does Kate go back to school?' 'The holidays don't end for another three weeks.'

So the Copes all went to Mrs Lacey's second party, which began exactly as the first had done: everything was the same. The women whisked their children into the improvised dormitory without showing even a formal uneasiness. One of them said: 'It is nice to be free of them for once, isn't it?' and Kate saw Mrs Lacey looking humorous before she turned away her face. That evening Mrs Lacey wore a dress of dim green transparent stuff, as innocent and billowing, though as subtly indiscreet as the white one. And the women – save for Mrs Cope – were in attempts at evening dress.

Mrs Lacey saw Kate standing uncertainly in the passage, grasped her by the shoulder, and pushed her gently into the room where all the people were. 'I shall find you a boyfriend,' she stated gaily; and Kate looked apprehensively towards her parents, who were regarding her, and everyone else, with helpless disapproval. Things had gone beyond their censure already: Mrs Lacey was so sure of herself that she could defy them about their own daughter before their eyes. But Kate found herself seated next to a young assistant recently come to the district, who at eighteen was less likely to be tolerant of little girls than an older man might have been. Mrs Lacey had shown none of her usual shrewdness in the choice. After a few painful remarks, Kate saw this young man turn away from her, and soon she tried to slip away. Mr Hackett, noticing her, put his arm round her and said, 'Don't run away, my dear,' but the thought of her watching parents stiffened her to an agony of protest. He dropped his arm, remarked humorously to the rest of the room – for everyone was looking over at them and laughing: 'These girlish giggles!' and turned his attention to the bottle he was holding. Kate ran to the kitchens. Soon she fled from there, as people came in. She crept furtively to the baby's cot, but he was asleep; and it was not long before Mrs Lacey glanced in and said: 'Do leave him alone, Kate,' before vanishing again. Kate took herself to that set of rooms that Mrs Lacey had not touched at all. They were still roughly whitewashed, and the cement floors, though polished, were bare. Saddles of various patterns hung in rows in one room; another was filled with beautifully patterned belts with heavy silver buckles and engraved holsters. There were, too, rows and rows of guns of all kinds, carved, stamped, twisted into strange shapes. They came from every part of the world, and were worth a fortune, so people said.

These rooms were where Mr Lacey and Mr Hackett liked to sit; and they had heavy leather armchairs, and a cupboard with a private supply of whisky and siphons. Kate sat stiffly on the edge of one of the chairs, and looked at the rows of weapons: she was afraid the men might be angry to find her there. And in fact it was not long before Mr Lacey appeared in the doorway, gave an exclamation, and withdrew. He had not been alone. Kate, wondering who the lady was, and whether Mrs Lacey would mind, left the house altogether and sat in the back of their car. Half asleep, she watched the couples dancing along the verandah, and saw how at one end a crowd of natives gathered outside in the dark, pressing their noses to the wire gauze, in curious admiration at the white people enjoying themselves. Sometimes a man and a woman would come down the steps, their arms about each other, and disappear under the trees; or into the cars. She shrank back invisibly, for in the very next car were a couple who were often visitors at their house, though as members of their own families; and she did not want them to have the embarrassment of knowing she was there. Soon she stuck her fingers in her ears; she felt sick, and she was also very hungry.

But it was not long before she heard shouts from the house, and the shouts were angry. Peering through the back window of the car she could see people standing around two men who were fighting. She saw legs in riding breeches, and then Mrs Lacey came and stood between them. 'What nonsense,' Kate heard her exclaim, her voice still high and gay, though strained. Almost immediately Kate heard her name called, and her mother appeared, outlined against the light. Kate slipped from the car so that the couple in the next car might not see her and ran to tug at her mother's arm.

'So there you are!' exclaimed Mrs Cope in a relieved voice. 'We are going home now. Your father is tired.'

In the car Kate asked: 'What were Mr Hackett and Mr Lacey fighting about?' There was a pause before Mrs Cope replied: 'I don't know, dear.' 'Who won?' insisted Kate. Then, when she got no answer, she said: 'It's funny, isn't it, when in the daytime they are such friends?' In the silence the sound of her own words tingled in her ears, and Kate watched something unexpected, yet familiar, emerge. Here it was again, the other pattern. It was of Mr Hackett that she thought as the car nosed its way through the trees to their own farm, and her wonder crystallized at last into exclamation: 'But they are so much alike!' She felt as she would have done if she had seen a little girl, offered a doll, burst into tears because she had not been given another that was identical in every way. 'Don't bother your head about it,' soothed Mrs Cope. 'They aren't very nice people. Forget about it.'

The next Sunday was Church Sunday. The ministers came in rotation: Presbyterian, Church of England, Roman Catholic. Sometimes there was a combined service. The

Copes never missed the Church of England Sundays.

The services were held in the district hall, near the station. The hall was a vast barn of a place, and the small group of worshippers crowded at one end, near the platform, where Nan Fowler perched to play the hymns, like a thin flock of birds in a very large tree. The singing rose meagrely over the banging of the piano and dissolved in the air above their heads: even from the door the music seemed to come from a long way off.

The Laceys and Mr Hackett arrived late that day, tiptoeing uncomfortably to the back seats and arranging themselves so that Mrs Lacey sat between the men. This was the first time they had been to church. Kate twisted her neck and saw that for once the men were not in riding things; released, thus, from their uniform, looking ordinary in brown suits, it was easier to see them as two different people. But even so, they were alike, with the same flat slouching bodies and lean humorous faces. They hummed tunelessly, making a bumblebee noise, and looked towards the roof. Mrs Lacey, who held the hymn book for all three of them, kept her eyes on the print in a manner which seemed to be directing the men's attention to it. She looked very neat and sober today, and her voice, a pretty contralto, was stronger than anyone's, so that in a little while she was leading the singing. Again, irresistibly, the subterranean laughter bubbled in Kate, and she turned away, glancing doubtfully at her mother, who hissed in her ear: 'It's rude to stare.'

When the service was over, Mrs Lacey came straight to Mrs Cope and held out her hand. 'How are you?' she asked winningly. Mrs Cope replied stiffly: 'It is nice to see you at church.' Kate saw Mrs Lacey's face twitch, and sympathy told her that Mrs Lacey, too, was suffering from the awful need to laugh. However, her face straightened, and she glanced at Mr Cope and flushed. She stood quietly by and watched while Mrs Cope issued invitations to everyone who passed to come home to Sunday lunch. She was expecting an invitation too, but none was offered. Mrs Cope finally nodded, smiled, and climbed into the car. There was suddenly a look of brave defiance about Mrs Lacey that tugged at Kate's heart: if it had not been for the stoic set of her shoulders as she climbed into the car with her two men, Kate would have been able to bear the afternoon better. When lunch was over, things arranged themselves as usual with the men on one side of the room and the women on the other. Kate stood for a while behind her father's chair; then, with burning cheeks, she moved over to the women who had their heads together around her mother's chair. They glanced up at her, and then behaved as grown-up people do when they wish to talk and children are in the way; they simply pretended she was not there. In a few moments Kate sped from the house and ran through the bush to her place of refuge, which was a deep hollow over which bushes knotted and tangled. Here she flung herself and wept.

Nobody mentioned the Laceys at supper. People seemed to have been freed from something. There was a great deal of laughter at the comfortable old jokes at which they had been laughing for years. The air had been cleared: something final had happened, or was going to happen. Later, when these farmers and their wives, carrying their children rolled in blankets, went to find their cars, Kate lifted the curtain and looked over at the cluster of lights on the opposite ridge, and wondered if Mrs Lacey was watching the headlights of the cars swing down the various roads home, and if so, what it was she was thinking and feeling.

Next morning a basket arrived at the back door, full of fresh vegetables and roses. There was also a note addressed to Miss Catherine Cope. It said: 'If you have nothing better to do, come and spend the day. I have been looking over some of my old dresses for you.' Kate read this note, feeling her mother's reproachful eyes fixed on her, and reluctantly handed it over. 'You are not going, surely!' exclaimed Mrs Cope. 'I might as well, for the last time,' said Kate. When she heard what it was she had said, the tears came into her eyes, so that she could not turn round to wave goodbye to her mother.

That last day she missed nothing of the four miles' walk: she felt every step.

The long descent on their side was through fields which were now ploughed ready for the wet season. A waste of yellow clods stretched away on either side, and over them hung a glinting haze of dust. The road itself was more of a great hogsback, for the ditches on either side had eroded into cracked gullies fifteen feet deep. Soon, after the rains, this road would have to be abandoned and another cut, for the water raced turbulently down here during every storm, swirling away the soil and sharpening the ridge. At the vlei, which was now quite dry, the gullies had cut down into a double pothole, so that the drift was unsafe even now. This time next year the old road to the Laceys would be a vivid weal down the slope where no one could walk.

On the other side the soil changed: here it was pale and shining, and the dews of each night hardened it so that each step was a small crusty subsidence. Because the lands had not been farmed for years and were covered with new vegetation, the scars that had been cut down this slope, too, were healing, for the grasses had filmed over them and were gripping the loose soil.

Before Kate began to ascend this slope she took off her cretonne hat that her mother had made to 'go' with her frock, and which stuck up in angles round her face, and hid it in an antbear hole, where she could find it on the way home; she could not bear Mrs Lacey to see her in it.

Being October, it was very hot, and the top of her head began to feel as if a weight were pressing on it. Soon her shoulders ached too, and her eyes dazzled. She could hardly see the bright swift horses in the bushy paddock for glare, and her tight smile at Mr Hackett and Mr Lacey was more like a grimace of pain. When she arrived on the verandah, Mrs Lacey, who was sewing, gave her a concerned glance, and exclaimed: 'What have you done with your hat?' 'I forgot it,' said Kate.

On the sewing table were piles of Mrs Lacey's discarded frocks. She said kindly: 'Have a look at these and see which you would like.' Kate blinked at the glare outside and slid thankfully into a chair; but she did not touch the frocks. After a while her head cleared and she said: 'I can't take them. My mother wouldn't like it. Thank you all the same.' Mrs Lacey glanced at her sharply, and went on sewing for a while in silence. Then she said lightly: 'I don't see why you shouldn't, do you?' Kate did not reply. Now that she had recovered, and the pressure on her head had gone, she was gazing about her, consciously seeing everything for the last time, and wondering what the next lot of people would be like.

'Did you have a nice time yesterday?' asked Mrs Lacey, wanting to be told who had spent the day with the Copes, what they had done, and – most particularly – what they had said. 'Very nice, thank you,' said Kate primly; and saw Mrs Lacey's face turn ugly with annoyance before she laughed and asked: 'I am in disgrace, am I?'

But Kate could not now be made an ally. She said cautiously: 'What did you expect?'

Mrs Lacey said, with amused annoyance: 'A lot of hypocritical old fogeys.' The word 'hypocrite' isolated itself and stood fresh and new before Kate's eyes; and it seemed to her all at once that Mrs Lacey was wilfully misunderstanding.

She sat quietly, watching the sun creep in long warm streaks towards her over the shining floor, and waited for Mrs Lacey to ask what she so clearly needed to ask. There would be some question, some remark, that would release her, so that she could go home, feeling a traitor no longer: she did not know it, but she was waiting for some kind of an apology, something that would heal the injustice that burned in her: after all, for Mrs Lacey's sake she had let her own parents dislike her.

But there was no sound from Mrs Lacey, and when Kate looked up, she saw that her face had changed. It was peaked,

and diminished, with frail blue shadows around the mouth
and eyes. Kate was looking at an acute, but puzzled fear, and
could not recognize it; though if she had been able to search
inside herself, now, thinking of how she feared to return
home, she would have found pity for Mrs Lacey.

After a while she said: 'Can I take the baby for a walk?' It
was almost midday, with the sun beating directly downwards; the baby was never allowed out at this hour; but after
a short hesitation Mrs Lacey gave her an almost appealing
glance and said: 'If you keep in the shade.' The baby was
brought from the nursery and strapped into the pram. Kate
eased the pram down the steps, but instead of directing her
steps towards the avenue, where there might possibly have
been a little shade, even at this hour, went down the road to
the river. On one side, where the bushes were low, sun-glare
fell about the grass-roots. On the other infrequent patches of
shade stood under the trees. Kate dodged from one patch to
the next, while the baby reclined in the warm airless cave
under the hood.

She could not truly care: she knew Mrs Lacey was watching
her and did not turn her head; she had paid for this by weeks
of humiliation. When she was out of sight of the house she
unstrapped the baby and carried it a few paces from the road
into the bush. There she sat, under a tree, holding the child
against her. She could feel the sweat running down her face,
and did not lift her hand to find whether tears mingled with
it: her eyes were smarting with the effort of keeping her lids
apart over the pressure of tears. As for the baby, beads of
sweat stood all over his face. He looked vaguely about and
reached his hands for the feathery heads of grasses and
seemed subdued. Kate held him tight, but did not caress him;
she was knotted tight inside with tears and anger. After a
while she saw a tick crawl out of the grass on to her leg, and
from there to the baby's leg. For a moment she let it crawl;
from that dark region of her mind where the laughter
spurted, astonishingly, came the thought: He might get tick
fever. She could see Mrs Lacey very clearly, standing beside a

tiny oblong trench, her head bent under the neat brown hat. She could hear women saying, their admiration and pity heightened by contrition: 'She was so brave, she didn't give way at all.'

Kate brushed off the tick and stood up. Carefully keeping the sun off the child – his cheek was already beginning to redden – she put him back in the pram, and began wheeling it back. Whatever it was she had been looking for, satisfaction, whether of pain, or love, she had not been given it. She could see Mrs Lacey standing on the verandah shading her eyes with her hand as she gazed towards them. Another thought floated up: she vividly saw herself pleading with Mrs Lacey: 'Let me keep the baby, you don't want him, not really.'

When she faced Mrs Lacey with the child, and looked up into the concerned eyes, guilt swept her. She saw that Mrs Lacey's hands fumbled rapidly with the straps; she saw how the child was lifted out, with trembling haste, away from the heat and the glare. Mrs Lacey asked: 'Did you enjoy the walk?' but although she appeared to want to make Kate feel she had been willingly granted this pleasure, Mrs Lacey could not help putting her hand to the baby's head and saying: 'He's very hot.'

She sat down beside her sewing-table; and for the first time Kate saw her actually hold her child in her arms, even resting her cheek against his head. Then the baby wriggled round towards her and put his arms around her neck and burrowed close, gurgling with pleasure. Mrs Lacey appeared taken aback; she looked down at her own baby with amazement in which there was also dismay. She was accepting the child's cuddling in the way a woman accepts the importunate approaches of someone whose feelings she does not want to hurt. She was laughing and protesting and putting down the baby's clutching arms. Still laughing, she said to Kate: 'You see, this is all your doing.' The words seemed to Kate so extraordinary that she could not reply. Through her mind floated pictures of women she had known from the district, and they flowed together to make one picture – her idea, from experience, of a mother. She saw a plump smiling woman holding a baby to her face for the pleasure of its touch. She remembered Nan Fowler one mail day at the station, just after the birth of her third child. She sat in the front seat of the car, with the bundled infant on her lap, laughing as it nuzzled to get to her breasts, where appeared two damp patches. Andrew Wheatley stood beside the car talking to her, but her manner indicated a smiling withdrawal from him. 'Look,' she seemed to be saying – not at all concerned for her stretched loose body and those shameless patches of milk – 'as you observe, I can't be really with you for the moment, but I'd like to see you later.'

Kate watched Mrs Lacey pull her baby's arms away from her neck, and then gently place it in the pram. She was frowning. 'Babies shouldn't be messed about,' she remarked; and Kate saw that her dislike of whatever had just happened was stronger even than her fear of Kate's parents.

Kate got up, saying: 'I feel funny.' She walked blindly through the house in the direction of the bedroom. The light had got inside her head: that was how it felt; her brain was swaying on waves of light. She got past Mrs Lacey's bed and collapsed on the stool of the dressing-table, burying her face in her arms. When she lifted her eyes, she saw Mrs Lacey standing beside her. She saw that her own shoes had left brownish patches on the carpet, and that along the folds of the crystalline drapery at the windows were yellowish streaks.

Gazing into the mirror, her own face stared back. It was a narrow face, pale and freckled; a serious lanky face, and incongruously above it perched a large blue silk bow from which pale lanky hair straggled. Kate stood up and looked at her body in shame. She was long, thin, bony. The legs were a boy's legs still, flat lean legs set on to a plumping body. Two triangular lumps stood out from her tight child's bodice. Kate turned in agony from this reflection of herself, which seemed to be rather of several different young boys and girls haphazardly mingled, and fixed her attention to Mrs Lacey, who was frowning as she listened to the baby's crying from the verandah: this time he had not liked being put down. 'There!' she exclaimed angrily, 'that's what happens if you give in to them.' Something rose in a wave to Kate's head: 'Why did they say the baby is exactly like Mr Hackett?' she demanded, without knowing she had intended to speak at all. Looking wonderingly up at Mrs Lacey she saw the shadows round her mouth deepen into long blue lines that ran from nose to chin; Mrs Lacey had become as pinched and diminished as her room now appeared. She drew in her breath violently: then held herself tight, and smiled. 'Why, what an extraordinary thing for them to say,' she commented, walking away from Kate to fetch a handkerchief from a drawer, where she stood for a while with her back turned, giving them both an opportunity to recover. Then, turning, she looked long and closely at Kate, trying to determine whether the child had known what it was she had said.

Kate faced her with wide and deliberately innocent eyes; inside she was gripped with amazement at the strength of her own desire to hurt the beloved Mrs Lacey, who had hurt her so badly: it was this that the innocence was designed to conceal.

They both moved away from the room to the verandah, with the careful steps of people conscious of every step, every action. There was, however, not a word spoken.

As they passed through the big room Mrs Lacey took a photograph album from a bookstand and carried it with her to the chairs. When Kate had seated herself, the album was deposited on her lap; and Mrs Lacey said: 'Look at these; here are pictures of Mr Lacey when he was a baby; you can see that the baby is the image of him.' Kate looked dutifully at several pages of photographs of yet another fat, smiling, contented baby, feeling more and more surprised at Mrs Lacey. The fact was that whether the baby did or did not look like Mr Hackett was not the point; it was hard to believe that Mrs Lacey did not understand this, had not understood the truth, which was that the remark had been made in the first place as a sort of stick snatched up to beat her with. She put down the album and said: 'Yes, they do look alike, don't they?' Mrs Lacey remarked casually: 'For the year before the baby was born I and Mr Lacey were living alone on a ranch. Mr Hackett was visiting his parents in America.' Kate made an impatient movement which Mrs Lacey misinterpreted. She said reproachfully: 'That was a terrible thing to say, Kate.' 'But I didn't say it.' 'No matter who said it, it was a terrible thing.' Kate saw that tears were pouring down Mrs Lacey's cheeks.

'But . . .'

'But what?'

'It isn't the point.'

'What isn't the point?'

Kate was silent: there seemed such a distance between what she felt and how Mrs Lacey was speaking. She got up, propelled by the pressure of these unsayable things, and began wandering about the verandah in front of Mrs Lacey. 'You see,' she said helplessly, 'we've all been living together so long. We all know each other very well.'

'You are telling me,' commented Mrs Lacey, with an unpleasant laugh. 'Well?'

Kate sighed. 'Well, we have all got to go on living together, haven't we? I mean, when people have *got* to live together . . .' She looked at Mrs Lacey to see if she had understood.

She had not.

Kate had, for a moment, a vivid sense of Mrs Sinclair standing there beside her; and from this reinforcement she gained new words: 'Don't you see? It's not what people do, it's how they do it. It can't be broken up.'

Mrs Lacey's knotted forehead smoothed, and she looked ruefully at Kate: 'I haven't a notion of what I've done, even now.' This note, the playful note, stung Kate again: it was as if Mrs Lacey had decided that the whole thing was too childish to matter.

She walked to the end of the verandah, thinking of Mrs

Sinclair. 'I wonder who will live here next?' she said dreamily, and turned to see Mrs Lacey's furious eyes. 'You might wait till we've gone,' she said. 'What makes you think we are going?'

Kate looked at her in amazement: it was so clear to her that the Laceys would soon go.

Seeing Kate's face, Mrs Lacey's grew sober. In a chastened voice she said: 'You frighten me.' Then she laughed, rather shrilly.

'Why did you come here?' asked Kate unwillingly.

'But why on earth shouldn't we?'

'I mean, why *this* district. Why so far out, away from everything?'

Mrs Lacey's eyes bored cruelly into Kate's. 'What have they been saying? What are they saying about us?'

'Nothing,' said Kate, puzzled, seeing that there was a new thing here, that people could have said.

'I suppose that old story about the money? It isn't true. It isn't true, Kate.' Once again tears poured down Mrs Lacey's face and her shoulders shook.

'No one has said anything about money. Except that you must have a lot,' said Kate. Mrs Lacey wiped her eyes dry and peered at Kate to see if she were telling the truth. Then her face hardened. 'Well, I suppose they'll start saying it now,' she said bitterly.

Kate understood that there was something ugly in this, and directed at her, but not what it could be. She turned away from Mrs Lacey, filled again with the knowledge of injustice.

'Aren't I ever to have a home? Can't I ever have a home?' wept Mrs Lacey.

'Haven't you ever had one?'

'No, never. This time I thought I would be settled for good.'

'I think you'll have to move again,' said Kate reasonably. She looked around her, again trying to picture what would happen to Old John's Place when the new people came.

Seeing that look, Mrs Lacey said quickly: 'That's superstition. It isn't possible that places can affect people.'

'I didn't say they did.'

'What are you saying, then?'

'But you get angry when I do say. I was just thinking that . . .'

'Well?'

Kate stammered: 'You ought to go somewhere where . . . that has your kind of people.' She saw this so clearly.

Mrs Lacey glared at her and snapped: 'When I was your age I thought of nothing but hockey.' Then she picked up her sewing as she might have swallowed an aspirin tablet, and sat stitching with trembling, angry fingers.

Kate's lips quivered. Hockey and healthy games were what her own mother constantly prescribed as prophylactics against the little girl she did not want Kate to be.

Mrs Lacey went on: 'Don't you go to school?'

'Yes.'

'Do you like it?'

Kate replied: Yes, knowing it was impossible to explain what school meant to her: it was a recurring episode in the city where time raced by, since there was nothing of importance to slow it. School had so little to do with this life, on the farm, and the things she lived by, that it was like being taken to the pictures as a treat. One went politely, feeling grateful, then sat back and let what happened on the screen come at you and flow over you. You left with relief, to resume a real life.

She said slowly to Mrs Lacey, trying to express that injustice that was corroding her: 'But if I had been – like you want – you wouldn't have been able to – find out what you wanted, would you?'

Mrs Lacey stared. 'If you were mine I'd . . .' She bit off her thread angrily.

'You'd dress me properly,' said Kate sarcastically, quivering with hate, and saw Mrs Lacey crimson from throat to hairline.

'I think I'd better be going home,' she remarked, sidling to the door.

'You must come over again sometime,' remarked Mrs Lacey brightly, the fear lying deep in her eyes.

'You know I can't come back,' said Kate awkwardly.

'Why not?' said Mrs Lacey, just as if the whole conversation had never happened.

'My parents won't let me. They say you are bad for me.'

'Do you think I am bad for you?' asked Mrs Lacey, with her high, gay laugh.

Kate stared at her incredulously. 'I'm awfully glad to have met you,' she stammered finally, with embarrassment thick in her tongue. She smiled politely, through tears, and went away down the road to home.

'Leopard' George

George Chester did not earn his title for some years after he first started farming. He was well into middle age when people began to greet him with a friendly clout across the shoulders and the query: 'Well, what's the score now?' Their faces expressed the amused and admiring tolerance extorted by a man who has proved himself in other ways, a man entitled to eccentricities. But George's passion for hunting leopards was more than a hobby. There was a period of years when the District Notes in the local paper were headed, Friday after Friday, by a description of his week-end party: 'The Four Winds' Hunt Club bag this Sunday was four jackals and a leopard' – or a wild dog and two leopards, as the case might be. All kinds of game make good chasing; the horses and dogs went haring across the veld every week after whatever offered itself. As for George, it was a recognized thing that if there was a chance of a leopard, the pack must be called off its hare, its duiker, its jackal, and directed after the wily spotted beast, no matter what the cost in time or patience or torn dogs. George had been known to climb a kopje alone, with a wounded leopard waiting for him in the tumbled chaos of boulder and tree; they told stories of how he walked once into a winding black cave (his ammunition finished and his torch smashed) and finally clouted the clawing spitting beast to death with the butt of his rifle. The scars of that fight were all over his body. When he strode into the post office or store, in shorts, his sleeves rolled up, people looked at the flesh that was raked from shoulder to knuckle and from thigh to ankle with great white weals, and quickly turned their eyes away. Behind his back they might smile, their lips compressed forbearingly.

But that was when he was one of the wealthiest men in the

district; one of those tough, shrewd farmers who seem ageless, for sun and hard work and good eating have shaped their bodies into cases of muscle that time can hardly touch.

George was the child of one of the first settlers. He was bred on a farm, and towns made him restless. When the First World War began he set off at once for England where he joined up in a unit that promised plenty of what he called fun. After five years of fighting he had collected three decorations, half a dozen minor wounds, and the name 'Lucky George'. He allowed himself to be demobilized with the air of one who does not insist on taking more than his fair share of opportunities.

When he returned to Southern Rhodesia, it was not to that part of it he had made his own as a child; that was probably because his father's name was so well known there, and George was not a man to be the mere son of his father.

He saw many farms before finally choosing Four Winds. The agent was a man who had known his father well: this kind of thing still counts for more than money in places where there is space and time for respect of the past, and George was offered farms at prices which broke the agent's businessman's heart. Besides, he was a war hero. But the agent was defeated by George. He had been selling farms long enough to recognize the look that comes into a man's face when he is standing on land that appeals to him, land which he will shape and knead and alter to the scale of his own understanding – the look of the creator. That look did not appear on George's face.

After months of visiting one district after another, the agent took George to a farm so beautiful that it seemed impossible he could refuse to buy it. It was low lying and thickly covered with trees, and the long fat strip of rich red land was held between two rivers. The house had gardens running away on two sides to vistas of water. Rivers and richness and unspoiled trees and lush grass for cattle – such farms are not to be had for whistling in Africa. But George stood there on a rise between the stretches of water where they ran close to each other, and moved his shoulders restlessly in a way which the agent had grown to understand. 'No good?' he said, sounding disgruntled. But by now there was that tolerance in him for George which he was always to make people feel: his standards were different. Incomprehensible they might be; but the agent at last saw that George was not looking for the fat ease promised by this farm. 'If you could only tell me what you *are* looking for,' he suggested, rather irritably.

'This is a fine farm,' said George, walking away from it, holding his shoulders rigid. The agent grabbed his elbow and made him stop. 'Listen to me,' he said. 'This must be one of the finest farms in the country.'

'I know,' said George.

'If you want me to get you a farm, you'll have to get your mind clear about what you need.'

George said: 'I'll know it when I see it.'

'Have I got to drive you to every free farm in a thousand miles of Africa? God damn it, man,' he expostulated, 'be reasonable. This is my job. I am supposed to be earning my living by it.'

George shrugged. The agent let go his arm, and the two men walked along beside each other, George looking away over the thick dark trees of the river to the slopes on the other side. There were the mountains, range on range of them, rising high and glistening into the fresh blue sky.

The agent followed that look, and began to think for himself. He peered hard at George. This man, in appearance, was what one might expect after such a childhood, all freedom and sunlight, and after five years of such fighting. He was very lean and brown, with loose broad shoulders and an easy swinging way of moving. His face was lean and angled, his eyes grey and shrewd, his mouth hard but also dissatisfied. He reminded the agent of his father at the same age; George's father had left everything familiar to him, in an old and comfortable country, to make a new way of living with new people. The agent said tentatively: 'Good to get away from people, eh? Too many people crowded together over there in the Old Country?' exactly as he might have done to the older man. George's face did not change: this idea seemed to mean nothing to him. He merely continued to stare, his eyes tightened, at the mountains. But now the agent knew what he had to do. Next day he drove him to Four Winds, which had just been surveyed for sale. It was five thousand acres of virgin bush, lying irregularly over the lower slopes of a range of kopjes that crossed high over a plain where there were still few farms. Four Winds was all rocky outcrops, scrubby trees and wastes of shimmering grass, backed by mountains. There was no house, no river, not so much as a fence; no one could call it a desirable farm. George's face cleared to content as he walked over it, and on it came that look for which the agent had been waiting.

He slouched comfortably all through that day over those bare and bony acres, rather in the way a dog will use to make a new place its own, ranging to pick up a smell here or a memory there, anything that can be formed into a shell of familiarity for comfort against strangeness. But white men coming to Africa take not only what is there, but also impose on it a pattern of their own, from other countries. This accounts for the fine range of variation one can find in a day's travelling from farm to farm across any district. Each house will be different, suggesting a different country, climate, or way of speech.

Towards late afternoon, with the blaze of yellow sunlight falling directly across his face and dazzling into his eyes, and glazing the wilderness of rock and grass and tree with the sad glitter of sunset, George stopped suddenly in a place where gullies ran down from all sides into a flat place among bushes. 'There should be water here, for a borehole,' he said. And, after a moment: 'There was a windmill I caught sight of in Norfolk from a train. I liked the look of it. The shape of it, I mean. It would do well here . . .'

It was in this way that George said he was buying the farm, and showed his satisfaction at the place. The restless, rather wolfish look had gone from the long bony face.

'Your nearest neighbour is fifteen miles away,' was the last warning the agent gave.

George answered indifferently: 'This part of the country is opening up, isn't it?' And the next day he signed the papers.

He was no recluse after all, or at least, not in the way the agent had suspected.

He went round to what farms there were, as is the custom, paying his respects, saying he had bought Four Winds, and would be a neighbour, though not a near one. And the house he built himself was not a shack, the sort of house a man throws together to hold off the weather for a season.

He intended to live there, though it was not finished. It looked as if it had been finely planned and then cut in half. There were, to begin with, three large rooms, raftered with that timber that sends out a pungent fragrance when the weather changes, and floored with dark red wood. These were furnished properly, there were no makeshifts here, either. And he was seen at the station on mail days, not often, but often enough, where he was greeted in the way proper not only to his father's son and to his war record, but because people approved what he was doing. For after both wars there has been a sudden appearance of restless young men whose phrases: 'I want to be my own boss,' and 'I'm not going to spend my life wearing out the seat of my trousers on a stool,' though clichés, still express the spirit that opened up the country in the first place. Between wars there is a different kind of immigrant, who use their money as spades to dig warm corners to sleep in. Because of these people who have turned an adventurous country into a sluggish one, and because of the memory of something different, restless young men find there is no need to apologize for striking out for themselves. It is as if they are regarded as a sort of flag, or even a conscience. When people heard that George had bought Four Winds, a bare, gusty, rocky stretch of veld on the side of a mountain, they remarked, 'Good luck to him,' which is exactly how they speak when a returning traveller says: 'There is a man on the shores of Lake Nyasa who has lived alone in a hut by himself for twenty years,' or 'I heard of someone who has gone native in the Valley – he goes away into the bush if a white person comes near him.' There is no condemnation, but rather a recognition of something in themselves to which they pay tribute by proxy.

George's first worry was whether he would get sufficient native labour; but he had expected an anxious time, and, knowing the ropes, he sat tight, built his house, sank his borehole and studied his land. A few natives did come, but they were casual labourers, and were not what he was waiting for. He was more troubled, perhaps, than he let himself know. It is so easy to get a bad name as an employer. A justly dismissed man can spitefully slash a tree on the boundary of a farm where the migrating natives walk, in such a way that they read in the pattern of the gashes on the bark: This is a bad farm with a bad master. Or there may be a native in the compound who frightens or tyrannizes over the others, so that they slowly leave, with excuses, for other farms, while the farmer himself never finds out what is wrong. There can be a dozen reasons why a fair man, just to his natives according to the customs of the time, can get a bad name without ever knowing the reason for it.

George knew this particular trouble was behind him when one day he saw coming up the road to his front door an old native who had worked many years for his own father. He waited on the steps, smoking comfortably, smiling his greeting.

'Morning,' he said.

'Morning, baas.'

'Things go well with you, old Smoke?'

'Things go well, baas.'

George tapped out his pipe, and motioned to the old man to seat himself. The band of young men who had followed Smoke along the road, were waiting under some trees at a short distance for the palaver to finish. George could see they had come a long way, for they were dusty, weary with the weight of their big bundles. But they looked a strong lot and good for work, and George settled himself in the big chair he used for audiences with satisfaction growing in him.

'You have come a long way?' he asked.

'A long way, baas. I heard the Little Baas had come back from the war and was wanting me. I have come to the Little Baas.'

George smiled affectionately at old Smoke, who looked not a day older now than he had ten years, or even twenty years back, when he had lifted the small boy for rides on the mealie wagon, or carried him, when he was tired, on his back. He seemed always to have been a very old man, with grizzling hair and filming eyes but as light and strong and erect as a youth.

'How did you know I had come back?'

'One of my brothers told me.'

George smiled again, acknowledging that this was all he would ever be told of the mysterious way the message had travelled from mouth to mouth across hundreds of miles. 'You will send messages to all your brothers to work for me? I need a great many boys.'

'I have brought twenty. Later, others will come. I have other relations coming after the rains from Nyasaland.'

'You will be my bossboy, Smoke? I need a bossboy.'

'I am too old, much too old, baas.'

'Do you know how old you are?' asked George, knowing he would get no satisfactory answer, for natives of Smoke's generation had no way of measuring their age.

'How should I know, baas? Perhaps fifty. Perhaps a hundred. I remember the days of the fighting well, I was a young man.' He paused, and added carefully, having averted his eyes: 'Better we do not remember those days, perhaps.'

The two men laughed, after a moment during which their great liking for each other had time to take the unpleasantness from the reminder of war. 'But I need a bossboy,' repeated George. 'Until I find a younger man as capable as you are, will you help me?'

'But I am too old,' protested Smoke again, his eyes brightening.

Thus it was settled, and George knew his labour troubles were over. Smoke's brothers would soon fill his compound. It must be explained that relationships, among Africans, are not understood as they are among white people. A native can travel a thousand miles in strange country, and find his clan brothers in every village, and be made welcome by them.

George allowed these people a full week to build themselves a village, and another week as earnest of good feeling. Then he pulled the reins tight and expected hard work. He got it. Smoke was too old to work hard himself; also he was something of an old rascal with his drinking and his women – he had got his name because he smoked dagga, which bleared his eyes and set his hands shaking – but he held the obedience of the younger men, and because of this was worth any amount of money to George.

Later, a second man was chosen to act as bossboy under Smoke. He was a nephew, and he supervised the gangs of natives, but it was understood that Smoke was the real chief. When George held his weekly palavers to discuss farm matters, the two men came up from the compound together, and the younger man (who had in fact done the actual hard work) deferred to the older. George brought a chair from the house to the foot of the great flight of stone steps that led up to the living-rooms, and sat there at ease smoking, while Smoke sat cross-legged on the ground before him. The nephew stood behind his uncle, and his standing was not so much an act of deference to George – though of course it was that too – as respect for his tribal superior. (This was in the early 'twenties, when a more gentle, almost feudal relationship was possible between good masters and their servants: there was space, then, for courtesy, bitterness had not yet crowded out affection.)

During these weekly talks it was not only farm matters that

were discussed, but personal ones also. There was always a short pause when crops, weather, plans, had been finished; then Smoke turned to the young man behind him and spoke a few dismissing words. The young man said, 'Good night, baas,' to George, and went away.

George and Smoke were then free to talk about things like the head driver's quarrels with his new wife, or how Smoke himself was thinking of taking a young wife. George would laugh and say: 'You old rascal. What do you want with a wife at your age?' And Smoke would reply that an old man needed a young body for warmth during the cold weather.

Nor was old Smoke afraid of becoming stern, though reproachful, as if he momentarily regarded himself as George's father, when he said: 'Little Baas, it is time you got married. It is time there was a woman on this farm.' And George would laugh and reply that he certainly agreed he should get married, but that he could find no woman to suit him.

Once Smoke suggested: 'The baas will perhaps fetch himself a wife from England?' And George knew then that it was discussed in the compound how he had a photograph of a girl on his dressing-table: old Smoke's son was cookboy in George's house.

The girl had been his fiancée for a week or so during the war, but the engagement was broken off after one of those practical dissecting discussions that can dissolve a certain kind of love like mist. She was a London girl, who liked her life, with no desire for anything different. There was no bitterness left after the affair; at least, not against each other. George remained with a small bewildered anger against himself. He was a man, after all, who liked things in their proper place. It was the engagement he could not forgive himself: he had been temporarily mad; it was that he could not bear to think of. But he remembered the girl sometimes with an affectionate sensuality. She had married and was living the kind of life he could not imagine any sane person choosing. Why he kept her picture – which was a very artificial posed affair – he did not ask himself. For he had cared for other women more, in his violent intermittent fashion.

However, there was her picture in his room, and it was seen not only by the cookboy and the houseboys but by the rare visitors to the house. There was a rumour in the district that George had a broken heart over a woman in England; and this explanation did as well as any other for George's cheerful but determined self-isolation, for there are some people the word loneliness can never be made to fit. George was alone, and seemed not to know it. What surprised people was that the frame of his life was so much larger than he needed, and for what he was. The three large rooms had been expanded, after a few years, into a dozen. It was the finest house for many miles. Outhouses, storehouses, wash-houses and poultry yards spread about the place, and he had laid out a garden, and paid two boys handsomely to keep it beautiful. He had scooped out the soil between a cluster of boulders, and built a fine natural swimming pool over which bamboos hung, reflecting patterns of green foliage and patches of blue sky. Here he swam every morning at sun-up, summer or winter, and at evening, too, when he came from the day's work. He built a row of stables, sufficient to house a dozen beasts, but actually kept only two, one of which was ridden by old Smoke (whose legs were now too feeble to carry him far) and one which he used himself. This was a mare of great responsiveness and intelligence but with no beauty, chosen with care after weeks of attending sales and following up advertisements: she was for use, not show. George rode her round the farm, working her hard, during the day, and when he stabled her at night patted her as if he were sorry she could not come into the house with him. After he had come from the pool, he sat in the glow from the rapidly fading sunset, looking out over the wild and beautiful valley, and ceremoniously drinking beside a stinkwood table laden with decanters and siphons. Nothing here of the bachelor's bottle and glass on a tin tray; and his dinner was served elaborately by two uniformed men, with whom he chatted or kept silence, as he felt inclined. After dinner coffee was brought to him, and having read farming magazines for half an hour or so, he went to bed. He was asleep every night by nine, and up before the sun.

That was his life. It was his life for years, one of exhausting physical toil, twelve hours a day of sweat and effort in the sun, but surrounded by a space and comfort that seemed to ask for something else. It asked, in short, for a wife. But it is not easy to ask of such a man, living in such a way, what it is he misses, if he misses anything at all.

To ask would mean entering into what he feels during the long hours riding over the ridges of kopje in the sunshine, with the grass waving about him like blond banners. It would mean understanding what made him one of mankind's outriders in the first place.

Even old Smoke himself, ambling beside him on the other horse, would give him a long look on certain occasions, and quietly go off, leaving him by himself.

Sloping away in front of the house was a three-mile-long expanse of untouched grass, which sprang each year so tall that even from their horses the two men could not see over it. There was a track worn through it to a small knoll, a cluster of rocks merely, with trees breaking from the granite for shade. Here it was that George would dismount and, leaning his arm on the neck of his mare, stand gazing down into the valley which was in itself a system of other hills and valleys, so high did Four Winds stand above the rest of the country. Twenty miles away other mountains stood like blocks of tinted crystal, blocking the view; between there were trees and grass, trees and rocks and grass, with the rivers marked by lines of darker vegetation. Slowly, as the years passed, this enormous reach of pure country became marked by patches of cultivation; and smudges of smoke showed where new houses were going up, with the small glittering of roofs. The valley was being developed. Still George stood and gazed, and it seemed as if these encroaching lives affected him not at all. He would stay there half the morning, with the crooning of the green-throated wood pigeons in his ears, and when he rode back home for his meal, his eyes were heavy and veiled.

But he took things as they came. Four Winds, lifted high into the sky among the great windswept sun-quivering mountains, tumbled all over with boulders, offering itself to storms and exposure and invasion by baboons and leopards – this wilderness, this pure, heady isolation, had not affected him after all.

For when the valley had been divided out among new settlers, and his neighbours were now five miles, and not fifteen, away, he began going to their houses and asking them to his. They were very glad to come, for though he was an eccentric, he was harmless enough. He chose to live alone: that piqued the women. He had become very rich; which pleased everyone. For the rest, he was considered mildly crazy because he would not allow an animal to be touched on his farm; and any native caught setting traps for game would be beaten by George himself and then taken to the police afterwards: George considered the fine that he incurred for beating the native well worth it. His farm was as good as a game reserve; and he had to keep his cattle in what were practically stockades for fear of leopards. But if he lost an occasional beast, he could afford it.

George used to give swimming parties on Sundays; he kept open house on that day, and everyone was welcome. He was a good host, the house was beautiful, and his servants were the envy of every housewife; perhaps this was what people found it difficult to forgive him, the perfection of his servants. For they never left him to go 'home' as other people's boys did; their home was here, on this farm, under old Smoke, and the compound was a proper native village, and not the usual collection of shambling huts about which no one cared, since no one lived in them long enough to care. For a bachelor to have such well-trained servants was a provocation to the women of the district; and when they teased him about the perfection of his arrangements, their voices had an edge on them. They used to say: 'You damned old bachelor, you.' And he would reply, with calm good-humour: 'Yes, I must think about getting me a wife.'

Perhaps he really did feel he ought to marry. He knew it was suspected that this new phase of entertaining and being entertained, was with a view to finding himself a girl. And the girls, of course, were only too willing. He was nothing, if not a catch; and it was his own fault that he was regarded, coldly, in this light. He would sometimes look at the women sprawled half-naked around the swimming pool under the bamboos – sprawling with deliberate intent, and for his benefit – and his eyes would narrow in a way that was not pleasant. Nor was it even fair, for if a man will not allow himself to be approached by sympathy and kindness, there is only one other approach. But the result of all this was simply that he set that photograph very prominently on the table beside his bed; and when girls remarked on it he replied, letting his eyelids half-close in a way which was of course exasperatingly attractive: 'Ah yes, Betty – now *there* was a woman for you.'

At one time it was thought he was 'caught' after all. One of his boundaries was shared with a middle-aged woman with two grown daughters; she was neither married, nor unmarried, for her husband seemed not to be able to make up his mind whether to divorce her or not, and the girls were, in their early twenties, horse-riding, whisky-drinking, flat-bodied tomboys who were used to having their own way with the men they fancied. They would make good wives for men like George, people said: they would give back as good as they got. But they continued to be spoken of in the plural, for George flirted with them both, and they were extraordinarily similar. As for the mother, she ran the farm, for her husband was too occupied with a woman in town to do this, and drank a little too much, and could be heard complaining fatalistically: 'Christ, why did I have daughters? After all, sons are *expected* to behave badly.' She used to complain to George, who merely smiled and offered her another drink. 'God help you if you marry either of them,' she would say gloomily. 'May I be forgiven for saying it, but they are fit for nothing but enjoying themselves.' 'At their age, Mrs Whately, that seems reasonable enough.' Thus George retreated, into a paternally indulgent attitude that nevertheless had a hint in it of cruel relish for the girls' discomfiture.

He used to look for Mrs Whately when he entered a room, and stay beside her for hours, apparently enjoying her company; and she seemed to enjoy his. She did all the talking, while he stretched himself beside her, his eyes fixed thoughtfully on his glass, which he swung lightly between finger and thumb, occasionally letting out an amused grunt. She spoke chiefly of her husband whom she had turned from a liability into an asset, for the whole room would become silent to hear her humorous, grumbling tales of him. 'He came home last week-end,' she would say, fixing wide astonished eyes on George, 'and do you know what he said? My God, he said, I don't know what I'd do without you, old girl. If I can't get out of town for a spot of fresh air, sometimes, I'd go mad. And there I was, waiting for him with my grievances ready to air. What can one do with a man like that?' 'And are you prepared to be a sort of week-end resort?' asked George. 'Why, Mr Chester!' exclaimed Mrs Whately, widening her eyes to an incredibly foolish astonishment, 'after all, he's my husband, I suppose.' But this handsome, battered matron was no fool, she could not have run the farm so capably if she had been; and on these occasions George would simply laugh and say: 'Have another drink.'

At his own swimming parties Mrs Whately was the only woman who never showed herself in a swimming suit. 'At my age,' she explained, 'it is better to leave it to one's daughters.' And with an exaggerated sigh of envy she gazed across at the girls. George would gaze, too, non-committally; though on the whole it appeared he did not care for the spare and boyish type. He had been known, however, during those long hot days when thirty or forty people lounged for hours in their swimming suits on the edge of the pool, eating, drinking, and teasing each other, to rise abruptly looking inexplicably irritated, and walk off to the stables. There he saddled his mare – who, one would have thought, should have been allowed her Sunday's rest, since she was worked so hard the rest of the week – swung himself up, and was off across the hillsides, riding like a maniac. His guests did not take this hardly; it was the sort of thing one expected of him. They laughed – most particularly the women – and waited for him to come back, saying: 'Well, old George, you know . . .'

They used to suggest it would be nice to go riding together, but no one ever succeeded in riding with George. Now that the farms had spread up from the valley over the foothills, George often saw people on horses in the early morning, or at evening; and on these occasions he would signal a hasty greeting with his whip, rise in his stirrups and flash out of sight. This was another of the things people made allowances for: George, that lean, slouching, hard-faced man, riding away along a ridge with his whip raised in perfunctory farewell was positively as much a feature of the landscape as his own house, raised high on the mountain in a shining white pile, or the ten-foot high notices all along the boundaries saying: Anyone found shooting game will be severely prosecuted.

Once, at evening, he came on Mrs Whately alone, and as instinctively he turned his horse to flee, heard her shout: 'I won't bite.' He grinned unamiably at her expectant face, and shouted back: 'I'm no more of a fool than you are, my dear.'

At the next swimming party she acknowledged this incident by saying to him thoughtfully, her eyes for once direct and cool: 'There are many ways of being a fool, Mr Chester, and you are the sort of man who would starve himself to death because he once overate himself on green apples.'

George crimsoned with anger. 'If you are trying to hint that there are, there really *are*, some *sweet*, *charming* women, if I took the trouble to look, I promise you women have suggested that before.'

She did not get angry. She merely appeared genuinely surprised. 'Worse than I thought,' she commented amicably. And then she began talking about something else in her familiar, rather clowning manner.

It was at one of these swimming parties that the cat came out of the bag. Its presence had of course been suspected, and accorded the usual tolerance. In fact, the incident was not of importance because of his friends' reactions to it, but because of George's own reactions.

It was one very warm December morning, with the rains due to break at any moment. All the farmers had their seed-beds full of tobacco ready to be planted out, and their attention was less on the excellence of the food and drink and the attractions of the women, than on the sky, which was filled with heavy masses of dull cloud. Thunder rolled behind the kopjes, and the air was charged and tense. Under the bamboos round the pool, whose fronds hung without a quiver, people tended to be irritable because of the feeling of waiting; for the last few weeks before the season are a bad time in any country where rain is uncertain.

George was sitting dressed on a small rock: he always dressed immediately he had finished bathing. The others were still half-naked. They had all lifted their heads and were looking with interested but non-committal expressions past him into the trees when he noticed the direction of their gaze, and turned himself to look. He gave a brief exclamation; then said, very deliberately: 'Excuse me,' and rose. Everyone watched him walk across the garden, and through the creeper-draped rocks beyond to where a young native woman stood, hand on hips provocatively, swinging herself a little as if wishing to dance. Her eyes were lowered in the insolently demure manner of the native woman; and she kept them down while George came to a standstill in front of her and began to speak. They could not make out from his gestures or from his face, what he was saying; but after a little while the girl looked sulky, shrugged, and then moved off again towards the compound, which could be seen through trees and past the shoulder of a big kopje, perhaps a mile away. She walked dragging her feet, and swinging her hands to loosely clutch at the grass-heads; it was a beautiful exhibition of unwilling departure; that was the impression given, that this was not only how she felt, but how she intended to show she felt. The long ambiguous look over her bare shoulder (she wore native-style dress, folded under the armpits) directed at the group of white people, could be interpreted in a variety of ways. No one chose to interpret it. No one spoke; and eyes were turned carefully to sky, trees, water or fingernails, when George returned. He looked at them briefly, without any hint of apology, then sat himself down again and reached for his glass. He took a swallow, and went on speaking where he had left off. They were quick to answer him; and in a moment conversation was general, though it was a conscious and controlled conversation: these people were behaving as if for the benefit of an invisible observer who was standing somewhere at a short distance and chuckling irresistibly as he called out: 'Bravo! Well done!'

What they felt towards George – an irritation which was a reproach for not preserving appearances – was not allowed to appear in their manner. The women, however, were noticeably acid; and George's acknowledgement of this was a faint smile, so diminishing of their self-respect that by that evening, when the party broke up (it would rain before midnight and they would all have to be up early for a day's hard planting) relations were as usual. In fact, George would be able to count on their saying, or implying: 'Oh, George! Well, it is all very well for him, I suppose.'

But that did not end the matter for him. He was very angry. He summoned old Smoke to the house when the visitors had gone, and this showed how angry he was, for it was a rule of his never to disturb the labourers on a Sunday.

The girl was Smoke's daughter (or grand-daughter, George did not know), and the arrangement – George's attitude towards the thing forbade any other term – had come about naturally enough. The only time it had ever been mentioned between the two men was when shortly after the girl set herself in George's path one evening when he was passing from swimming pool to house, Smoke had remarked, without reproach, but sternly enough, that a half-caste child would not be welcome among his people. George had replied, with equal affability, that he gave his assurance there would be no child. The old man replied, half-sighing that he understood the white people had means at their disposal. There the thing had ended. The girl came to George's room when he sent for her, two or three time a week. She used to arrive when George's dinner was finished, and she left at sun-up, with a handful of small change. George kept a supply of sixpences and threepenny bits under his handkerchiefs, for he had noticed she preferred several small coins to one big one. The discrimination was the measure of his regard for her, of her needs and nature. He liked to please her in these little ways. For instance, recently, when he had gone into town and was down among the Kaffir-truck shops buying a supply of aprons for his houseboys, he had made a point of buying her a head-cloth of a colour she particularly liked. And once, she had been ill, and he drove her himself to hospital. She was not afraid to come to him to ask for especial favours to her family. This had been going on for five years.

Now, when old Smoke came to the house, with the lowered eyes and troubled manner that showed he knew of the incident, George said simply that he wished the girl to be sent away; she was making trouble. Smoke sat crosslegged before George for some minutes before replying, looking at the ground. George had time to notice that he was getting a very old man indeed. He had a shrunken, simian appearance; even the flesh over his skull was crinkled under dabs of white wool; his face was withered to the bone; and his small eyes peered with difficulty. At last he spoke, and his voice was resigned and trembling: 'Perhaps the Little Baas could speak to the girl? She will not do it again.'

But George was not taking the chance of it happening again.

'She is my child,' pleaded the old man.

George, suddenly irritable, said: 'I cannot have this sort of thing happening. She is a very foolish girl.'

'I understand, baas, I understand. She is certainly a foolish girl. But she is also young, and my child.' But even this last appeal, spoken in the old wheezy voice, did not move George.

It was finally arranged that George should pay the expenses of the girl at mission school, some fifty miles off. He would not see her before she left, though she hung about the back step for days. She even attempted to get into his bedroom the night before she was to set off, accompanied by one of her brothers for escort, for the long walk to her new home. But George had locked his door. There was nothing to be said. In a way he blamed himself. He felt he might have encouraged the girl: one did not know, for example, how the matter of the head-cloth might rearrange itself in a primitive woman's mind. He had been responsible, at any rate, for acting in a way that had 'put ideas into her head'. That appearance of hers at the swimming pool had been an act of defiance, a deliberate claiming of him, a provocation, whose implications appalled him. They appalled him precisely because the thing could never have happened if he had not treated her faultily.

During the week after she left, one evening, before going to bed, he suddenly caught the picture of the London girl off his dressing-table, and tossed it into a cupboard. He was thinking of old Smoke's daughter – grand-daughter, perhaps – with an uncomfortable aching of the flesh, for some weeks before another girl presented herself for his notice.

He had been waiting for this to happen: for he had no intention of incurring old Smoke's reproach by enticing a woman to him.

He was sitting on his verandah one night, smoking, his legs propped on the verandah wall, gazing at the great yellow moon that was rising over a long wooded spur to one side of the house, when a furtive, softly-gliding shape entered the corner of his vision. He sat perfectly still, puffing his pipe, while she came up the steps, and across the patch of light from the lamp inside. For a moment he could have sworn it was the same girl, but she was younger, much younger, not more than about sixteen. She was naked above the waist, for his inspection, and she wore a string of blue beads around her neck.

This time, in order to be sure of starting on the right basis, he pulled out a handful of small coins and laid them on the verandah wall before him. Without raising her eyes, the girl leaned over sideways, picked them up, and caused them to disappear in the folds of her skirt. An hour later she was turned out of the house, and the doors were locked for the night. She wept and pleaded to be allowed to stay till the first light came (as the other girl had always done) for she was afraid to go home by herself through the dark bush that was full of beasts and ghosts and the ancient terrors that were her birthright. George replied simply that if she came at all, she must resign herself to leaving when the business of the occasion was at an end. He remembered the nights with the other one, which had been spent wrapped close in each other's arms – *that* was where he had made his mistake, perhaps? In any case, it was not going to be allowed to happen again.

This girl wept pitifully the first night, and even more violently the second. George suggested that one of her brothers should come for her. She was shocked at the idea, so shocked that he understood things were with her as with him; the thing was permissible provided it was possible decently to ignore it. But she was sent home; and George did not allow himself to picture her gliding through the dark shadows of the moonlit path, and whimpering with fear, as she had done in his arms before leaving him.

At their next weekly palaver, George waited for Smoke to speak for he knew that he would. It was with a conscious determination not to show guilt (a reaction which surprised and annoyed him) that George watched the old man dismiss the nephew, wait for him to get well on his way on the path to the compound, and turn back to face him, in appeal. 'Little Baas,' he said, 'there are things that need not be said between us.' George did not answer. 'Little Baas, it is time that you took a wife from your own people.'

George replied: 'The girl came to me, of her own accord.'

Smoke said, as if it were an insult that he was forced to say such an obvious thing: 'If you had a wife, she would not have come.' The old man was deeply troubled; far more so than George had expected. For a while he did not answer. Then he said: 'I shall pay her well.' It seemed to him that he was speaking in that spirit of honesty that was in everything he said, or did, with this man who had been the friend of his father, and was his own good friend. He could not have said anything he did not feel. 'I'm paying her well; and will see that she is looked after. I am paying well for the other one.'

'Aie, aie,' sighed the old man, openly reproachful now, 'this is not good for our women, baas. Who will want to marry her?'

George moved uncomfortably in his chair. 'They both came to me, didn't they? I didn't go running after them.' But he stopped. Smoke so clearly considered this argument irrelevant that he could not pursue it, even though he himself considered it valid. If he had gone searching for a woman among those at the compound, he would have felt himself responsible. That old Smoke did not see things in this light made him angry.

'Young girls,' said Smoke reproachfully, 'you know how they are.' Again there was more than reproach. In the feeble ancient eyes there was a deeper trouble. He could not look straight at George. His gaze wavered this way and that, over George's face, away to the mountains, down to the valley, and his hands were plucking at his garments.

George smiled, with determined cheerfulness: 'And young men, don't you make allowances for them?'

Smoke suddenly flashed into anger: 'Young men, little boys, one expects nonsense from them. But you, baas, you – you should be married, baas. You should have grown children of your own, not spoiling mine . . .' the tears were running down his face. He scrambled to his feet with difficulty, and said, very dignified: 'I do not wish to quarrel with the son of my old friend, the Old Baas. I ask you to think, only, Little Baas. These girls, what happens to them? You have sent the other one to the mission school, but how long will she stay? She has been used to your money and to . . . she has been used to her own way. She will go into the town and become one of the loose women. No decent man will have her. She will get herself a town husband, and then another, and another. And now there is this one . . .' He was now grumbling, querulous, pathetic. His dignity could not withstand the weight of his grief. 'And now this one, this one! You, Little Baas, that you should take this woman . . .' A very old, tottering scarecrow man, he swayed off down the path.

For a moment George was impelled to call him back for it was the first time one of their palavers had ended in unkindness, without courteous exchange in the old manner. But he watched the old man move uncertainly past the swimming pool through the garden, along the rockeries, and out of sight.

He was feeling uncomfortable and irritated, but at the same time he was puzzled. There was a discrepancy between what had happened and what he had expected that he felt now as a sharp intrusion – turning over the scene in his mind, he knew there was something that did not fit. It was the old man's emotion. Over the first girl reproach could be gathered from his manner but a reproach that was fatalistic, and related not to George himself but rather to circumstances, some view of life George could not be expected to share. It had been an impersonal grief, a grief against life. This was different; Smoke had been accusing him, George, directly. It had been like an accusation of disloyalty. Reconstructing what had been said, George fastened upon the recurring words: 'wife' and 'husband'; and suddenly an idea entered George's head that was intolerable. It was so ugly that he rejected it, and cast about for something else. But he could not refuse it for long; it crept back, and took possession of him, for it made sense of everything that had happened: a few months before old Smoke had taken to himself a new young wife.

After a space of agitated reflection George raised his voice and called loudly for his houseboy. This was a young man brought to the house by old Smoke himself years before. His relations with George were formal, but warmed slightly by the fact that he knew of George's practical arrangements and treated them with an exquisite discretion. All this George now chose to throw aside. He asked directly: 'Did you see the girl who was here last night?'

'Yes, baas.'

'Is she old Smoke's new wife?'

His eyes directed to the ground, the youth replied: 'Yes, baas.'

George smothered an impulse to appeal: 'I didn't know she was,' an impulse which shocked him, and said: 'Very well, you can go.' He was getting more and more angry; the situation infuriated him; by no fault of his own he was in a cruel position.

That night he was in his room reading when the girl entered smiling faintly. She was a beautiful young creature, but for George this fact had ceased to exist.

'Why did you not tell me you were Smoke's new wife?' he asked.

She was not disconcerted. Standing just inside the door, still in that pose of shrinking modesty, she said: 'I thought the baas knew.' It was possible that she had thought so; but George insisted: 'Why did you come when you knew I didn't know?'

She changed her tone, and pleaded: 'He is an old man, baas,' seeming to shudder with repugnance.

George said: 'You must not come here again.'

She ran across the room to him, flung herself down, and embraced his legs. 'Baas, baas,' she murmured, 'don't send me away.'

George's violent anger, that had been diffused within him, now focused itself sharply, and he threw her away from him, and got to his feet. 'Get out,' he said. She slowly got to her feet, and stood as before, though now sullenness was mingled with her shrinking humility. She did not say a word. 'You are not to come back,' he ordered; and when she did not move, he took her arm with the extreme gentleness that is the result of controlled dislike, and pushed her out of the front door. He locked it, and went to bed.

He always slept alone in the house, for the cookboy and the houseboys went back to the compound every night after finishing the washing-up, but one of the garden boys slept in a shed at the back with the dogs, as a guard against thieves. George's garden boys, unlike his personal servants, were not permanent, but came and went at short intervals of a few months. The present one had been with him for only a few weeks, and he had not troubled to make a friend of him.

Towards midnight there was a knock at the back door, and when George opened it he found this garden boy standing there, and there was a grin on his face that George had never seen on the face of a native before – at least, not directed at himself. He indicated a shadowy human shape that stood under a large tree which rose huge and glittering in the strong moonlight, and said intimately: 'She's there, baas, waiting for you.' George promptly cuffed him, in order to correct his expression, and then strode out into the moonlight. The girl neither moved nor looked at him. A statue of grief, she stood waiting, with her hands hanging at her sides. Those hands – the helplessness of them – particularly infuriated George. 'I told you to get back to where you belong,' he said, in a low angry voice. 'But, baas, I am afraid.' She began to cry again.

'What are you afraid of?'

The girl, her eyeballs glinting in the gleams of moonlight that fell strong through the boughs overhead, looked along to the compound. It was a mile of bush, with kopjes rising on either side of the path, big rocks throwing deep shadows all the way. Somewhere a dog was howling at the moon; all the sounds of night rose from the bush, bird noises, insect noises, animal noises that could not be named: here was a vast protean life, and a cruel one. George, looking towards the compound, which in this unreal glinting light had shrunk back, absorbed, into the background of tree and rock, without even a glow of fire to indicate its presence, felt as he always did; it was the feeling which had brought him here so many years before. It was as if, while he looked, he was flowing softly outwards, diffused into the bush and the moonlight. He knew no terror; he could not understand fear; he contained that cruelty within himself, shut safe in some deep place. And this girl, who was bred of the bush and of the wildness, had no right to tremble with fright. That, obscurely, was what he felt.

With the moonlight pouring over him, showing how his lips were momentarily curled back from his teeth, he pulled the girl roughly towards him out of the shade, turned her round so that she faced the compound, and said: 'Go, now.'

She was trembling, in sharp spasms, from heat to foot. He could feel her convulse against him as if in the convulsions of love, and he pushed her away so that she staggered. 'Go,' he ordered, again. She was now sobbing wildly, with her arm across her eyes. George called to the garden boy who was standing near the house watching the scene, his face expressing an emotion George did not choose to recognize. 'Take this woman back to the compound.'

For the first time in his life George was disobeyed by a native. The youth simply shook his head, and said with a directness that was not intended to be rude, but was rather a rebuke for asking something that could not be asked: 'No, baas.' George understood he could not press the point. Impatiently he turned back to the girl and dismissed the matter by saying: 'I'm not going to argue with you.'

He went indoors, and to bed. There he listened futilely for sounds of conversation: he was hoping that the two people outside might come to some arrangement. After a few moments he heard the scraping of chains along earth, and the barking of dogs; then a door shut. The garden boy had gone back to his shed. George repressed a desire to go to the window and see if the girl was still there. He imagined that she might perhaps steal into one of the outhouses for shelter. Not all of them were locked.

It was hours before he slept. It was the first night in years that he had difficulty in sleeping. He was still angry, yes; he was uncomfortable because of his false relationship to old Smoke, because he had betrayed the old man; but beyond these emotions was another; again he felt that discrepancy, something discordant which expressed itself through him in a violent irritation; it was as if a fermenting chemical had been poured into a still liquid. He was intolerably restless, and his limbs twitched. It seemed as if something large and challenging were outside himself saying: And how are you going to include *me*? It was only by turning his back on that challenge that he eventually managed to sleep.

Before sunrise next day, before the smoke began to curl up from the huts in the compound, George called the garden boy, who emerged sleepy and red-eyed from the shed, the dogs at his heels, and told him to fetch old Smoke. George felt he had to apologize to him; he must put himself right with that human being to whom he felt closer than he had ever felt to anyone since his parents died.

He dressed while waiting. The house was quite empty, as the servants had not yet come from the compound. He was in a fever of unrest for the atonement it was necessary for him to make. But the old man delayed his coming. The sun was blazing over the kopjes, and the smells of coffee and hot fat were pervading the house from the kitchen when George, waiting impatiently on the verandah, saw a group of natives coming through the trees. Old Smoke was wrapped in a blanket, and supported on each side by a young man; and he moved as if each step were an effort to him. By the time the three natives had reached the steps, George was feeling like an accused person. Nor did any of his accusers look at him directly.

He said at once: 'Smoke, I am very sorry. I did not know she was your wife.' Still they did not look at him. Already irritation was growing inside him, because they did not accept his contrition. He repeated sternly: 'How was I to know? How could I?'

Instead of answering directly, Smoke said in the feeble and querulous tones of a very old man: 'Where is she?'

This George had not foreseen. Irritation surged through him with surprising violence. 'I sent her home,' he said angrily. It was the strength of his own anger that quieted him. He did not know himself what was happening within him.

The group in front of him remained silent. The two young men, each supporting Smoke with an arm under his shoulders, kept their eyes down. Smoke was looking vaguely beyond the trees and over the slopes of grass to the valley; he was looking for something, but looking without hope. He was defeated.

With a conscious effort at controlling his voice, George said: 'Till last night I did not know she was your wife.' He paused, swallowed, and continued, dealing with the point which he understood now was where he stood accused: 'She came to me last night, and I told her to go home. She came late. Has she not returned to you?'

Smoke did not answer: his eyes were ranging over the kopjes tumbled all about them. 'She did not come home,' said one of the young men at last.

'She has not perhaps gone to the hut of a friend?' suggested George futilely.

'She is not in the compound,' said the same young man, speaking for Smoke.

After a delay, the old man looked straight at George for the first time, but it was as if George were an object, a thing, which had nothing to do with him. Then he moved himself against the arms of the young men in an effort towards independence; and, seeing what he wanted, his escort turned gently round with him, and the three moved slowly off again to the compound.

George was quite lost; he did not know what to do. He stood on the steps, smoking, looking vaguely about him at the scenery, the familiar wild scenery, and down to the valley. But it was necessary to do something. Finally he again raised his voice for the servant. When he came, orders were given that the garden boy should be questioned. The houseboy returned with a reflection of the garden boy's insolent grin on his face, and said: 'The garden boy says he does not know what happened, baas. He went to bed, leaving the girl outside – just as the baas did himself.' This final phrase showed itself as a direct repetition of the insolent accusation the garden boy had made. But George did not act as he would have done even the day before. He ignored the insolence.

'Where is she?' he asked the houseboy at last.

The houseboy seemed surprised; it was a question he thought foolish, and he did not answer it. But he raised his eyes, as Smoke had done, to the kopjes, in a questing hopeless way; and George was made to admit something to his mind he had been careful not to admit.

In that moment, while he stood following the direction of his servant's eyes with his own, a change took place in him; he was gazing at a towering tumbling heap of boulders that stood sharp and black against a high fresh blue, the young blue of an African morning, and it was as if that familiar and loved shape moved back from him, reared menacingly like an animal and admitted danger – a sharp danger, capable of striking from a dark place that was a place of fear. Fear moved in George; it was something he had not before known; it crept along his flesh with a chilling touch, and he shivered. It was so new to him that he could not speak. With the care that one uses for a fragile, easily destroyable thing he took himself inside for breakfast, and went through the meal conscious of being sustained by the ceremony he always insisted on. Inside him a purpose was growing, and he was shielding it tenderly; for he did not know what it was. All he knew was, when he had laid down his coffee cup, and rung the bell for the servants, and gone outside to the verandah, that there the familiar landscape was outside of him, and that something within him was pointing a finger at it. In the now strong sunlight he shivered again; and crossed his arms so that his hand cupped his shoulders: they felt oddly frail. Till lately they had included the pushing strength of mountains; till this morning his arms had been branches and the birds sang in them; within him had been that terror which now waited outside, and which he must fight.

He spent the day doing nothing, sitting on his verandah with his pipe. His servants avoided the front part of the house.

Towards sundown he fetched his rifle which he used only on the rare occasion when there was a snake that must be killed, for he had never shot a bird or a beast with it, and cleaned it, very carefully. He ordered his dinner for an hour earlier than usual, and several times during that meal went outside to look at the sky. It was clear from horizon to horizon, and a luminous glow was spreading over the rocks. When a heavy yellow moon was separated from the highest boulder of the mountain by a hairline, he said to the boys that he was going out with his gun. This they accepted as a thing he must do; nor did they make any move to leave the house for the compound: they were waiting for him to return.

Geroge passed the ruffling surface of the swimming pool, picked his way through the rock garden, and came to where his garden merged imperceptibly, in the reaching tendrils of the creepers, with the bush. For a few yards the path passed through short and trodden grass, and then it forked, one branch leading off to the business part of the farm, the other leading straight on through a grove of trees. Through the dense shadows George moved steadily; for the grass was still short, and the tree trunks glimmered low to the ground. Between the edge of this belt of trees and the half mile of path that wound in and around the big boulders of the kopje was a space filled with low jagged rocks, that seemed higher and sharper than they were because of the shadows of the moon. Here it was clear moving. The moon poured down its yellow flood; and his shadow moved beside him, lengthening and shortening with the unevenness of the ground. Behind him were the trees in their gulf of black, before him the kopjes, the surfaces of granite showing white and glittering, like plates of crusted salt. Between, the broken shadows, of a dim purple colour, dappled with moonlight. To the left of him the rocks swept up sharply to another kopje; on the other side the ground fell away into a gulley which in its turn widened into the long grass slope, which, moving gently in the breeze, presented a gently gleaming surface, flattening and lifting so that there was a perpetual sweeping movement of light across miles of descending country. Far below was the valley, where the lights of homesteads gleamed steadily.

The kopje in front of him was silent, dead silent. Not a bird stirred, and only insects kept up their small shrilling. George moved into the shadows with a sharp tug of the heart, holding his fear in him cold and alive, like a weapon. But his rifle he handled carelessly.

With cautious, directed glances he moved along and up the path as it rose through the boulders on the side of the kopje. As he went he prayed. He was praying that the enemy might present itself and be slain. It was when he was on the height of the path so that half a mile behind showed the lit verandah of his house, and half a mile in front the illuminated shapes of the huts in the compound, that he stopped and waited. He remained quite still, and allowed his fear to grow inside him, a controlled fear, so that while his skin crept and his scalp tingled, yet his hands remained steady on the rifle. To one side of him was a large rock, leaning forward and over him in a black shelf. On the other was a rock-encumbered space, girt by a tangle of branches and foliage. There were, in fact, trees and rocks all about him; the thing might come from any side. But this was the place; he knew it by instinct. And he kept perfectly still for fear that his enemy might be scared away. He did not have to wait long. Before the melancholy howling of the moonstruck dogs in the compound had had time to set the rhythm of his nerves, before his neck had time to ache with the continual alert movements of his head from side to side, he saw one of the shadows a dozen paces from him lengthen gradually, and at last separate itself from the rock. The low, ground-creeping thing showed a green glitter of eyes, and a sheen of moonlight shifted with the moving muscles of the flank. When the shape stilled and flattened itself for a spring, George lifted his rifle and fired. There was a coughing noise, and the shape loosened. George lowered the rifle and looked at it, almost puzzled, and stood still. There lay the enemy, dead, not a couple of paces from him. Sprawled almost at his feet was the leopard, its body tensing and convulsing in death. Anger sprang up again in George; it had all been so easy, so easy! Again he looked in wonder at his rifle; then he kicked the unresisting flesh of the leopard, first with a kind of curiosity, then brutally. Finally he smashed the butt of the rifle, again and again, in hard, thudding blows, against the head. There was no resistance, no sound, nothing.

Finally, as the smell of blood and flesh began to fill him, he desisted, weak and helpless. He was let down. He had not been given what he had come for. When he finally left the beast lying there, and walked home again, his legs were weak under him and his breath was coming in sobs; he was crying the peevish, frustrated tears of a disappointed man.

The houseboys went out, without complaint, into the temporarily safe night to drag the body into the homestead. They began skinning the beast by lamplight. George slept heavily; and in the morning found the skin pegged in the sunshine, flesh side uppermost, and the fine papery inner skin was already blistering and puffing in the heat. George went to the kopje, and after a morning's search among thorn and blackjack and stinging-nettle, found the mouth of a cave. There were fresh human bones lying there, and the bones of cattle, and smaller bones, probably of buck and hare.

But the thing had been killed; and George was still left empty, a hungry man without possibility of food. He did not know what satisfaction it was he needed.

The farm boys came to him for instructions; and he told them, impatiently, not to bother him, but to go to old Smoke.

In a few days old Smoke himself came to see him, an evasive, sorrowful, dignified figure, to say he was going home: he was too old now to work for the Old Baas's son.

A few days later his compound was half empty. It was the urgent necessity of attracting new labour that pulled George together. He knew that an era was finished, for him. While not all old Smoke's kinsmen had left, there was now no focus, no authority, in his compound. He himself, now, would have to provide that focus, with his own will, his own authority; and he knew very well the perpetual strain and worry he must face. He was in the position of his neighbours.

He patched things up, as he could; and while he was re-ordering his life, found that he was behaving towards himself as he might to a convalescent. For there was a hurt place in him, and a hungry anger that no work could assuage.

For a while he did nothing. Then he suddenly filled his stables with horses; and his home became a centre for the horse-loving people about him. He ran a pack of dogs, too, trained by himself; and took down those notices along his boundaries. For 'Leopard' George had been born. For him, now, the landscape was simply a home for leopards. Every weekend his big house was filled with people, young, old, male and female, who came for various reasons; some for the hospitality, some for love of George, some, indeed, for the fun of the Sunday's hunting, which was always followed by a gigantic feast of food and drink.

Quite soon George married Mrs Whately, a woman who

had the intelligence to understand what she could and could not do if she wished to remain the mistress of Four Winds.

Winter in July

The three of them were sitting at their evening meal on the verandah. From behind, the living-room shed light on to the table, where their moving hands, the cutlery, the food, showed dimly, but clear enough for efficiency. Julia liked the half-tones. A lamp or candles would close them into a soft illuminated space, but obliterate the sky, which now bent towards them through the pillars of the verandah, a full deep sky, holding a yellowy bloom from an invisible moon that absorbed the stars into a faint far glitter.

Sometimes Tom said, grumbling humorously: 'Romantic, that's what she is'; and Kenneth would answer, but with an abrupt rather grudging laugh: 'I like to see what I am eating.' Kenneth was altogether an abrupt person. That quick, quickly-checked laugh, the swift critical look he gave her (which she met with her own eyes, as critical as his) were part of the long dialogue between them. For Kenneth did not accept her. He resisted her. Tom accepted her, as he accepted everything. For Julia it was not a question of preference: the two men supported her in their different manners. And the things they said, the three of them, seemed hardly to matter. The real thing was the soft elastic tension that bound them close.

Her liking for the evening hour, before moving indoors to the brightly-lit room, was expression of her feeling for them. The mingling lights, half from the night-sky, half from the lamp, softened their faces and subdued their voices, and she was free to feel what they were, rather than rouse herself by listening. This state was a continuation of her day, spent by herself (for the men were most of the time on the lands) in an almost trance-like condition where the soft flowing of the hours was marked by no necessities of action strong enough to wake her. As for them, she knew that returning to her was an entrance into that condition. Their day was hard and vigorous, full of practical details and planning. At sundown they entered her country, and the evening meal, where the outlines of fact were blurred by her passivity no less than by the illusion of indistinctness created by sitting under a roof which projected shadow-like into the African night, was the gateway to it.

They used to say to her sometimes: 'What do you do with yourself all day? Aren't you bored?' She could not explain how it was she could never become bored. All restlessness had died in her. She was content to do nothing for hours at a time; but it depended on her feeling of being held loosely in the tension between the two men. Tom liked to think of her content and peaceful in his life; Kenneth was irritated.

This particular evening, half-way through the meal, Kenneth rose suddenly and said: 'I must fetch my coat.' Dismay chilled Julia as she realized that she, too, was cold. She had been cold for several nights, but had put off the hour of recognizing the fact. Her thoughts were confirmed by Tom's remark: 'It's getting too cold to eat outside now, Julia.'

'What month is it?'

He laughed indulgently. 'We are reaping.'

Kenneth came back, shrugging himself quickly into the coat. He was a small, quick-moving, vital man; dark, dark-eyed, impatient; he did everything as if he resented the time he had to spend on it. Tom was large, fair, handsome, in every way Kenneth's opposite. He said with gentle persistence to Julia, knowing that she needed prodding: 'Better tell the boys to move the table inside tomorrow.'

'Oh, I suppose so,' she grumbled. Her summer was over: the long luminous warm nights, broken by swift showers, or obscured suddenly by heavy driving clouds – the tumultuous magical nights – were gone and finished for this year. Now, for the three months of winter, they would eat indoors, with the hot lamp over the table, the cold shivering about their legs, and outside a parched country, roofed by dusty freezing stars.

Kenneth said briskly: 'Winter, Julia, you'll have to face it.'

'Well,' she smiled, 'tomorrow you'll be able to see what you are eating.'

There was a slight pause; then Kenneth said: 'I shan't be here tomorrow night. I'm taking the car into the town in the morning.'

Julia did not reply. She had not heard. That is to say, she felt dismay deepening in her at the sound of his voice; then she wondered at her own forebodings, and then the words: 'Town. In the morning,' presented themselves to her.

They very seldom went into the city, which was fifty miles away. A trip was always planned in advance, for it would be a matter of buying things that were not available at the local store. The three of them had made the journey only last week. Julia's mind was now confronting and absorbing the fact that on that day Kenneth had abruptly excused himself and gone off on some business of his own. She remembered teasing him, a little, in her fashion. To herself she would have said (disliking the knowledge) that she controlled jealousy, like many jealous women, by becoming an accomplice, as it were, in Kenneth's adventures: the tormenting curiosity was eased when she knew what he had been doing. Last week he had disliked her teasing.

Now she looked over at Tom for reassurance, and saw that his eyes were expressing disquiet as great as her own. Doubly deserted, she gazed clearly and deliberately at both men; and because Kenneth's bald statement of his intentions seemed to her so gross a betrayal of their real relations, chose to say nothing, but in a manner of waiting for an explanation. None was offered, though Kenneth appeared uneasy. They finished their meal in silence and went indoors, passing through the stripped dining-room, which tomorrow would appear in its winter guise of arranged furniture and candles and bowls of fruit, into the living-room.

The house was built for heat. In the winter cold struck up

from the floor and out of the walls. This room was very bare, very high, of dull red brick, flagged with stone. Tomorrow she would put down rugs. There was a large stone fireplace, in which stood an earthenware jar filled with Christ-thorn. Julia unconsciously crossed to it, knelt, and bent to the little glowing red flowers, holding out her hands as if to the comfort of fire. Realizing what she was doing, she lifted her head, smiled wryly at the two men, who were watching her with the same small smile, and said: 'I'll get a fire put in.' Shaking herself into a knowledge of what she did by action, she walked purposefully to the door, and called to the servants. Soon the houseboy entered with logs and kindling materials, and the three stood drinking their coffee, watching him as he knelt to make the fire. They were silent, not because of any scruples against letting their lives appear falsely to servants, but because they knew speech was necessary, and that what must be said would break their life together. Julia was trembling; it was as if a support had been cut away beneath her. Held as she was by these men, her life made for her by them, her instincts were free to come straight and present themselves to her without the necessity for disapproval or approval. Now she found herself glancing alternatively from Tom, that large gentle man, her husband, whose very presence comforted her into peace, to Kenneth, who was frowning down at his coffee cup, so as not to meet her eyes. If he had simply laughed and said what was needed! – he did not. He drank what remained in the cup with two large gulps, seemed to feel the need of something to do, and then went over to the fireplace. The native still knelt there, his bare legs projecting loosely behind him, his hands hanging loose, his body free and loose save for head and shoulders, into which all his energy was concentrated for the purpose of blowing up the fire, which he did with steady, bellow-like breathing. 'Here,' said Kenneth, 'I'll do that.' The servant glanced at him, accepted the white man's whim, and silently left the room, leaving the feeling behind him that he had said: 'White men can't make fires'; just as Julia could feel her cook saying, when she was giving orders in the kitchen: 'I can make better pastry than you.'

Kenneth knelt where the servant had knelt and began fiddling with the logs. But he was good with his hands, and in a moment the sparse beginnings of a fire flowered in the wall; while the crock of prickly red thorn blossoms, Julia's summer fire, was set to one side.

'Now,' said Kenneth, rather off-hand, rather too loudly: 'You can warm your hands, Julia.' He gave his quick, grudging laugh. Julia found it offensive; and met his eyes. They were hostile. She flushed, walked slowly over to the fireplace, and sat down. The two men followed her example. For a while they did nothing; that unoffered explanation hung in the air between them. After a while Kenneth reached for a magazine and began to read. Julia looked over at her husband, whose kind blue eyes had always accepted everything she was, and raised her brows humorously. He did not respond, for he had turned again to Kenneth's now purposely bent head.

The fact that Kenneth had not spoken, that Tom was troubled, made Julia, thrown back on herself, ask: 'Why should you be so resentful? Surely he has a right to do as he pleases?' No, she answered herself. Not in this way. He shouldn't suddenly withdraw, shutting us out. Either one thing or the other. Doing it this way means that all our years together have been a lie; he simply repudiates them. But that *was* Kenneth, this continuous alternation between giving and withdrawal. Julia felt tears welling up inside her from a place that for a long time had remained dry. They were the tears of trembling insecurity. The thin, cold air in the great stone room, just beginning to be warmed by the small fire, was full of menace for Julia. But Kenneth did not speak: he was reading as if his future depended on the advertisements for tractors; and Tom soon began to read too, ignoring Julia.

She pulled herself together, and lay back in her chair, making herself think. She was thinking consciously of her life and what she was. There had been no need for her to consider herself for so long, and she hated having to do it.

She was the daughter of a small-town doctor in the North of England. To say that she had been ambitious would be false: the word ambition implies purpose; she was rather critical and curious, and her rebellion against the small-town atmosphere, and the prospect of marrying into it was no more conscious than the rebellion of most young people who think vaguely: Surely life can be better than this?

Yet she escaped. She was clever: at the end of her schooling she was better educated than most. She learned French and German because languages came easily to her, but mostly because at eighteen she fell in love with a French student, and at twenty became secretary to a man who had business connections in Germany, and she liked to please men. She was an excellent secretary, not merely because she was competent, but because of her peculiar fluid sympathy for the men she worked with. Her employers found that she quickly, intuitively, fitted herself in with what they wanted: it was a sort of directed passivity, a receptiveness towards people. So she earned well, and soon had the opportunity of leaving her home town and going to London.

Looking back now from the age she had reached (which was nearly forty) on the life she had lived (which had been varied and apparently adventurous) she could not put her finger on any point in her youth when she had said to herself: 'I want to travel; I want to be free.' Yet she had travelled widely, moving from one country to the next, from one job to the next; and all her relations with people, whether men or women, had been coloured by the brilliance of imper-manence. When she left England she had not known it would be final. It was on a business trip with her employer, and her relations with him were almost those of a wife with a husband, excepting for sex: she could not work with a man unless she offered a friendly, delicate sympathy.

In France she fell in love, and stayed there for a year. When that came to an end, the mood took her to go to Italy – no, that is the wrong way of putting it. When she described it like that to herself, she scrupulously said: That's not the truth. The fact was that she had been very seriously in love; and yet could not bring herself to marry. Going to Italy (she had not wanted to go in the least) had been a desperate but final way of ending the affair. She simply could not face the idea of marriage. In Italy she worked in a travel agency; and there she met a man whom she grew to love. It was not the desperate passion of a year before, but serious enough to marry. Later, she moved to America. Why America? Why not? – she was offered a good job there at the time she was looking for some place to go.

She stayed there two years, and had, as they say, a wonderful time. She was now a little bit more cautious about falling in love; but nevertheless there was a man who almost persuaded her to stay in New York. At the last moment a wild, trapped feeling came over her; what have I got to do with this country? she asked herself. This time, leaving the man was a destroying effort; she did not want to leave him. But she went south to the Argentine, and her state of mind was not a pleasant one.

Also, she found she was not as efficient as she had been. This was because she had become more wary, less adaptable. Afraid of falling in love, she was conscious of pulling away from the people she worked for; she gave only what she was paid to give, and this did not satisfy her. What, then, was going to satisfy her? After all, she could not spend all her life moving from continent to continent; yet there seemed no reason why she should settle in one place rather than another, even why it should be one man rather than another. She was tired. She was very tired. The springs of her feeling had run dry. This particular malaise is not so easily cured.

And now, for the first time, she had an affair with a man for whom she cared nothing: this was a half-conscious choice, for she understood that she could not have chosen a man whom she would grow to love. And so it went on, for perhaps two years. She was associating only with people who moved her not at all; and this was because she did not want to be moved.

There came a point when she said to herself that she must decide now, finally, what she wanted, and make sacrifices to get it. She was twenty-eight. She had spent the years since leaving school moving from hotel to furnished flat, from one job to the next, from one country to another. She seemed to have a tired affectionate remembrance of so many people, men and women, who had once filled her life. Now it was time to make something permanent. But what?

She said to herself that she was getting hard; yet she was not hard; she was numbed and tired. She must be very careful, she decided; she must not fall in love, lightly, again. Next time, it must matter.

All this time she was leading a full social life: she was attractive, well-dressed, amusing. She had the reputation of being brilliant and cold. She was also very lonely and she had never been lonely before, since there had always been some man to whom she gave warmth, affection, sympathy.

There was one morning when she had a vision of evil. It was at the window of a large hotel, one warm summer's day, when she was looking down through the streets of the attractive modern city in South America, with the crowds of people and the moving traffic . . . it might have been almost any city, on a bright warm day, from a hotel window, with the people blowing like leaves across her vision, as rootless as she, as impermanent, their lives meaning as little. For the first time in her life, the word, evil, meant something to her: she looked at it, coldly, and rejected it. This was sentiment, she said; the result of being tired, and nearly thirty. The feeling was not related to anything. She could not feel – why should one feel? She disliked what she was – well, it was at any rate honest to accept oneself as unlikeable. Her brain remarked dispassionately that if one lived without rules, one should be prepared to take the consequences, even if that meant moments of terror at hotel windows, with death beckoning below and whispering: Why live? Anyway, who was responsible for the way she was? Had she ever planned it? Why should one be one thing rather than another?

It was chance that took her to Cape Town. At a party she met a man who offered her a job as his secretary on a business trip, and it was easy to accept, for she had come to hate South America.

During the trip over she found, with a groan, that she had never been more efficient, more responsible, more gently responsive. He was an unhappy man, who needed sympathy . . . she gave it. At the end of the trip he asked her to marry him; and she understood she would have felt much the same if he had asked her to dinner. She fled.

She had enough money saved to live without working, so for months she stayed by herself, in a small hotel high over Cape Town, where she could watch the ships coming and going in the harbour and think: they are as restless as I am. She lived gently, testing every emotion she felt, making no contact save the casual ones inevitable in a hotel, walking by herself for hours of every day, soaking herself in the sea and the sun as if the beautiful peninsula could heal her by the power of its beauty. And she ran away from any possibility of liking some other human being as if love itself were poisoned.

One warm afternoon when she was walking high along the side of a mountain, with the blue sea swinging and lifting below, and a low sun sending a sad red pathway from the horizon, she was overtaken by two other walkers. There was no one else in sight, and it was inevitable they should continue together. She found they were farmers on holiday from Rhodesia, half-brothers, who had worked themselves into prosperity; this was the first holiday they had taken for years, and they were in a loosened, warm, adventurous mood. She sensed they were looking for wives to take back with them.

She liked Tom from the first, though for a day or so she flirted with Kenneth. This was an automatic response to his laughing, challenging antagonism. It was Kenneth who spoke first, in his brusque, off-hand way, and she felt attracted to him: theirs was the relationship of people moving towards a love affair. But she did not really want to flirt; with Kenneth it seemed anything else was impossible. She was struck by the way Tom, the elder brother, listened while they sparred, smiling uncritically, almost indulgently: his was an almost protective attitude. It was more than protective. A long while afterwards she told Tom that on that first afternoon he had reminded her of the peasant who uses a bird to catch fish for him. Yet there was a moment during the long hike back to the city through the deepening evening, when Julia glanced curiously at Tom and saw his warm blue glance resting kindly on her in a slow, speculative way, and she chose him, then, in her mind, even while she continued the exchange with Kenneth. Because of that kindness, she let herself sink towards the idea of marriage. It was what she wanted, really; and she did not care where she lived. Emotionally there was no country of which she could say: this is my home.

For several days the three of them went about together, and all the time she bantered with Kenneth and watched Tom. That defensive, grudging thing she could feel in Kenneth, which attracted her, against her will, was what she was afraid of: she was watching, half-fearfully, half-cynically, for its appearance in Tom. Then, slowly, Kenneth's treatment of her grew more off-hand and brutal: he knew he was being made use of. There came a point when in his sarcastic frank way he shut himself off from her; and for a while the three of them were together without contact. It had been Kenneth and she, with Tom as urbane onlooker; now it was she, by herself, drifting alone, floating loose, waiting, as it were, to be gathered in; and it was possible to mark the point when Tom and Kenneth looked at each other sardonically, in understanding, before Tom moved into Kenneth's place, in his warm and deliberate fashion, claiming her.

He was nicer than she had believed possible. There was

suddenly no conflict. He listened to her tales about her life with detached interest, as if they could not possibly concern him. He remarked once, in his tender, protective way: 'You must have been hurt hard at some time. That's the trouble with you independent women. Actually, you are quite a nice woman, Julia.' She laughed at him scornfully, as an arrogant male who has to make some kind of a picture of a woman so as to be able to fit her into his life. He treated her laughter tolerantly. When she said things like this he found it merely a sort of piquancy, a sign of her wit. Half-laughingly, half-despairingly, she said to Kenneth: 'You do realize that Tom hasn't an idea of what I'm like? Do you think it's fair to marry him?'

'Well, why not, if he wants to be married?' returned Kenneth briskly. 'He's romantic. He sees you as a wanderer from city to city, and from bed to bed, because you are trying to heal a broken heart or something of the kind. That appeals to him.'

Tom listened to this silently, smiling with disquiet. But there were times when Julia liked to think she had a broken heart; it certainly felt bruised. It was restful to accept Tom's idea of her. She said in a piqued way to Kenneth: 'I suppose *you* understand perfectly easily why I've lived the way I have?'

Kenneth raised his brows. 'Why? Because you enjoyed it of course. What better reason?'

She could not help laughing, even while she said crossly, feeling misunderstood: 'The fact is, you are as bad as Tom. You make up stories about women, too, to suit yourself. You like thinking of women as hard and decided, cynically making use of men.'

'Certainly,' said Kenneth. 'Much better than letting yourself be made use of. I like women to know what they want and get it.'

This kind of conversation irritated and saddened Julia: it was rather like a froth whipping on the surface of the sea, with the currents underneath dark and unknown.

She did not like being reminded how much better Kenneth understood her than Tom did. She was pleased to get the business of the ceremony over. Tom married her in a purposeful, unhurrying way; but he remarked that it must be before a certain date because he wanted to start planting soon.

Kenneth attended as best man with a glint of malice in his eye, and the air of a well-wishing onlooker, interested to see how things would turn out. Julia and he exchanged a glance of pure understanding, very much against their wills, for their attitude towards each other was now one of brisk friendship. From the security of Tom's arms, she allowed herself to think that if Kenneth were not the kind of man to feel protective towards a woman simply because he enjoyed feeling protective, then it was so much the worse for him. This was slightly vindictive in her: but on the whole good-natured enough – good-nature was necessary; the three of them would be living together in one house, on the same farm, seeing other people seldom.

It was quite easy, after all. Kenneth did not have to efface himself. Tom effortlessly claimed Julia as his wife, from his magnificent, lazy self-assurance, and she was glad to be claimed. Kenneth and she maintained a humorous understanding. He was given three rooms to himself in one wing of the house; but it was not long before they became disused. It seemed silly for him to retire after dinner by himself. In the evenings, the fact that Julia was Tom's wife was marked by their two big chairs set side by side, with Kenneth's opposite. He used to sit there watching them with his observant, slightly sarcastic smile.

After a while Julia understood she was feeling uneasy; she put it down to the fact that she had expected subtle antagonism between the two men, which she would have to smooth over, while in fact there was no antagonism. It went deeper than that. Those first few nights, when Kenneth tactfully withdrew to his rooms, but looking amused, Tom was restless: he missed Kenneth badly. Julia watched them;

and saw with a curious humorous sinking of the heart that they were so close to each other they could not bear to be apart for long. In the evenings it was they who talked, in the odd bantering manner they used even when serious: particularly when serious. Tom liked it when Kenneth sat there opposite, looking shrewd and sceptical about this marriage: they would tease each other in a way that, had they been man and woman, would have seemed positively flirtatious. Listening to them, Julia felt an extraordinary unease, as at a perversity. She chose not to think about it. Better to be affectionately amused at Tom's elder-brother attitude towards Kenneth; there was often something petulant, rebellious, childish, in Kenneth's attitude towards Tom. Why, Tom was even elder-brotherish to her, who had been managing her own life, so efficiently, for years all over the world. Well, and was not that why she had married him?

She accepted it. They all accepted it. They grew into a silent comfortable understanding. Tom, so to speak, was the head of the family, commanding, strong, perhaps a little obtuse, as authority has to be; and Julia and Kenneth deferred to him, with the slightest hint of mockery, to gloss the fact that they were glad to defer: how pleasant to let the responsibility rest on someone else!

Julia even learned to accept the knowledge that when Tom was busy, and she walked with Kenneth, or swam with Kenneth, or took trips into town with Kenneth, it was not only with Tom's consent; more, he liked it, even needed it. Sometimes she felt as if he were urging her to be with his brother. Kenneth felt it and rebelled, shying away in his petulant younger-brother manner. He would exclaim: 'Good Lord, man, Julia's your wife, not mine.' And Tom would laugh uneasily and say: 'I don't like the idea of being possessive.' The thought of Tom being possessive was so absurd that Julia and Kenneth began giggling helplessly, like conspiring and wise children. And when Tom had departed, leaving them together, she would say to Kenneth, in her troubled serious fashion: 'But I don't understand any of it. It flies in the face of nature.'

'So it does,' Kenneth would return easily. He looked at her with a quizzical glint. 'You must take things as they come, my dear sister-in-law.' But Julia felt she had been doing just that: she had relaxed, without thinking, drifting warmly and luxuriously inside Tom's warm and comfortable grasp; which was also Kenneth's, and because Tom wanted it that way.

In spite of Tom, she maintained with Kenneth a slight but strong barrier, because they were people who could be too strongly attracted to each other. Once or twice, when they had been left alone together by Tom, Kenneth would fly off irritably: 'Really, why I bother to be loyal in the circumstances I can't think.'

'But what *are* the circumstances?' Julia asked, puzzled.

'Oh *Lord*, Julia . . .' Kenneth expostulated irritably.

Once, when he was brutal with irritability, he made the curious remark: 'The fact is, it was just about time Tom and I had a wife.' He began laughing, not very pleasantly.

Julia did not understand. She thought it sounded ugly.

Kenneth regarded her ironically and said: 'Fortunately for Tom, he doesn't know anything at all about himself.'

But Julia did not like this said about her husband, even though she felt it to be true. Instinctively this particular frontier in their mutual relations was avoided in future; and she was careful with Kenneth, refusing to discuss Tom with him.

From time to time during those two years before Tom left for the war, Kenneth investigated (his own word) the girls on surrounding farms, with a view to marrying. They bored him. He had a prolonged affair with a married woman whose husband bored her. To Julia and Tom he made witty remarks about his position as a lover. Sometimes the three of them would become helpless with laughter at his descriptions of himself being gallant: the lady was romantic, and liked being courted. Kenneth was not romantic, and his interest in the lady was confined to an end which he could not prevent himself describing in his pungent, sour, resigned fashion during those long evenings with the married couple. Again, Julia got the uneasy feeling that Tom was really too interested – no, that was not the word; it was not the easygoing interest of an amused outsider that Tom displayed; while he listened to Kenneth being witty about his affair, it was almost as if he were participating himself, as if he were silently urging Kenneth on to further revelations. On these occasions Julia felt a revulsion from Tom. She said to herself that she was jealous, and repressed the feeling.

When the war started Tom became restless; Julia knew that he would soon go. He volunteered before there was conscription; and she watched, with a humorous sadness, the scene (an uncomfortable one) between her two men, when it seemed that Tom felt impelled to apologize to Kenneth for taking the advantage of him in grasping a rare chance of happiness. Kenneth was unfit; the two brothers had come to Africa in the first place because of Kenneth's delicate lungs. Kenneth did not at all want to go to the war. 'Lord!' he exclaimed to Tom, 'there's no need to sound so apologetic. You're welcome. I'm not a romantic. I don't like getting killed unless in a good cause. I can't see any point in the thing.' In this way he appeared to dismiss the war and the world's turmoil. As for Tom, he didn't really care about the issues of the war, either. It was sufficient that there was a war. For both men it was axiomatic that it was impossible England could ever be beaten in a war; they might laugh at their own attitude (which they did, when Julia, from her liberal travelled internationalism, mocked at them), but that was what they felt, nevertheless.

As for Julia, she was more unhappy about the war than either of them. She had grown into security on the farm; now the world, which she had wanted to shut out, pressed in on her again; and she thought of her many friends, in so many countries, in the thick of things, feeling strange partisan emotions which seemed to her absurd. For she thought in terms of people, not of nations or issues; and the war, to her, was a question of mankind gone mad, killing each other pointlessly. Always the pointlessness of everything! And now she was not allowed to forget it.

To do her credit, all her unhappiness and female resentment at being so lightly abandoned by Tom at the first sound of a bugle calling adventure down the wind was suppressed. She merely said scornfully to him: 'What a baby you are! As if there hadn't been the last war! And look at all the men in the district, pleased as punch because something exciting is going to happen. If you really cared two hoots about the war, I might respect you. But you don't. Nor do most of the people we know.'

Tom did not like this. The atmosphere of war had stirred him into a superficial patriotism. 'You sound like a newspaper leader,' Julia mocked him. 'You don't really believe a word you say. The truth is that most people like us, in all the countries I've been in, haven't a notion what we believe about anything. We don't believe in the slogans and the lies. It makes me sick, to see the way you all get excited the moment war comes.'

This made Tom angry, because it was true; and because he had suddenly remembered his sentimental attachment to England, in the Rupert Brooke fashion. They were on edge with each other, in the days before he left: he was glad to go, particularly as Kenneth was being no less caustic. This was the first time the two men had ever been separated; and Julia felt that Kenneth was as hurt as she because Tom left them so easily. In fact, they were all pleased when Tom was able to leave the farm, and put an end to the misery of their tormenting each other.

But after he had gone, Julia was very unhappy. She missed him badly. Marrying had been a greater peace than she had imagined possible for her. To let the restless critical part of one die; to drift; to relax; to enjoy Africa as a country, the way it looked and the way it felt; to enjoy the physical things slowly, without haste – learning all this had, she imagined, healed her. And now, without Tom, she was nothing. She was unsupported and unwarmed; and she knew that marrying had after all cured her of nothing. She was still floating rootlessly, without support; she belonged nowhere; and even Africa, which she had grown to love, meant nothing to her really: it was another country she had visited as lightly as a migrant bird.

And Kenneth was no help at all. With Tom on the farm she might have been able to drift with the current, to take the conventional attitude towards the war. But Kenneth used to switch on the wireless in the evenings and pungently translate the news of the war into the meaningless chaotic brutality which was how she herself saw it. He spoke with the callous cynicism that means people are suffering, and which she could hear in her own voice.

'It's all very well,' she would say to him. 'It's all very well for us. We sit here out of it all. Millions of people are suffering.'

'People like suffering,' he would retort angrily. 'Look at Tom. There he sits in the desert, bored as hell. He'll be talking about the best years of his life in ten years' time.'

Julia could hear Tom's voice, nostalgically recalling adventure, only too clearly. At the same time Kenneth made her angry, because he expressed what she felt, and she did not like the way she felt. She joined the local women's groups and started knitting and helping with district functions; and flushed up when she saw Kenneth's cold angry eyes resting on her. 'By God, Julia, you are as bad as Tom . . .'

'Well, surely, one must be part of it, surely, Kenneth?' She tried hard to express what she was feeling.

'Just what are you fighting *for*?' he demanded. 'Can you tell me that?'

'I feel we ought to find out . . .'

He wouldn't listen. He flounced off down the farm saying: 'I'm going to make a new dam. Unless they bomb it, it's something useful done in all this waste and chaos. You can go and knit nice woollies for those poor devils who are getting themselves killed and listen to the dear women talking about the dreadful Nazis. My God, the hypocrisy. Just tell them to take a good look at South Africa, from me, will you?'

The fact was, he missed Tom. When he was approached to subscribe to war charities he gave generously, in Tom's name, sending the receipts carefully to Tom, with sarcastic intention. As the war deepened and the dragging weight of death and suffering settled in their minds, Julia would listen at night to angry pacing footsteps up and down, up and down the long stone passages of the house, and going out in her dressing-gown, would come on Kenneth, his eyes black with anger, his face tense and white: 'Get out of my way, Julia. I shall kill you or somebody. I'd like to blow the whole thing up. Why not blow it up and be finished with it? It would be good riddance.'

Julia would gently take him by the arm and lead him back to bed, shutting down her own cold terror at the world. It was necessary for one of them to remain sane. Kenneth at that time was not quite sane. He was working fourteen hours a day; up long before sunrise, hastening back up the road home after sundown, for an evening's studying: he read scientific stuff about farming. He was building dams, roads, bridges; he planted hundreds of acres of trees; he contour-ridged and drained. He would listen to the news of so many thousands killed and wounded, so many factories blown up, and turn to Julia, his face contracted with hate, saying: 'At any rate I'm building not destroying.'

'I hope it comforts you,' Julia would remark, mildly sarcastic, though she felt bitter and futile.

He would look at her balefully and stride out again, away on some work for his hands.

They were quite alone in the house. For a short while after Tom left they discussed whether they would get an assistant, for conventional reasons. But they disliked the idea of a stranger, and the thing drifted. Soon, as the men left the farms to go off to the war, many women were left alone, doing the work themselves, or with assistants who were unfit for fighting, and there was nothing really outrageous in Kenneth and Julia living together by themselves. It was understood in the district, that for the duration of the war, this kind of situation should not be made a subject for gossip.

It was inevitable they should be lovers. From the moment Tom left they both knew it.

Tom was away three years. She was exhausted by Kenneth. His mood was so black and bitter and she knew that nothing she could do or say might help him, for she was as bad herself.

She became the kind of woman he wanted: he did not want a warm, consoling woman. She was his mistress. Their relationship was a complicated fencing game, conducted with irony, tact, and good sense – except when he boiled over into hatred and vented it on her. There were times when suddenly all vitality failed her, and she seemed to sink swiftly, unsupported, to lie helpless in the depths of herself, looking up undesirously at the life of emotion and warmth washing gently over her head. Then Kenneth used to leave her alone, whereas Tom would have gently coaxed her into life again.

'I wish Tom would come back, oh dear Christ, I wish he'd come back,' she would sigh.

'Do you imagine I don't?' Kenneth would enquire bitterly. Then, a little piqued, but not much: 'Don't I do?'

'Well enough, I suppose.'

'What do you want then?' he enquired briefly, giving what small amount of attention he could spare from the farm to the problem of Julia, the woman.

'Tom,' Julia replied simply.

He considered this critically. 'The fact is, you and I have far more in common than you and Tom.'

'I don't see what "in common" has to do with it.'

'You and I are the same kind of animal. Tom doesn't know the first thing about you. He never could.'

'Perhaps that's the reason.'

Dislike began welling between them, tempered, as always,

by patient irony. 'You don't like women at all,' complained Julia suddenly. 'You simply don't like me. You don't trust me.'

'Oh if it comes to liking . . .' He laughed resentfully. 'You don't trust me either, for that matter.'

It was the truth; they didn't trust each other; they mistrusted the destructive nihilism that they had in common. Conversations like these, which became far more frequent as time went on, left them hardened against each other for days, in a condition of watchful challenge. This was part of their long, exhausting exchange, which was a continual resolving of mutual antagonism in tired laughter.

Yet, when Tom wrote saying he was being demobilized, Kenneth, in a mood of tenderness, asked Julia to marry him. She was shocked and astonished. 'You know quite well you don't want to marry me,' she expostulated. 'Besides, how could you do that to Tom?' Catching his quizzical glance, she began laughing helplessly.

'I don't know whether I want to marry you or not,' admitted Kenneth honestly, laughing with her.

'Well, I know. You don't.'

'I've got used to you.'

'I haven't got used to you. I never could.'

'I don't understand what it is Tom gives you that I don't.'

'Peace,' said Julia simply. 'You and I fight all the time, we never do anything else.'

'We don't fight,' protested Kenneth. 'We have never, as they say, exchanged a cross word.' He grimaced. 'Except when I get wound up, and that's a different thing.'

Julia saw that he could not imagine a relationship with a woman that was not based on antagonism. She said, knowing it was useless: 'Everything is so easy with Tom.'

'Of course it's easy,' he said angrily. 'The whole damn thing is a lie from beginning to end. However, if that's what you like . . .' He shrugged, his anger evaporating. He said drily: 'I imagined I was qualifying as a husband.'

'Some men can't ever be husbands. They'll always be lovers.'

'I thought women liked that?'

'I wasn't talking about women, I was talking about me.'

'Well, I intend to get married, for all that.'

After that they did not discuss it. Speaking of what they felt left them confused, angry, puzzled.

Before Tom came back Kenneth said: 'I ought to leave the farm.'

She did not trouble to answer, it was so insincere.

'I'll get a farm over the other side of the district.'

She merely smiled. Kenneth had written long letters to Tom every week of those three years, telling him every detail of what was happening on the farm. Plans for the future were already worked out.

It was arranged that Julia should go and meet Tom in town, where they would spend some weeks before the three began life together again. As Kenneth said, sarcastically, to Julia: 'It will be just like a second honeymoon.'

It was. Tom returned from the desert toughened, sunburnt, swaggering a little because he was unsure of himself with Julia. But she was so happy to see him that in a few hours they were back where they had been. 'About Kenneth . . .' began Tom warily, after they had edged round this subject for some days.

'Much better not talk about it,' said Julia quickly.

Tom's blue eyes rested on her, not critically, but appealingly. 'Is it going to be all right?' he asked after a moment. She could see he was terrified she might say that Kenneth had decided to go away. She said drily: 'I didn't want you to go off to the wars like a hero, did I?'

'There's something in that,' he admitted; admitting at the same time that they were quits. Actually, he was rather subdued because of his years as a soldier. He was quick to drop the subject. It would not be just yet that he would begin talking about the happiest years of his life. He had still to forget how bored he had been and how he had missed his farm.

For a few days there was awkwardness between the three.

Kenneth was jealous because of the way Julia had gladly turned back to Tom. But there was so much work to do, and Kenneth and Tom were so pleased to be back together, that it was not long before everything was as easy as before. Julia thought it was easier; now that her attraction for Kenneth, and his for her, had been slaked, the restlessness that had always been between them would vanish. Perhaps not quite . . . Julia and Kenneth's eyes would meet sometimes in that instinctive, laughing understanding that she could never have with Tom, and then she would feel guilty.

Sometimes Kenneth would 'take out' a girl from a near farm; and they would afterwards discuss his getting married. 'If only I could fall in love,' he would complain humorously. 'You are the only woman I can bear the thought of, Julia.' He would say this before Tom, and Tom would laugh; they had reached such a pitch of complicity.

Very soon there were plans for expanding the farm. They bought several thousands of acres of land next door. They would grow tobacco on a large scale; this was the time of the tobacco boom. They were getting very rich.

There were two assistants on the new farm, but Tom spent most of his days there. Sometimes his nights, too. Julia, after three days spent alone with Kenneth, with the old attraction strong between them, said to him: 'I wish you would let Kenneth run that farm.'

Tom, who was absorbed and fascinated by the new problems, said rather impatiently: 'Why?'

'Surely that's obvious.'

'That's up to you, isn't it?'

'Perhaps it isn't, always.'

It was the business of the war over again. He seemed a slow, deliberate man, without much fire. But he liked new problems to solve. He got bored. Kenneth, the quick, lively, impatient one, liked to be rooted in one place, liked to develop what he had.

Julia had the helpless feeling again that Tom simply didn't care about herself and Kenneth. She grew to accept the knowledge that really, it was Kenneth that mattered to him. Except for the war, they had never been separated. Tom's father had died, and his mother married Kenneth's father. Tom had always been with Kenneth, he could not remember a time when he had not been protectively guarding him. Once Julia asked him: 'I suppose you must have been very jealous of him, that was it, wasn't it?' and she was astonished at his quick flare of rage at the suggestion. She dropped the thing: what did it matter now?

The two boys had gone through various schools and to university together. They had started farming in their early twenties, when they hadn't a penny between them, and had to borrow money to support their mother, for whom they shared a deep love, which was also half-exasperated admiration; she had apparently been a helpless, charming lady with many admirers who left her children to the care of nurses.

When Tom was away one evening, and would not be back till next day, Kenneth said brusquely, with the roughness that is the result of conflict: 'Coming to my room tonight, Julia?'

'How can I?' she protested.

'Well, I don't like the idea of coming to the marriage bed,' he said practically, and they began to laugh. To Julia, Kenneth would always be the laughter of inevitability.

Tom said nothing, though he must have known. When Julia again appealed that he should stay on this farm and send Kenneth to the other, he turned away, frowning, and did not reply. His manner to her did not change. And she still felt: this is my husband, and compared to that feeling, Kenneth was nothing. At the same time a grim anxiety was taking possession of her: it seemed that in some perverse way the two men were brought even closer together, for a time, by sharing the same woman. That was how Julia put it, to herself: the plain and brutal fact.

It was Kenneth who pulled away in the end. Not from Julia: from the situation. There came a time when it was possible for Kenneth to say, as he stood smiling sardonically opposite Julia and Tom, who were sitting like an old married couple on their side of the fire: 'You know that it is quite essential I should get married. Things can't go on like this.'

'But you can't marry without being in love,' protested Julia; and immediately checked herself with an annoyed laugh – she realized that what she was protesting against was Kenneth going away from her.

'You must see that I should.'

'I don't like the idea,' said Tom, as if it were his marriage that was under discussion.

'Look at you and Tom,' said Kenneth peaceably, but not without maliciousness. 'A very satisfactory marriage. You weren't in love.'

'Weren't we in love, Julia?' asked Tom, rather surprised.

'Actually, I was "in love" with Kenneth,' said Julia, with the sense that this was an unnecessary thing to say.

'You wanted a wife. Julia wanted a husband. All very sensible.'

'One can be "in love" once too often,' said Julia, aiming this at Kenneth.

'Are you in love with Kenneth now?'

Julia did not answer; it annoyed her that Tom should ask it, after virtually handing her over to Kenneth. After a moment she remarked: 'I suppose you are right. You really ought to get married.' Then, thoughtfully: 'I couldn't be married to you, Kenneth. You destroy me.' The word sounded heightened and absurd. She hurried on: 'I didn't know it was possible to be as happy as I have been with Tom.' She smiled at her husband and reached over and took his hand: he returned the pressure gratefully.

'Ergo, I have to get married,' said Kenneth caustically.

'But you say so yourself.'

'I don't seem to be feeling what I ought to feel,' said Tom at last, laughing in a bewildered way.

'That's what's wrong with the three of us,' said Julia; then, feeling as if she were on the edge of that dangerous thing that might destroy them, she stopped and said: 'Let's not talk about it. It doesn't do any good to talk about it.'

That conversation had taken place a month ago. Kenneth had not mentioned getting married since; and Julia had secretly hoped he had shelved it. Not long since, during that trip to town, he had spent a day away from Tom and herself – and with whom? Tomorrow he was making the trip again, and for the first time for years, since they had been together, it was not the three of them, close in understanding, but Tom and Julia, with Kenneth deliberately excluding himself and putting up barriers.

Kenneth did not open his mouth the whole evening; though both Tom and Julia waited for him to break the silence. Julia did not read; she moiled over the facts of her life unhappily; and from time to time looked over at Tom, who smiled back affectionately, knowing she wanted this of him.

In spite of the fire, that now roared and crackled in the wall, Julia was cold. The thin frosty air of the high veld was of an electric dryness in the big bare room. The roof was crackling with cold; every time the tin snapped overhead it evoked the arching, myriad-starred, chilly night outside, and the drying, browning leaves, the tall waving grass that was now a dull parched colour. Julia's skin crinkled and stung with dryness.

Suddenly she said: 'It won't do, Kenneth. You can't behave like this.' She got up, and stood with her back to the fire, gazing levelly at them. She felt herself to be parching and withering within; she felt no heavier than a twig; the sap did not run in her veins. Because of Kenneth's betrayal, she was wounded in some place she could not name. She had no substance. That was how she felt.

What they saw was a tall, rather broad woman, big-framed, the bones of her face strongly supporting the flesh. Her eyes were blue and candid, now clouded by trouble, but still humorously troubled. She was forcing them to look at her; to make comparisons; she was challenging them. She was forcing them even to break the habit of loyalty which, blithely tender, continually recreative, blinds the eyes of lovers to change.

They saw this strong, ageing woman, the companion of their lives, standing there in front of them, still formed in the shape of beauty, for she was pleasant to look at, but with the light of beauty gone. They remembered her, perhaps, on that afternoon by the sea when they had first encountered her, or when she was newly arrived at the farm; young, vivid, a slender and rather boyish girl, with sleek, close-cropped hair and quick amused blue eyes.

Now, around the firm and bony face the soft hair fell in dressed waves, she wore a soft flowery dress; they saw a disquieting incongruity between this expression of femininity and what they knew her to be. They were irritated. To stand there, reminding them (when they did not want to be reminded) that she was facing the sorrowful abdication of middle age, and facing it alone, seemed to them irrelevant, even unfair.

Kenneth said resentfully: 'Oh, Lord, you are very much a woman, after all, Julia. Must you make a scene?'

Her quick laugh was equally resentful. 'Why shouldn't I make a scene? I feel entitled to it.'

Kenneth said: 'We all know there's got to be a change. Can't we go through with it without this sort of thing?'

'Surely,' she said helplessly, 'everything can't be changed without some sort of explanation . . .' She could not go on.

'Well, what sort of explanation do you want?'

She shrugged hopelessly. After a moment she said, as if continuing an old conversation: 'Perhaps I should have had children, after all?'

'I always said so,' remarked Tom mildly.

'You are nearly forty,' said Kenneth practically.

'I wouldn't make a good mother,' she said. 'I couldn't compete with yours. I wouldn't have the courage to take it on, knowing I should fail by comparison with your so perfect mother.' She was being sarcastic, but there were tears in her voice.

'Let's leave our mother out of it,' said Tom coldly.

'Of course, we always leave everything important out of it.'

Neither of them said anything; they were closed away from her in hostility. She went on: 'I often wonder, why did you want me at all, Tom? You didn't really want children particularly.'

'Yes, I did,' said Tom, rather bewildered.

'Not enough to make me feel you cared one way or the other. Surely a woman is entitled to that, to feel that her children matter. I don't know what it is you took me into your life *for*?'

After a moment Kenneth said lightly, trying to restore the comfortable surface of flippancy: 'I have always felt that we ought to have children.'

Neither Tom nor Julia responded to this appeal. Julia took a candle from the mantelpiece, bent to light it at the fire, and said: 'Well, I'm off to bed. The whole situation is beyond me.'

'Very well then,' said Kenneth. 'If you must have it: I'm getting married soon.'

'Obviously,' said Julia drily.

'What did you want me to say?'

'Who is it?' Tom sounded so resentful that it changed the weight of the conversation: now it was Tom and Kenneth as antagonists.

'Well, she's a girl from England. She came out here a few months ago on this scheme for importing marriageable women to the Colonies . . . well, that's what the scheme amounts to.'

'Yes, but the girl?' asked Julia, amused in spite of herself at Kenneth's invincible distaste at the idea of marrying.

'Well . . .' Kenneth hesitated, his dark bright eyes on Julia's face, his mouth already beginning to twist into dry amusement. 'She's fair. She's pretty. She seems capable. She wants to be married . . . what more do I want?' That last phrase was savage. They had come to a dead end.

'I'm going to bed!' exclaimed Julia suddenly, the tears pouring down her face. 'I can't bear this.'

Neither of them said anything to prevent her leaving. When she had gone, Kenneth made an instinctive defensive movement towards Tom. After a moment Tom said irritably, but commandingly: 'It's absurd for you to get married when there's no need.'

'Obviously there's a need,' said Kenneth angrily. He rose, taking another candle from the mantelpiece. As he left the room – and it was clear that he left in order to forestall the scene Tom was about to make – he said: 'I want to have children before I get an old man. It seems to be the only thing left.'

When Tom went into the bedroom, Julia was lying dry-eyed on the pillow, waiting for him. She was waiting for him to comfort her into security of feeling. He had never failed her. When he was in bed, she found herself comforting him; it gave her such a perverse, topsy-turvy feeling she could not sleep.

Soon after breakfast Kenneth left for town. He was dressed smartly; normally he did not care how he looked, and his clothes seemed to have been put on in the spirit of one picking up tools for a job. All three acknowledged his appearance with small, constricted smiles; and Kenneth reddened as he got into the car. 'I might not be back tonight,' he called back, driving away without looking back.

Tom and Julia watched the big car nose its way through the trees, and turned back to face each other. 'Like to come down the lands with me?' he asked. 'Yes, I would,' she accepted gratefully. Then she saw, and was thrown back on to herself by the knowledge of it, that he was asking her, not for her comfort, but for his own.

It was a windy, sunlit morning, and very cold; winter had taken possession of the veld overnight.

The house was built on a slight ridge, with the country falling away on either side. The landscape was dulling for the dry season into olive green and thin yellows; there was that extraordinary contrast of limpid, sparkling skies, with sunshine pouring down like a volatile spirit, and dry cold

206

parching the face and hands that made Julia uneasy in winter. It was as if the dryness tightened the cold into rigid fetters on her, so that a perpetual inner shivering had to be suppressed. She walked beside Tom over the fields with hunched shoulders and arms crossed tight over her chest. Yet she was not cold, not in the physical sense. Around the house the mealie fields, now a gentle silvery-gold colour, swept into runnels of light as the wind passed over them, and there was a dry tinkling of parched leaves moving together, like rat's feet over grass. Tom did not speak; but his face was heavy and furrowed. When she took his hand he responded, but listlessly. She wanted him to turn to her, to say: 'Now he's going to make something of his own, you must come to me, and we'll build up again.' She wanted him to claim her, heal her, make her whole. But he was uneasy and restless; and she said at last diffidently: 'Why should you mind so much? It ought to be me who's unhappy.'

'Don't you?' he asked, sounding like a person angry at dishonesty.

'Yes, of course,' she said; and tried to find the words to say that if only he could take her gently into his own security, as he had years ago, things would be right for them.

But that security no longer existed in him.

All that day they hardly spoke, not because of animosity between them, but because of a deep, sad helplessness. They could not help each other.

That night Kenneth did not come back from town. Next day Tom went off by himself to the second farm, leaving her with a gentle apologetic look, as if to say: 'Leave me alone, I can't help it.'

Kenneth telephoned in the middle of the morning from town. His voice was offhand; it was also subtly defensive. That small voice coming from such a distance down the wires, conjured up such a clear vision of Kenneth himself, that she smiled tenderly.

'Well?' she asked warily.

'I'll be back sometime. I don't know when.'

'That means it's definite?'

'I think so.' A pause. Then the voice dropped into dry humour: 'She's such a nice girl that things take a long time, don't you know.' Julia laughed. Quickly he added: 'But she really is, you know, Julia. She's awfully nice.'

'Well, you must do as you think,' she said cautiously.

'How's Tom?' he asked.

'I suddenly don't know anything about Tom,' she answered.

There was such a long silence that she clicked the telephone.

'I'm still here,' said Kenneth. 'I was trying to think of the right things to say.'

'Has it come to the point where we have to think of the right things?'

'Looks like it, doesn't it?'

'Good-bye,' she said quickly, putting down the receiver. 'Let me know when you're coming and I'll get your things ready.'

As usual in the mornings, she passed on a tour of inspection from room to room of the big bare house, where the windows stood open all day, showing blocks of blue crystal round the walls, or views of veld, as if the building, the very bricks and iron, were compounded with sky and landscape to form a new kind of home. When she had made her formal inspection, and found everything cleaned and polished and arranged, she went to the kitchen. Here she ordered the meals, and discussed the state of the pantry with her cook. Then she went back to the verandah; at this hour she would normally read, or sew, till lunch-time.

The thought came into her mind, with a destroying force, that if she were not in the house, Tom would hardly notice it, from a physical point of view: the servants would create comfort without her. She suppressed an impulse to go into the kitchen and cook, or tidy a cupboard, to find some work for the hands; that was not what she sought, a temporary salve for feeling useless. She took her large light straw hat from the nail in the bare, stone-floored passage, and went out into the garden. As she did not care for gardening, the ground about the house was arranged with groups of shrubs, so that there would be patches of blossom at any time of the year. The garden boy kept the lawns fresh and green. Over the vivid emerald grass spread the flowers of dryness, the poinsettias, loose scattering shapes of bright scarlet, creamy pink, light yellow. On the fine, shiny-brown stems fluttered light green leaves. In a swift gusty wind the quickly moving blossoms and leaves danced and shook; they seemed to her the very essence of the time of year, the essence of dry cold, of light thin sunshine, of high cold-blue skies.

She passed quietly down the path through the lawns and flowers to the farm road, and turned to look back at the house. From the outside it appeared such a large, assertive, barn of a place, with its areas of shiny tin roof, the hard pink of the walls, the glinting angled shapes of the windows. Although shrubs grew sparsely around it, and it was shaded by a thick clump of trees, it looked naked, raw, crude. 'That is my home,' said Julia to herself, testing the word. She rejected it. In that house she had lived ten years – more. She turned away from it, walking lightly through the sifting pink dust of the roads like a stranger. There had always been times when Africa rejected her, when she felt like a critical ghost. This was one of those times. Through the known and loved scenes of the veld she saw Buenos Aires, Rome, Cape Town – a dozen cities, large and small, merging and mingling as the country rose and fell about her. Perhaps it is not good for human beings to live in so many places? But it was not that. She was suffering from an unfamiliar dryness of the senses, an unlocated, unfocused ache that, if she were young, would have formed itself about a person or place, but now remained locked within her. 'What am I?' she kept saying to herself as she walked through the veld, in the moving patch of shade that fell from the large drooping hat. On either side the long grass moved and whispered sibilantly; the doves throbbed gently from the trees; the sky was a flower-blue arch over her – it was, as they say, a lovely morning.

She passed like a revenant along the edges of the mealie fields, watching the working gangs of natives; at the well she paused to see the women with their groups of naked children; at the cattle sheds she leaned to touch the wet noses of the thrusting soft-headed calves which butted and pushed at her legs. There she stayed for some time, finding comfort in these young creatures. She understood at last that it was nearly lunch-time. She must go home, and preside at the lunch-table for Tom, in case he should decide to return. She left the calves thinking: Perhaps I ought to have children? She knew perfectly well that she would not.

The road back to the house wound along the high hogsback between two vleis that fell away on either side. She walked slowly, trying to recover that soft wonder she had felt when she first arrived on the farm and learned how living in cities had cheated her of the knowledge of the shapes of sky and land. Above her, in the great bright bell of blue sky, the wind currents were marked by swirls of cloud, the backwaters of the air by heavy sculptured piles of sluggish white. Around her the skeleton of rock showed under the thin covering of living soil. The trees thickened with the fall or rise of the ground, with the running of underground rivers; the grass – the long blond hair of the grass – struggled always to heal and hold whatever wounds were made by hoof of beast or thoughtlessness of man. The sky, the land, the swirling air, closed around her in an exchange of water and heat, and the deep multitudinous murmuring of living substance sounded like a humming in her blood. She listened, half-passively, half-rebelliously, and asked: 'What do I contribute to all this?'

That afternoon she walked again, for hours; and throughout the following day; returning to the house punctually for meals and greeting Tom across the distance that puts itself between people who try to support themselves with the mental knowledge of a country, and those who work in it. Once Tom said, with tired concern, looking at her equally tired face: 'Julia, I didn't know you would mind so much. I suppose it was conceit. I always thought I came first.'

'You do,' she said quickly, 'believe me, you do.'

She went to him, so that he could put his arms about her. He did, and there was no warmth in it for either of them. 'We'll come right again,' he promised her. But it was as though he listened to the sound of his own voice for a message of assurance.

Kenneth came back unexpectedly on the fourth evening. He was alone; and he appeared purposeful and decided. During dinner no one spoke much. After dinner, in the bare, gaunt, firelit room, the three waited for someone to speak.

At last Julia said: 'Well, Kenneth?'

'We are getting married next month.'

'Where?'

'In church,' he said. He smiled constrictedly. 'She wants a proper wedding. I don't mind, if she likes it.' Kenneth's attitude was altogether brisk, down-to-earth and hard. At the same time he looked at Julia and Tom uneasily: he hated his position.

'How old is she?' asked Julia.

'A baby. Twenty-three.'

This shocked Julia. 'Kenneth, you can't do that.'

'Why not?'

Julia could not really see why not.

'Has she money of her own?' asked Tom practically, causing the other two to look at him in surprise. 'After all,' he said quickly, 'we must know about her, before she comes?'

'Of course she hasn't,' said Kenneth coldly. 'She wouldn't be coming out to the Colonies on a subsidized scheme for importing marriageable women, would she?'

Tom grimaced. 'You two are brutal,' he remarked.

Kenneth and Julia glanced at each other; it was like a shrug. 'I didn't mention money in the first place,' he pointed out. 'You did. Anyway, what's wrong with it? If I were a surplus woman in England I should certainly emigrate to find a husband. It's the only sensible thing to do.'

'What is she living on now?' asked Julia.

'She has a job in an office. Some such nonsense.' Kenneth dismissed this. 'Anyway, why talk about money? Surely we have enough?'

'How much have we got?' asked Julia, who was always rather vague about money.

'A hell of a lot,' said Tom, laughing. 'The last three years we've made thousands.'

'How many thousands?'

'Difficult to say, there's so much going back into the farms. Fifty thousand perhaps. We'll make a lot more this year.'

Julia smiled. The words 'fifty thousand' could not be made to come real in her mind. She thought of how she had earned her living for years, in offices, budgeting for everything she spent. 'I suppose we could be described as rich?' she asked wonderingly at last, trying to relate this fact to the life she lived, to the country around them, to their future.

'I suppose we could,' agreed Tom, snorting with amused laughter. He liked it when Julia made it possible for him to think of her as helpless. 'Most of the credit goes to Kenneth,' he added. 'All the work he did during the war is reaping dividends now.'

Julia looked at him; then sardonically at Kenneth, who was shifting uncomfortably in his chair. Tom persisted with good-natured sarcasm, getting his own back for Kenneth's gibes over the war: 'This is getting quite a show-place; I got a letter from the Government asking me if they could bring a collection of distinguished visitors from Home to see it, next week. You'll have to act as hostess. They're coming to see Kenneth's war effort.' He laughed. 'It's also been very profitable.'

Kenneth shut his mouth hard; and kept his temper. 'We are discussing my future wife,' he said coldly.

'So we are,' said Julia.

'Well, let's finish with the thing. I shall give the girl a thumping, expensive honeymoon in the most glossy and awful hotels in the sub-continent,' continued Kenneth grimly. 'She'll love it.'

'Why shouldn't she?' asked Julia. 'I should have loved it too, at her age.'

'I didn't say she shouldn't.'

'And then?' asked Julia again. She was wanting to hear what sort of plans Kenneth had for another farm. He looked at her blankly. 'And then what?'

'Where will you go?'

'Go?'

It came to her that he did not intend to leave the farm. This was such a shock she could not speak. She collected herself at last, and said slowly: 'Kenneth, surely you don't intend to live here?'

'Why not?' he asked quickly, very much on the defensive.

The atmosphere had tightened so that Julia saw, in looking from one man to the other, that this was the real crisis of the business, something she had not expected, but which they had both been waiting, consciously or unconsciously, for her to approach.

'Good God,' she said slowly in rising anger. 'Good God.' She looked at Tom, who at once averted his eyes. She saw that Tom was longing uneasily for her to make it possible for Kenneth to stay.

She understood at last that, if it had occurred to either of them that another woman could not live here, it was a knowledge neither of them was prepared to face. She looked at these two men and hated them for the way they took their women into their lives, without changing a thought or a habit to meet them.

She got up, and walked away from them slowly, standing with her back to them, gazing out of the window at the heavily-starred winter's night. She said: 'Kenneth, you are marrying this girl because you intend to have a family. You don't care tuppence for her, really.'

'I've got to be very fond of her,' protested Kenneth.

'At bottom, you don't care tuppence.'

He did not reply. 'You are going to bring her here to me. She'll feel with her instinct if not with her head that she's being made use of. And you bring her here to me.' It seemed to her that she had made her sense of outrage clear enough. She turned to face them.

'The prospect of bringing her "to you" doesn't seem to me as shocking as apparently it does to you,' said Kenneth drily.

'Can't you see?' she said desperately. 'She couldn't compete . . .'

'You flatter yourself,' said Kenneth briskly.

'Oh, I don't mean that. I mean we've been together for so long. There's nothing we don't know about each other. Have I got to say it . . .'

'No,' said Kenneth quietly. 'Much better not.'

Through all this Tom, that large, fair, comfortable man, leaned back in his chair, looking from his wife to his half-brother with the air of one suddenly transported to a foreign country.

He said stubbornly: 'I don't see why you shouldn't adjust yourself, Julia. After all, both Kenneth and I have had to adjust ourselves to . . .'

'Quite,' said Kenneth quickly, 'quite.'

She turned on Kenneth furiously. 'Why do you always cut the conversation short? Why shouldn't we talk about it? It's what's real, isn't it, for all of us?'

'No point talking about it,' said Kenneth, with a sullen look.

'No,' she said coldly. 'No point.' She turned away from them, fighting back tears. 'At bottom neither of you really cared tuppence. That's what it is.' At the moment this seemed to her true.

'What do you mean by "really caring"?' asked Kenneth.

Julia turned slowly from the window, jerking the light summer curtains across the stars. 'I mean, we don't care. We just don't care.'

'I don't know what you are talking about,' said Tom, sounding bewildered and angry. 'Haven't you been happy with me? Is that what you are saying, Julia?'

At this both Kenneth and Julia began laughing with an irresistible and painful laughter.

'Of course I've been happy with you,' she said flatly, at last.

'Well then?' asked Tom.

'I don't know why I was happy then and why I'm unhappy now.'

'Let's say you're jealous,' said Kenneth briskly.

'But I don't think I am.'

'Of course you are.'

'Very well then, I am. That's not the point. What are we going to do to the girl?' she asked suddenly, her feeling finding expression.

'I shall make her a good husband,' said Kenneth. The three of them looked at each other, with raised brows, with humorous, tightened lips.

'Very well then,' amended Kenneth. 'But she'll have plenty of nice children. She'll have you for company, Julia, a nice intelligent woman. And she'll have plenty of money and pretty clothes and all that sort of nonsense, if she wants them.'

There was a silence so long it seemed that nothing could break it.

Julia said slowly and painfully: 'I think it is terrible we shouldn't be able to explain what we feel or what we are.'

'I wish you'd stop trying to,' said Kenneth. 'I find it unpleasant. And quite useless.'

Tom said: 'As for me, I would be most grateful if you'd try to explain what you are feeling, Julia. I haven't an idea.'

Julia stood up with her back to the fire and began gropingly: 'Look at the way we are. I mean, what do we add up to? What are we doing here, in the first place?'

'Doing where?' asked Tom kindly.

'Here, in Africa, in this district, on this land.'

'Ohhh,' groaned Tom humorously.

'Oh *Lord*, Julia,' protested Kenneth impatiently.

'I feel as if we shouldn't be here.'

'Where should we be, then?'

'We've as much right as anybody else.'

'I suppose so,' Julia dismissed it. It was not her point, after all, it seemed. She said slowly: 'I suppose there are comparatively very few people in the world as secure and as rich as we are.'

'It takes a couple of bad seasons or a change in the international set-up,' said Kenneth. 'We could get poor as easily as we've got rich. If you want to call it easy. We've worked hard enough, Tom and I.'

'So do many other people. In the meantime we've all the money we want. Why do we never talk about money, never think about it? It's what we are.'

'Speak for yourself, Julia,' said Tom. 'Kenneth and I spend all our days thinking and talking about nothing else. How else do you suppose we've got rich?'

'How to make it. Not what it all adds up to.'

The two men did not reply; they looked at each other with resignation. Kenneth lit a cigarette, Tom a pipe.

'I've been getting a feeling of money the last few days. Perhaps not so much money as . . .' She stopped. 'I can't say what I feel. It's no use. What do our lives add up to? That's what I want to know.'

'Why do you expect us to tell you?' asked Kenneth curiously at last.

This was a new note. Julia looked at him, puzzled. 'I don't know,' she said at last. Then, very drily: 'I suppose I should be prepared to take the consequences for marrying the pair of you.' The men laughed uneasily though with relief that the worst seemed to be over. 'If I left this place tomorrow,' she said sadly, 'you simply wouldn't miss me.'

'Ah, you love Kenneth,' groaned Tom suddenly. The groan was so sudden, coming just as the flippant note had been struck, and successfully, that Julia could not bear it. She continued quietly, lightly, to wipe away the naked pain of Tom's voice: 'No, I don't. I wish you wouldn't talk about love.'

216

'That's what all this is about,' said Kenneth. 'Love.'

Julia looked at him scornfully. She said: 'What sort of people are we? Let's use bare words for bare facts, just for once.'

'Must you?' breathed Kenneth.

'Yes, I must. The fact is that I have been a sort of high-class concubine for the two of you . . .' She stopped at once. Even the beginning of the tirade sounded absurd in her own ears.

'I hope that statement has cleared your mind for you,' said Kenneth ironically.

'No, it hasn't. I didn't expect it would.' But now Julia was fighting hard against that no-man's-land of feeling in which she had been living for so long, that under-sea territory where one thing confuses with another, where it is so easy to drift at ease according to the pull of the tides.

'I should have had children,' she said at last, quietly. 'That's where we went wrong, Tom. It was children we needed.'

'Ah,' said Kenneth from his chair, suddenly deeply sincere, 'now you are talking sense.'

'Well,' said Tom, 'there's nothing to stop us.'

'I'm too old.'

'Other women of forty have children.'

'I'm too – tired. It seems to me, to have children, one needs . . .' She stopped.

'What does one need?' asked Tom.

Julia's eyes met Kenneth's; they exchanged deep, ironic, patient understanding.

'Thank God you didn't marry me,' he said suddenly. 'You were quite right. Tom's the man for you. In a marriage it's necessary for one side to be strong enough to create the illusion.'

'What illusion?' asked Tom petulantly.

'Necessity,' said Kenneth simply.

'Is that the office this girl is going to perform for you?' asked Tom.

'Precisely. She loves me, God help her. She really does,

217

you know . . .' Kenneth looked at them in a manner of inviting them to share his surprise at this fact. 'And she wants children. She knows why she wants them. She'll make me know it too, bless her. Most of the time,' he could not prevent himself adding.

Now it seemed impossible to go on. They remained silent, each face expressing tired and bewildered unhappiness. Julia stood against the mantelpiece, feeling the warmth of the fire running over her body, but not reaching the chill within.

Kenneth recovered first. He got up and said: 'Bed, bed for all of us. This doesn't help. We mustn't talk. We must get on, dealing with the next thing.' He said good night, and went to the door. There he turned, looked clear and full at Julia with his black, alert, shrewd eyes, and remarked: 'You must be nice to that girl, Julia.'

'You know very well I can be "nice" to her, but I won't be "nice" for her. You are deliberately submitting her to it. You won't even move two miles away on to the next farm. You won't even take that much trouble to make her happy. Remember that.'

Kenneth flushed, said hastily: 'Well, I didn't say I wouldn't go to the other farm,' and went out. Julia knew that it would take a lot of unhappiness for the four of them before he would consent to move himself. He thought of this house as his home; and he could not bear to leave Tom, even now.

'Come here,' said Tom gently, when Kenneth had left the room. She went to him, and slipped down beside him into his chair. 'Do you find me stupid?' he asked.

'Not stupid.'

'What then?'

She held him close. 'Put your arms round me.'

He held her; but she did not feel supported: the arms were as light as wind about her, and as unsure.

In the middle of the night she rose from her bed, slipped on her gown and went along the winding passages to Kenneth's bedroom, which was at the other end of the house.

It was filled with the brightness of moonlight. Kenneth was

sitting up against his pillows; he was awake; she could see the light glinting on his eyes.

She sat herself down on the foot of his bed.

'Well, Julia? It's no good coming to me, you know.'

She did not reply. The confusing dimness of the moon, which hung immediately outside the window, troubled her. She held a match to the candle, and watched a warm yellow glow fill the room, so that the moon retreated and became a small hard bright coin high among the stars.

She saw on the dressing-table a new framed photograph.

'If one acquires a wife,' she said sarcastically, 'one of course acquires a photo to put on one's dressing-table.' She went over and picked it up and returned to the bed with it. Kenneth watched her, alertly.

Slowly, Julia's face spread into a compassionate smile.

'What's the matter?' asked Kenneth quickly.

She was not twenty-three, Julia could see that. She was well over thirty. It was a pretty enough face, very English, with flat broad planes and small features. Fair neatly-waved hair fell away regularly from the forehead.

There was anxiety in those too-serious eyes; the mouth smiled carefully in a prepared sweetness for the photographer; the cheeks were thin. Turning the photograph to the light Julia could see how the neck was creased and furrowed. No, she was by no means a girl. She glanced at Kenneth; and was filled slowly by a sweet irrational tenderness for him, a delicious irresponsible gaiety.

'Why,' she said, 'you're in love, after all, Kenneth.'

'Whoever said I wasn't?' he grinned at her, lying watchfully back in his bed and puffing at his cigarette.

She grinned back affectionately, still lifted on a wave of delight; then she turned, and felt it ebb as she looked down at the photograph, mentally greeting this other tired woman, coming to the great rich farm, like the poor girl in the fairy story.

'What are you amused at?' asked Kenneth cautiously.

'I was thinking of you as a refuge,' she explained drily.

'I'm quite prepared to be.'

'You'd never be a refuge for anyone.'

'Not for you. But you forget she's younger.' He laughed: 'She'll be less critical.'

She smiled, without replying, looking at the pictured face. It was such a humourless, earnest, sincere face, the eyes so serious, so searching.

Julia sighed. 'I'm terribly tired,' she said to Kenneth, turning back to him.

'I know you are. So am I. That's why I'm marrying.'

Julia had a clear mental picture of this Englishwoman, who was soon coming to the farm. For a moment she allowed herself to picture her in various situations, arriving with nervous tact, hiding her longing for a home of her own, hoping not to find Julia an enemy. She would find not strife, or hostility, or scenes – none of the situations which she might be prepared to face. She would find three people who knew each other so well that for the most part they found it hardly necessary to speak. She would find indifference to everything she really was, a prepared, deliberate kindness. She would be like a latecomer to a party, entering a room where everyone is already cemented by hours of warmth and intimacy. She would be helpless against Kenneth's need for her to be something she could not be: a young woman, with the spiritual vitality to heal him.

Looking at the pretty girl in the frame which she held between her palms, the girl under whose surface prettiness Julia could see the anxious, haunted woman, the knowledge came to her of what word it was she sought: it was as though those carefully smiling lips formed themselves into that word. 'Do you know what we are?' she asked Kenneth.

'Not a notion,' he replied jauntily.

Julia accepted the word evil from that humourless, homeless girl. Twice in her life it had confronted her; this time she took it gratefully. After all, none other had been offered.

'I know what evil is,' she said to Kenneth.

'How nice for you,' he returned impatiently. Then he

added: 'I suppose, like most women who have lived their own lives, whatever that might mean, you are now beginning to develop an exaggerated conscience. If so, we shall both find you very tedious.'

'Is that what I'm doing?' she asked, considering it. 'I don't think so.'

He looked at her soberly. 'Go to bed, my dear. Do stop fussing. Are you prepared to do anything about it? You aren't, are you? Then stop making us all miserable over impossibilities. We have a pleasant enough life, taking it for what it is. It's not much fun being the fag-end of something, but even that has its compensations.'

Julia listened, smiling, to her own voice speaking. 'You put it admirably,' she said, as she went out of the room.

Doris Lessing

London Observed

Stories and Sketches

'Wise, compassionate, sharp-eyed.' *Financial Times*

'During that first year in England, I had a vision of London I cannot recall now . . . it was a nightmare city that I lived in for a year. Then, one evening, walking across the park, the light welded buildings, trees and scarlet buses into something familiar and beautiful, and I knew myself to be at home.'

Doris Lessing wrote these words in 1957, and since then she has continued to observe London and its inhabitants with the shrewd, sometimes critical, yet always affectionate and sensitive eye of an artist. Representing over three decades of fine writing, *London Observed* contains eighteeen perfect pen-portraits of Londoners and their city.

'Lessing's vision of London is a brilliant diorama of comedy, tragedy and squalor, lifted by moments of true delight.'

Cosmopolitan

'Explicit tenderness is a hallmark of many of these tales. Here's art holding up a mirror to life, to London, and declaring a vision untarnished, clear and steady.' *New Statesman and Society*

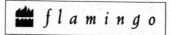

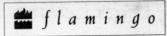
flamingo

Flamingo is a quality imprint publishing both fiction and non-fiction. Below are some recent titles.

Fiction
- [ ] News From a Foreign Country Came *Alberto Manguel* £4.99
- [ ] The Kitchen God's Wife *Amy Tan* £4.99
- [ ] Moon Over Minneapolis *Fay Weldon* £5.99
- [ ] Isaac and His Devils *Fernanda Eberstadt* £5.99
- [ ] The Crown of Columbus *Michael Dorris & Louise Erdrich* £5.99
- [ ] A Thousand Acres *Jane Smiley* £5.99
- [ ] Dirty Weekend *Helen Zahavi* £4.50
- [ ] Mary Swann *Carol Shields* £4.99
- [ ] Cowboys and Indians *Joseph O'Connor* £5.99
- [ ] The Waiting Years *Fumiko Enchi* £5.99

Non-fiction
- [ ] The Proving Grounds *Benedict Allen* £5.99
- [ ] The Quantum Self *Danah Zohar* £4.99
- [ ] Ford Madox Ford *Alan Judd* £6.99
- [ ] C. S. Lewis *A. N. Wilson* £5.99
- [ ] Into the Badlands *John Williams* £5.99
- [ ] Dame Edna Everage *John Lahr* £5.99
- [ ] Handel and His World *H. C. Robbins Landon* £5.99
- [ ] Taking It Like a Woman *Ann Oakley* £5.99

You can buy Flamingo paperbacks at your local bookshop or newsagent. Or you can order them from Fontana Paperbacks, Cash Sales Department, Box 29, Douglas, Isle of Man. Please send a cheque, postal or money order (not currency) worth the purchase price plus 24p per book (maximum postage required is £3.00 for orders within the UK).

NAME (Block letters)_____

ADDRESS_____

_____

_____

While every effort is made to keep prices low, it is sometimes necessary to increase them at short notice. Fontana Paperbacks reserve the right to show new retail prices on covers which may differ from those previously advertised in the text or elsewhere.